# Our Better Angels

by Kathleen Willett

Chapter 1

Whatever all her other faults, Lisa always tried to be politically correct. So when the word "crazy" came to mind to describe the latest events in her life, she deemed it to be too insensitive to just toss around. She also passed on the term "insane" although she heard people use that descriptor all the time.

Crazy and insane are indeed two very emotionally charged words. There are many words in the English language that are equally emotionally charged.

Lisa was pondering this as she sat and thought. She had had plenty of time and opportunity to do both: sit and think. A lot of people probably didn't do much of that in their daily lives anymore. You ask someone how they are and 99% of the time, they will tell you that they are busy. The other 1% reports to be very busy. Busy people don't have the luxury to sit and ponder emotionally-charged words. Words like commitment. Now there was one extremely charged word. Marriage was another. In-laws, Christmas, backward. Yup, there were tons of words that, when uttered, held a world-full charge when they landed with a boom and a fizz on the human ear drum. Animals didn't have this problem. You could say to the family pet, "Let's make a commitment to get married during the Christmas holidays so your backward in-laws can attend," and the only thing the dog would wonder about was what, if any of that, involved dog food going into a bowl. But you say the same thing to your prospective husband or wife, and it was prime time for an argument.

But that's not what Lisa had started out thinking about. In fact, she really hadn't planned at all to think about emotionally-charged words. It's just that it came to her as she was fishing around for a better word than crazy or insane to describe the latest chapter of her life.

When the notion had been floated that Lisa could be whisked away to a place with sun and sand, her mind immediately jumped to the idea of a beach resort like Hawaii. Ah, the land of volcanoes and surfing and fancy cocktails with tiny umbrellas... Beach Boy lyrics had floated through the mysterious gramophone in her mind. Didn't we all wish we could be California Girls...which didn't quite match up with Hawaii, but it was still the same notion.

So, it was Lisa's fault that she hadn't asked for more specifics, especially where beaches were concerned. The Witness Protection Program had gotten the sun and sand part right. The sun was the sun. The sand was more like prairie rather than St. Tropez. Not even Bridget Bardot would look sexy in this venue. Lisa hadn't been looking to be sexy. That wasn't the root of the complaint. The origin of her grumble bee attitude was that this was no place to kill time waiting for a member of the family to testify.

That sounded a lot more ominous than Lisa intended. As in Mob ominous. Mary wasn't part of the Mob by any stretch of the imagination. She wasn't even a part of the problem. She was part of the solution. Mary, Lisa's girlfriend, had stumbled upon a terror cell that had been literally days away from overthrowing the Pentagon. People had been tortured and killed in the process. Mary was a hero, even the President said so. THE President. And he would know. So now, Mary was holed up in some prison apartment out east for her own safety and Lisa was doing her best to be a chameleon in the Southwest American Desert.

It had been fun at first. Okay, that was a stretch. It had been interesting at first. Agent Smith, a grandfatherly gentleman, had made the first few days tolerable. Witness Protection was a tricky business. Most of the protected people were guilty of some slimy business that disgusted ordinary citizens and Federal Marshals. It should have made a huge difference that both Mary and Lisa were innocent. But old habits are hard to break. Maybe that's why Lisa's thoughts had drifted to mental illness. It was crazy that they were in this situation. Innocent of all charges. Guilty by association.

Lisa was feeling guilty, but for totally unrelated reasons. The complicated web of relationship had once again been in some sort of transition for her and those around her. Mary was her current girlfriend, but theirs was a strained relationship at best lately. Lisa had found herself drawn to Trish, one of Mitch's best friends. Mitch, who was Lisa's former girlfriend from a few years back, was now in a relationship with Rebecca, who was known most famously for being the former Governor of and Senator from Colorado. Coincidentally, she was also Mary's mother. It was an intricate web indeed. Whenever they all got together on rare occasions, the tension in the air was palpable. Lisa had committed the transgression of stealing Mitch's life savings when she left her and had worked hard to redeem herself in the eyes of Mitch first and foremost but also to everyone in the circle of friends and acquaintances. It had more often than not made her feel less than. Less than good enough or honest enough or trustworthy enough. So when Trish made her feel valued for her role in helping to care for Trish's disabled infant son Josh, it made it too difficult to resist her attraction to Trish. She didn't know whether she was in love or in love with the idea of being in love, but it felt too good to avoid. Hence the guilty feelings. The heart wants what it wants. And now, they were all scattered around the country. Lisa was in the desert, Mary was under the watchful eye of WITSEC out on the east coast, Trish was in Colorado and Mitch and Rebecca were currently nomads, bouncing between Colorado and Kansas. It was impossible to believe that this was in anyone's best interest, but Lisa was doing her best to cope.

Mary dealt out her thousandth hand of solitaire. It was fitting. She had been in solitary confinement for so long that not even books or newspapers held her interest anymore. So it was her and a well-worn deck of cards. She had pondered it like the old chicken versus egg question. Did the card game come before people were actually confined in solitary? Or after? And did it really matter or was it just something else to think about to keep her mind off her own screwed-up reality? Figuring out who the bad guys were was the easy part. Sorting out a personal life...that was the real bugger. Fawn, a fetching woman, had captured Mary's attention. It had felt like a shovel to the back of the head to find out that she was really Special Agent Fawn. Married Special Agent Fawn.

The only good thing about confinement so far had been the brief visits from Fawn. Which was still better than a thousand hands of solitaire. Of course, there were the depositions or whatever the legal experts called it. It was people asking nuanced questions to assure everyone involved that you knew what you were talking about. That was the innocent explanation. The bad angels would have you believe that they were just trying to trip you up. Trying to prove that you were as sinfully guilty as the next perp. Or, the worst possible scenario, you were the only truly guilty party and everyone else was an innocent bystander until you came along and dragged them down with you into the pit of crime.

This part had gotten really old really fast, and getting prickly about it only worsened the problem. It was a memory test, this much Mary had gleaned after having given a slightly different answer to the same question. It didn't seem like a big deal at the time to her, but the lawyers present had all rolled their eyes. No doubt, she was the topic of conversation over pricey drinks at whatever local bar they all liquored up at every day after work. Yeah, that lawyering stuff was hard work and she'd trade places with any of them for a day if it meant that she could leave her "apartment." Just one drink out with the group. It's believed that if you do the right thing, then the consequences are easier to accept. Mary was beginning to seriously doubt this truism. Seriously.


Rose couldn't find Trish. She wasn't frantic yet, but if this involved another trip to the cemetery to pull Trish away from Robbie's grave site, something that had already happened once before, she would need help. Not that there wasn't help to be found. They were supposed to be under some sort of guard. If Trish had left the premises, someone with a gun would know about it. This realization eased Rose's mind. Rose was a strong woman. She had survived the Holocaust. One missing person wasn't going to get the best of her. After enlisting Silver's help, Trish was located. She was downstairs in the haunted section of the house. Actually, that part of the house was no longer haunted, but you know how names can stick. A kid gets a nickname like Booger after an unfortunate incident in second grade with a tissue and the moniker stays forever. Rose didn't know if spirits walked the earth or not, but she understood how the dead

4

kept a hold on the living. If that's all it took to believe in ghosts, then count Rose among the believers.

"I was ready to fix dinner and wondered if you were hungry?" Rose asked.

Trish smiled. The first time she had met Rose and her husband, Max, lunch was dinner and dinner was supper. No matter what they called the meals, there was always plenty of food for everyone. Except Max. Max was on the cardiac diet. If it tasted good, you had to spit it out.

"I'm ready for a bite," Trish wasn't all that hungry but knew that she had to eat to keep up her strength. Since Lisa had been swallowed up by Federal Agents, Trish hadn't had much of an appetite. She had Josh, her son by Robbie, to keep her grounded and in the moment. But when he slept, Trish had taken to finding quiet places in the house to sit and ponder. Anyone else might have called it brooding, and they would be right. In one snap decision made necessary by events she had no control over, another person she loved had been taken from her. Robbie had committed suicide months ago and couldn't come back. Trish wasn't sure if Lisa could, either. Even if she did, Lisa wasn't Trish's to have and hold. Mary and Lisa would no doubt sort things out and be back together. Trish would love Lisa until they were all dead and buried, but that's about all she really knew right now. If brooding helped to sort it out and eventually deal with it, then it served a noble purpose. Meanwhile, it was time to eat.

"I said, I'll cook something if you'll eat it," Mitch repeated a variation of her question to Reb.

They had made it back to Kansas, but still weren't settled. It wasn't like being home, although there hadn't really been a home for them ever. There were plans and blueprints and fits and starts of building, but there wasn't a home yet. There would need to be one soon.

They were going to be parents. Parents! Talk about an emotionally-charged word. Parent was tops on the list of words that could easily send a chill down the back of the steadiest of persons.

"I'm sorry. Did you say something?" Reb asked.

Mitch wasn't at all irritated. It wasn't every day that your adult daughter was whisked away into Federal protection. But it had been many days now and not knowing had been the worst of it. Reb knew that Mary was alive and Mitch knew that Lisa was alive. That was about the extent of the knowing. Sometimes, you just didn't appreciate people until they were no longer a part of your life.

"I said, I'm going to cook!"
"Okay. You don't need to shout."
"For two." Mitch said quietly.
"I'll eat something."
"Good, because that's what I had planned to cook."
"Huh?" Reb had once again drifted to the island of not listening.
"I'll let you know when it's ready," Mitch patted Reb's shoulder. It was a loving gesture, about the only one they had shared lately. And that was okay. Life was like that sometimes. More so for them. Reb was paralyzed from the waist down and that affected their love life. They both worked diligently to fight this reality, but once in a while, reality won. Mitch set about to cook. Enough talking about it. Food didn't make life perfect, but it made it worthwhile. She cooked chicken and potatoes and broccoli. Okay, so she wasn't the most inspired of chefs lately. They had recently been to France and eaten enough fois gras to pave a driveway. Reb had the good grace to not give Mitch a bad time about her all-too-brief flirtation with veganism. It had been a good effort. Mitch had wanted to be strong and healthy in order to be the best help she could be for Reb. But she also wanted red meat. Not all the time. Just the occasional cheeseburger. And fries. And chocolate shake. Life is full of compromises. A little less prime rib. A little more asparagus.

Reb was truly pleased. By the time Mitch had gotten everything cooked and the table set, Reb's mood had lifted a little. She had convinced herself early on that Witness Protection wouldn't last forever. Not like the mobsters of old who had perished after years of bleak existences for doing the right thing. That's not what life had in store for her daughter. Life hadn't exactly made its intentions clear where Mary was concerned up to this point in her life anyway. But life rarely showed its hand where many people were concerned. It was the age-old question: Why am I here and why am I eating

6

chicken and potatoes and broccoli again?

"We should plan a trip to the grocery store," Reb said.
Mitch smiled. Reb was tired of chicken and potatoes and broccoli.
This was a good sign. It *had* been like living with Elvis. Meatloaf
for six months. Not that there was anything wrong with that.
Anybody with a voice like that could have meatloaf every day for six
years. Too bad it didn't keep all the other vices at bay. If this last
thought made Mitch feel any more evolved as a human being, she
didn't dwell on it.

"The grocery store?" Mitch asked just to make sure she heard
correctly.
"Your favorite outing," Reb had noticed the silly grin.
The grin wasn't all about the grocery store. Some of it involved the
spark of life that Reb was showing. Okay, so a lot of it involved
something other than chicken and potatoes and broccoli. Mitch was
only human, too.
"Are you going to make a list or should I?" Reb was all about tasks
pending.
"Maybe something fishy," Mitch said.
"Most of your suggestions do tend to have that quality," Reb stated
with just one eyebrow arched.
There was life in the old girl after all!

Everything is temporary. Lisa got that much about life. If that was
the case with normal life, then life in Witness Protection was
temporary on steroids. She had been rescued from a quiet life full of
impending danger to a motel that would give a dump a better
reputation by comparison. At least it wasn't burning down around
her. The house she and Mary shared in Denver had been torched by
the bad guys. Thankfully, no one was in it at the time. Lisa had
already had one life experience with burning buildings and once was
enough. Back to the motel she was stashed in. It, too, could
probably burn down in a heartbeat. The least the government could
do was to put you in a structure that was up to code. But they soon
moved again, they being Lisa and her entourage. Her reluctant
entourage. Another motel and then another and it was really so
conspicuously obvious that Stevie Wonder could've followed them

7

around. Still, there was no beach in sight. No crashing waves. The only water here was in bottles because the stuff out of the tap caused all sorts of intestinal distress.

Then, one day, they were there. Lisa knew this because Agent Smith showed up again, as gallant as ever. He knew things hadn't been good. He wasn't an idiot. But at least he was nice enough about it. It was just good fun to watch all the younger agents jump at his command. Especially where desserts had been concerned.

"When I say cheesecake, Field Agent, I don't mean out of the freezer case at the store!" he had barked to every probie on the detail. It didn't matter to him that they were in the middle of the Southwest desert. He knew that somewhere there was cheesecake that would bring tears to the eyes of any Manhattanite in the vicinity. And he didn't care who he had to growl at to make it so. You just didn't mess around with Agent Smith and expect a promotion anytime soon.

But to his charges, he was like the kindly grandfather that everyone wished they had. So it was with a measure of melancholy that Lisa received the news that they were at the end of their journey.

"We're breaking up, aren't we?" Lisa said to him with a sly smile. "You need someone younger," he held his hand over his heart. He knew her history. It wasn't all "don't ask don't tell" in government work. He had the good grace to not tell her she needed a younger man.
"And what is the plan from here?" Lisa knew better than to ask anyone else on the detail.
"You will have a cozy house."

It was just the way he said it that sent up red flags for Lisa. *Cozy* was one of those coded real estate words that translated to *dinky*. It didn't mean a cottage with a picket fence and a thatched roof. Not that that would be ideal either.
"Just how cozy?" Lisa got right to the point.
"The foreclosure market has been very good to WITSEC."
This sounded less thrilling every minute. Agent Smith took note of

the shift in mood.

"It won't be ideal. We can't put people in mansions. The taxpayers just don't like that sort of thing."

"I understand that you're doing your best. I've never doubted that."

"First thing tomorrow, we'll go to the site."

"So, we have one more night together after all," Lisa sounded more wistful than she meant to.

"You want to go out for a beer?"

"I thought you'd never ask."

"Okay, so you put salmon on the list, right?" Reb asked again. What was with her memory lately?

"Right after brown rice and before green beans," Mitch stated. "You want me to read through the list again?"

"No!" Reb replied sharply and then softened, "I'm not going senile."

"I never-"

"I know you didn't suggest it. I'm just distracted."

"I know. Let's just go to the store and pick out what looks good."

"The last time we did that, you bought out the bakery."

"Well, at least we had something to eat when we got home."

"Good thing we didn't take our blood sugar readings."

"Bread is the staff of life."

"Not when it's deep fried and dipped in chocolate icing."

"Can we go now? Please?"

They enjoyed their grocery shopping excursion. They always did once it got underway. The local grocery store liked it as well. For two people, they did more than their per capita share to keep the economy humming along.

"We're both eating for two," Mitch tried to explain it in terms that only she understood. People nodded, hoping to hear less rather than more. It wouldn't be too long before Miranda would be giving birth to Reb's sister's daughter's baby. In prison. It was complicated. Mitch had wondered in quiet moments if anything was ever going to

9

be simple. She had fallen in love with Lisa and now her old girlfriend was in hiding somewhere. Lisa and Mary, Reb's daughter, were a couple, sort of. Reb was Mitch's soul mate now, even if she had become disabled. And then, Reb's life had been saved by Lisa. Reb's niece, the previously mentioned Miranda, had tried to kill various family members and now she was serving time and pregnant by a prison guard.

So, if Mitch sought solace in chocolate-glazed doughnuts more than Reb approved, at least she wasn't medicating in other, more destructive ways. She stayed out of bars, totally rejected controlled substances unless she was being wheeled out of surgery, and even monitored her TV viewing. That left food. Everybody had to eat, right? Or was that, eat right? It was all in where you put the comma.

"Do you have to tell everyone that we're having a baby?" Reb broke through the reverie.
"Are you asking if that's the plan or just expressing your disapproval?"
"The checkout lady doesn't need to know that we're going to adopt."
"She'll know soon enough when we start loading up on diapers and formula."
"Just don't get ahead of yourself."
"What's going on?" was the best question Mitch could come up with at the moment.
"Going on?" Reb knew a couched question when she heard one.
This had davenport written all over it.
"I'm getting ready for a baby. What are you doing?"
"I'm trying not to jinx things."
"What are you talking about?"
"We don't have the baby yet."
Mitch stopped talking and started thinking. Not that she couldn't do both at the same time, but this was a special circumstance. Thinking seemed to take longer these days.
"You don't think this is going to work out the way we planned?"
"Nothing ever seems to work out the way we plan."
It was a general pronouncement meant to obfuscate a specific worry.
"When you're ready to be more specific, let me know," Mitch said

kindly.

"Has it dawned on you yet that we might not be allowed to adopt this baby?" Reb was ready to be more specific. When Reb got ready to be specific, it was a good idea to sit and listen. Mitch was ready to hear more. Reb paused so long that even Mitch now felt uncomfortable with the silence.

"Actually, no. That thought hadn't crossed my mind."

"Well, maybe it should. Just because Miranda has mentioned giving us custody of the baby doesn't mean that we can count on that. Things happen."

"Things?" Mitch prodded.

"Yes, things!" Reb was getting testy. This usually meant that she really wanted to share information that was emotional in nature.

"Keep talking, you're doing fine," Mitch nodded.

"Don't patronize me!"

Mitch never quite knew what this meant. What exactly was patronizing? Every time Reb used the word to describe Mitch, it was a case of Mitch trying her best to be agreeable. Which was no cause to make caustic remarks about her. Reb sensed the mood souring.

"I know enough about the law and judges and politicians to never take anything for granted," Reb explained her worries.

"You think that some politically-motivated right-wing judge is going to deny our adoption petition?"

"It's been known to happen."

"But it would be so illogical."

Reb smiled at Mitch. She was so trusting in the better angels that it didn't make sense to argue against her.

"What?" Mitch asked suspiciously after noticing the prolonged study by Reb.

"I'm just remembering now why I fell in love with you."

"Is it because of my fabulous cooking?" Mitch was still busy unpacking groceries.

"That's it! Absolutely!" Reb just smiled again.

Lisa had done her level best to prepare for this moment. When she had heard Agent Smith mention foreclosures, she was ready to tour

the Amityville of the west.  As in, the walls looked really nice…until
they started to ooze green slime.  They pulled up to the property in
cars with real estate logos painted on the doors to make this look as
normal as possible to any neighbors taking note.  Which there really
weren't any.  Neighbors, that is.  Not like in the city anyway.  When
someone new moved into a neighborhood, people took interest.
They might look on from windows or porches and perhaps peer
around hedges.  That wasn't the case here.  Here, there was no one to
check things out.  No humans anyway.  There were various animals
taking note, but that was the extent of the curiosity.
"We did have our reasons for selecting this place," Smith said.  He
was choosing his words carefully.  It sounded vaguely like an
apology.
"I'm sure you did," Lisa answered like she needed convincing.
"And the main reason wasn't to find a place that annoyed you."
Lisa had the good sense to laugh.  "I know you're doing your best,"
was her best non-answer of the day.
It was Smith's turn to chuckle.  "Our logic was that it would be hard
to sneak up on you in this place."
"Like a shogun," Lisa said wisely.
"A show gun?" Smith echoed, albeit incorrectly.
"Like in Japan.  That kind of shogun.  The leader would be in the
middle of a bamboo floor that would make noise if anyone tried to
sneak up on him."
"Well, do we have wooden floors for you!" Smith smiled like he had
hit a Las Vegas jackpot.
Lisa knew better than to envision glowing wooden floors polished to
a high shine.  Chestnuts roasting on an open fire.  Mel Torme
nipping at your ear…well, maybe not Mel.
"Are you ready to go in?" Smith asked.
It sounded like they were mounting an armed invasion.
"Sure," Lisa was resigned to the reality of the situation.  It didn't
matter if she liked the place or not.  She would be here for a while.
At least until Mary was done with the court case.  So for a few
months, she could endure anything.

One of the agents, looking quite ridiculous in a real estate blazer,
was trying to get the front door open.  He looked like he was about
ready to pull out his service revolver and shoot out the lock.  Smith

relieved him of the key and proceeded to unlock and open the door. You would've thought it was the miracle of the loaves and fishes. Lisa worried about the hair-trigger tempers of some law enforcement personnel. Was it more fun to shoot out a lock instead of gently finessing it into submission? Maybe it was just a way to feel like you've earned your paycheck. Lisa discounted this theory. Every bullet shot out of a Federal gun had to have some sort of paperwork attached. And seriously, who wanted more paperwork in their life? Certainly not these hot shot young agents. They had grown up watching one too many episodes of Walker Texas Ranger or other such fictional nonsense on TV.

Smith had a way with locks. Smith had a way with a lot of things. Lisa ached with the knowledge that the best aspect of this entire ordeal would soon be gone. Three agents went in first to do one final sweep of the house. Just in case what? A cockroach had ventured in to get out of the punishing heat? Lisa shifted from foot to foot. A trickle of sweat traveled down her back. Smith was dressed up like he was going on a fox hunt after this chore was complete. He gave definition to the concept of cool customer.
"Aren't you hot?" Lisa had to ask.
"All the ladies think so," was his dry reply.
"Seriously," Lisa said through a chuckle.
"I haven't been warm in five years."
It was an innocent reply that carried a huge implication. When the human body lost the ability to regulate its internal thermostat, something wasn't quite right. According to scientists who studied the human genetic condition, when that old DNA train goes up and down the replication track one too many times, things just naturally go wrong. Parts break, rust forms, joints get creaky.
Lisa shifted again, hoping that the sweat wasn't showing through.
"I heard they've been calling you names," Smith said out of the blue.
"Only when my back is turned," Lisa did her best to mask her reaction. This guy really knew everything that went on under his jurisdiction.
"They are all getting demoted and reassigned after this. I know it may be hard to believe, but after today, they will think of you as the lucky one."
"Where are you sending them? Siberia?"

Smith only smiled. He couldn't really say and Lisa really didn't care. As long as they never again called a burn victim Scarface, it was fine with her.

The fact that the search of the premises was taking as long as it was gave Lisa the impression that the house was bigger than it looked. With nothing close to lend perspective, it was a real-life optical illusion. Extended contemplation was interrupted by a rare show of emotion from Smith.
"Let's go interrupt their coffee break," he said irritably.
"Are you sure it's safe?"
"No. But I'm tired of waiting on the porch like a jilted prom date."
They went in single file. It was the only instance of Smith not being a total gentleman. He went first, just in case there might be gunplay involved. The first floor, all four rooms of it, was clear of the bad guys. What it wasn't clear of was dirt, dust and sand. The floor was, as Smith promised, made of wood. It was worn and torn up in many places. The holes weren't round, but rather long, narrow patches where the wood had splintered and torn away in thin strips. Not at all safe for bare feet nor, for that matter, socked feet. Shoes were a must. Boots preferable.

The walls were dark and brooding like a badly-written gothic novel. This place would creep out even the bravest vampire. Stuck against one wall was a poorly-constructed stairway that led to the second story. Lisa held out no hope that the upstairs level would be any better, due mostly to the dormer architecture. It would be smaller and cramped.

They could both hear the gentle creaking of the wood flooring upstairs as Smith posed to lead the charge.
"It's awfully quiet up there," he whispered to Lisa.
She realized that indeed it was deathly quiet and couldn't imagine why. They gingerly walked up the stairs. It all felt so absurd that Lisa would've laughed had she not been worried about spooking the bad guys. Since Smith had his gun drawn, they apparently weren't kidding around.

Once Smith had a clear view of what was exactly was transpiring, he started to chuckle. His supposedly crack team of agents were cornered by a snake. Lisa wasn't an expert on snakes. She knew there were big snakes and small snakes and both benign and poisonous snakes. That about summed up her knowledge. Further thought was interrupted by the loud retort of Smith's service revolver. With one bullet, he blew the snake's head up all over the place.

"You've done this before," Lisa stated.

"Nope."

"Never?"

"I'm not paid to kill snakes."

Everyone stood for a moment, almost out of respect. Maybe for the snake. Maybe for the marksmanship.

"Don't just stand there! Clean this up," Smith directed the command to his probies. To Lisa he said, "Let's go back downstairs and finish the tour."

They tramped back down the steps single file.

"I didn't know that snakes could go upstairs," Lisa admitted.

"Oh, sure. Big snakes have no problem with steps."

"That was quite a shot."

"Thanks."

He gave the impression that finding snakes in houses was humdrum stuff. Compared to dealing with mobsters, it probably was.

"I suppose you want to see the kitchen first?"

"Why would you suppose that?"

"You are a practical person. Practical people know their way around a kitchen."

Apparently it had nothing to do with being a female. It really had everything to do with safety. Going out to eat a lot on her own wasn't the best way to stay underground. Besides, Lisa wasn't called to eat a lot of fast food anymore. It didn't enhance her complexion.

The kitchen was sparse. Convents had better facilities. There was a tiny refrigerator, a two-burner stove that belonged in the Smithsonian and linoleum with most of its color worn away.

"It's going to take more than this to whip up a soufflé," Lisa remarked.

"I couldn't cook a soufflé in Julia Child's Cambridge kitchen,"

15

Smith said with a crooked smile.

"How am I going to buy groceries?"

"You'll have a stipend."

"How will I transport them is really my question."

"We'll find a beater."

Lisa wondered if somehow they were still talking about cooking.

"A what?"

"An old car. Something that won't stand out around these parts."

Smith had been far too kind for Lisa to grouse, but the prospect of driving something called a "beater" seemed grim at best. Over time, Lisa had become less materialistic. That was the result of having people in her life she cared about. This wasn't her reality here and now.

"You want to go car shopping?" Smith noticed the pall.

"I didn't see a dealership within a hundred miles."

"Come on. It's going to take them a while to clean up snake parts."

They walked back out into the driving sun and got into the pretend real estate vehicle. At least it had air conditioning. Lisa should've paid attention to where they were going. Soon, she would be expected to find her own way in this new territory. But right now, her eyes and mind were unfocused. The gravitas of her situation was becoming painfully apparent. It all looked so much more glamorous in the movies. Good guys on the run, living a new life on an allowance from WITSEC. In reality, it was all beginning to suck.

By the time it felt like they were going to drive off into the sunset, they were there. Wherever there was. It looked like just a shack in the middle of tumbleweeds with a jalopy gray truck parked in a weed-infested driveway.

"You can stay in the car if you want," Smith tried hard not to sound over protective.

"And miss out on meeting one of my distant neighbors?"

"Don't expect the welcome wagon."

"I never do."

They had parked a respectful distance away from the property and now were covering the remainder on foot. Smith knew the lay of the land, both literally and figuratively. There was no need to knock on the door. A man came out the front door to meet them in the yard. It wasn't green or lush. Nothing around here was.

"You Smith?" the man addressed his fellow man, completely ignoring Lisa.

"Yes Sir."

"Wanna smoke?" the man asked as he pulled out a pack of cigarettes that Lisa didn't even think they made anymore.

"Thank you, but no. Doctor's orders."

"Yeah, I'm not 'sposed to be doin this neither."

It didn't stop him from holding the pack up to his lips so he could extract one without using his fingers. If this was meant to impress the women folk, it fell way short. They stood in silence as he replaced the pack in his pocket and then lit a match. Smoke drifted from both the match and cigarette as the ritual ground to a halt.

"You wanna take it for a spin?"

"It's up to the lady," Smith replied.

It could've been laughter or a cancer-induced coughing fit that spewed forth from the man. It was hard to tell from the noise alone. Smith waited it out. Finally, the man spoke again, "She buying the truck?"

"I'm buying it for her."

"I see," he glanced over at Lisa like there was something unsavory about the entire transaction.

"I trust that the truck runs good. Cash okay?"

"Only cash."

"Cash it is."

For whatever male bonding reason existed, the two men had to huddle like it was a football game to exchange the money for the keys and title. Smith and Lisa made their way to the truck, which looked a whole lot worse up close. The climate was too dry for any rust damage, but the paint was sun bleached and the upholstery was shot. An old weather-beaten blanket covered the driver's side seat, masking the various cigarette burns arranged in random configuration. The engine turned over and actually coughed less than its previous owner. Lisa recognized a decent truck engine when she heard it.

"You want to drive the truck or the car back to the house?" Smith asked.

"I'll take the truck. I need to make friends with it sooner rather than later."

Reverse and first worked well enough to get it to the main road and the last thing Lisa saw in the rear-view mirror was the seller lighting up again and shaking his head. If he'd known a woman was going to end up with his truck, he might have never agreed to the sale. Smith probably paid double or triple the asking price. What could that be? Three-hundred bucks? Lisa did her best to ignore the reek of tobacco that had penetrated every porous millimeter of the vehicle. It ran good and would blend in when she went to the grocery store. Smith had kept his word. A gentleman through and through.

They drove a pretty good clip back to the house. Lisa had remembered more of the way than she would've guessed. It wasn't all that complicated. There weren't many roads to choose from. The agents on dead-snake-clean-up duty were done, or so they thought. It didn't pass muster with Smith, so he sent them to the nearest town with a list of things to buy. The front and back of a white piece of notebook paper was filled out with a little help from Lisa. Setting up a household, however preliminary, took a lot of items from the local grocer and hardware store. Hannibal probably took less supplies across the Alps. Whatever grumbling the agents might have voiced was quickly stemmed by a sharp look from Smith. Once the shoppers were dispatched, Smith sat Lisa down for a final conference.

"You have been provided with a house and vehicle, however humble," he acquiesced ahead of time.

"And I'm grateful, really I am," Lisa replied honestly.

"If I were you, I'd be about ten shades of angry."

"It wouldn't be constructive."

"If you were one of my kids, I'd be just as sick at heart as I am right now."

Lisa nodded. She respected his opinions. "It's okay. I know you're doing your best under the circumstances with regulations wrapped up in red tape."

"Well, I blame the English for red tape."

"I always thought red tape was a reference to Communism?"

"Henry VIII sent Pope Clement VII eighty petitions to annul his twenty-four-year marriage to Catherine of Aragon."

"And we all know how badly that turned out," Lisa interjected.

"Even worse for Anne Boleyn!"

"I suppose so," Lisa wasn't a history scholar. "But what does that have to do with red tape?"

"The petitions were bound with red tape, as was the custom in those days. Anyway, it's still one of the best examples of the history of the separation of church and state," Smith seemed to be mired in thought.

"And that's why we've ended up here," Lisa brought the conversation back to the present.

"Some people say that the wall of separation between church and state is a wonder of metaphorical architecture."

"I agree wholeheartedly!" Lisa was savoring this conversation. She felt it would be her last intelligent interaction for quite a while.

"Because of Mary and many other brave people, the wall stills stands here in America."

"She is a pretty special person," Lisa nodded.

When the shopping detail arrived with supplies, it was time to say goodbye to everyone. The agents were glad to be leaving, but Smith was almost tearful. He knew what Lisa was in for and it truly broke his heart. After they were gone, Lisa tried to stay busy unpacking groceries but it was an exercise in futility. She felt lost and alone. She was going to have to make do without the company of several special people for the duration of this trial. Mary, Reb, Mitch. Who was she kidding? She was missing Trish like crazy. She had never felt so lonely in all her life.

Trish stirred her coffee. It had been only a matter of days now without Lisa and the wearing-down effect was making sugared coffee a necessary, if bad, habit. It was socially acceptable to admit to the world that she was tired because she no longer had nanny help with Josh. And the world would've been sympathetic to that. What the world wouldn't be sympathetic to was the real circumstances: Trish was tearing apart on the inside because she missed Lisa so much and had no right to. No right to. A phrase Trish had heard in childhood. She had always associated it with a moral lesson. As in,

"You have no right to take something that doesn't belong to you," kind of morality.

So, Trish really had no right to long for Lisa night after night because she belonged to someone else. Another phrase left over from childhood. Did people really belong to each other simply because they were romantically entangled? After all, women used to be the property of men. So, under certain circumstances, belonging was yet another emotionally-charged word. If one's ancestors were slaves, then the concept of literally belonging to another human being was a repulsive concept. But having a sense of belonging in a community was a good thing. Trish felt that this was the sort of belonging she felt with Lisa, and the rest of society could just step off a cliff.

It was during the second cup of coffee with three more spoons of sugar that Rose came barreling into the kitchen.
"Max won't wake up," she said steadily.
"If I had my choice, I'd still be asleep, too," Trish yawned in reply.
"I'm serious. I need your help."
Immediately, Trish was on her feet and following Rose at a good clip through the house. Since all the bedrooms were on the main floor, it saved a lot of running up and down steps all the time. Before they even got close to his bed, Trish knew this wasn't going to be good. Not good at all. Max was too pale to be healthy. She was dialing 911 before Rose could concur and then handed the phone to Rose so she could convey the details to the emergency operator. Whatever was going wrong was out of the realm of their combined expertise. Then, Trish did the next best thing. She went in search of Silver and the security detail. They were trained in proper CPR technique. These guys didn't fool around. They had Max on the floor and were pumping his chest as the paramedics stormed in. Trish corralled Rose and began to prepare her for the trip to the hospital. It was a standard checklist: purse, coat, bodyguard. Well, maybe not standard for most people, but Rose was used to it by now.
"What about you?" Rose asked when she realized that Trish wasn't getting ready to go.
"I'm staying here to watch Josh."

It was at times like this that Lisa's presence was so much missed. If only Lisa was here, she could watch over the baby while Trish took care of everything else. Lisa had been the real rock of the household, although she would never have taken credit for the role. Rose sensed Trish's mood despite the panic over Max. "You do what you need to do here and don't worry."

Max was loaded into the ambulance without regaining consciousness. Everyone swept out of the premises as quickly as they had arrived and things were now emptier and lonelier than before. A couple of security people remained behind to guard Trish and Josh. She was used to it by now, but they were only strangers fulfilling a contracted obligation.

Trish checked on Josh. He was asleep. He was a good baby and an even better sleeper. Then, Trish sat down on the couch in the fireplace room and called the only person she could think of for support.

Chapter 2

Mitch had spent the better part of the morning once again looking over blueprints. For most of her relationship with Reb, they had lived like nomads, moving from one destination to another, going where they were called to serve. As sand had slipped through the proverbial hourglass, damage had occurred in their life. Mitch tried to not dwell too much on the destruction of several residences by arson, but she had seriously contemplated building a house out of something that couldn't easily catch fire and end up a gutted pile of ash. Didn't they build castles anymore? Reb's sole wry comment to this wonderment had been, "Well, we certainly have our court jester."
Mitch had chuckled. She figured that you either laugh or cry over events. Usually, she chose the former.
"And I certainly have my queen," she had replied kindly.

The architect kept his opinions to himself. Smart man. He had worked on and off again with them to design a house worthy of royalty and knew a fat paycheck was in the offing. He had left with a promise to contact them with any further questions, so when the phone rang, Mitch picked up on the first ring.
"Hello?"
"Mitch, it's Trish."
"What's wrong?"
Trish didn't bother to ask how Mitch knew immediately that there was a problem. They had been friends for far too long.
"It's Max. He's been taken to the hospital by ambulance."
Mitch listened for a couple more sentences, nodding along with the narrative. Reb observed the head motion and serious expression. She didn't even need to know the vocabulary to glean that one or both of them were going to need to pack a suitcase. When Mitch hung up, Reb awaited the edict.
"Should we fly or drive?" was Mitch spoken quandary.
"From the look on your face, I'm voting for a charter jet."
"Consider it chartered."

For the majority of ambulance transportation, the vehicle uses the sirens on the way to the residence and then travels at a slower rate once they have the patient somewhat stabilized and on board. Unfortunately, Max was not in the majority. His driver went as fast as humanly possible to the emergency room and the hospital staff were literally lined up to administer to him as soon as the gurney wheels hit the pavement. Rose, driven by Silver in the family SUV, had followed at a reasonable rate. Still, they had made good time and were seated in the waiting area when the doctor came searching for them. He looked grim.

"What do you need to tell me, Doctor?" Rose asked.

" Max, is in critical condition. He's had another heart attack."

"Worse than the one he had last time?"

"There's more damage to his heart this time."

Rose considered his answers carefully. She knew that he was a doctor, not an oracle. He couldn't tell her the future and was doing his best to explain the past and present. He had avoided using a lot of medical terms to couch the blow, which was appreciated.

"When can I see him?"

"Let's get him settled into the critical care unit and then we'll come and get you."

"Thank you, Doctor," Rose said steadily, but it was a good thing she was sitting down.

Silver, being her usual proactive self, asked, "Is there a more private area where we could wait?"

The doctor, God bless him, didn't quibble. "Come with me."

He led them over to the security guard in the waiting area, and after a moment's consultation, another guard arrived on the scene and escorted Rose and Silver to a secure location. Apparently, once you were under the purview of WITSEC, normally closed doors were opened, sometimes quite literally. This room was calming. It had a library motif and much more comfortable chairs. There was a table that would hold Thanksgiving dinner and a desk equipped with anything a computer user might need. Since Silver had left her guns back at the house, knowing full well that she would never have gotten them past security, she began to relax just a tad in the contained space. No use everyone being nervous as cats in the dog pound.

"Is there anything else I can do for you, Rose?"
"No, thank you, Silver."
They sat in companionable, if not restful, silence.


Mitch had decided to drive the van out to the airfield rather than to
rely on the well-known spotty reputation of the local taxi service.
One of the most famous videos in everyone's collective American
experience is a clip of multitudes of yellow cab cars clogging New
York City's Times Square. Here in Bible Belt Bread Basket Kansas,
two taxi cabs on the same street would've been a glut.
"Are you sure you want to leave the car? Aren't you worried
someone is going to steal it?" Reb asked.
"If it gets stolen, we'll just get another."
"But it's handicap equipped and not that easy to replace."
"So, we'll leave it in the hanger."
"Okay."
This answer satisfied Reb. Her van was important to her sense of
independence. It wasn't just another car. Besides, worrying about
these details served to keep their minds off the larger picture.
Trish's life was falling apart and she was running out of people she
could call upon to help in a crisis.


Mary had been moved. Not figuratively. Literally. From west to
east. It had happened in the dead of night. It hadn't done any good
to ask questions. The only thing Mary knew was that one day, she
had a two-section cell in a women's prison in Colorado and the next
afternoon, she had a three-section cell in some prison on the east
coast. It may have seemed laughable, but the extra space was a real
luxury. One room was a bathroom, one room a kitchen and the third
room was everything else. If Mary were the suspicious type, she
would've considered it a bribe. They probably needed something
more from her. Four-hundred extra square feet wasn't a substantial
enough of an offering, but the plane ride had been a welcome outing.
Whatever change of venue that had been granted had relocated
everything from Colorado to Washington DC. Apparently, the trial
of the century was about to get underway and Mary's testimony was
crucial.

As if to send the message that she really was still at the mercy of the system, she was left in solitary confinement for two days. On the third day, she had a visitor. A very lovely visitor.

"Good morning, Mary."

"Good morning, Agent O'Neal."

Fawn O'Neal, Special Agent in Charge, didn't bother to correct Mary on the title. Mary didn't mean any disrespect by this misstatement of authority.

"I see you had a safe journey out here."

Mary didn't answer. Surprisingly, even after not having a soul to talk to for days, she still wasn't in the mood for chit chat. Fawn waited just a beat for the reply that never materialized before going on.

"We thought you would enjoy your new accommodations."

"Really?" was Mary's honest retort.

"Well, it isn't exactly a room with a view..."

Fawn was trying so hard to be charming. Mary gave this serious consideration. It could've been a lot worse. She could be locked away with humorless people. Be thankful for small favors.

"Windows would be counter intuitive, of course," Mary smiled. She could play this game as well as anyone.

"Of course," Fawn agreed absently.

"So, why are you really here?" Mary figured that one of them should get down to business.

"The court proceedings are delayed."

So much for getting down to business.

"Delayed?" Mary knew right away that this wasn't going to be good.

"Probably not the news you wanted to hear."

"You guys moved me all the way out here to tell me that?"

There are moments of hesitation and then there are *moments* of *hesitation*. This was the latter.

"Sometimes in this process, actions need to be taken," was Fawn's best non answer to date.

Mary had no clue which actions she was referring to. Her silence spoke volumes.

"I wanted you to be closer. To have a nicer space to wait out things. A little more room and a TV is coming soon."

Mary didn't hear anything after Fawn had said that she wanted Mary

to be closer.  In fact, she had hardly breathed after hearing this.  Life in protective custody had pretty much sucked up until now.  The prospect of being closer to Fawn would make things tolerable.
"Did you hear what I said?" Fawn noted the comatose-like look in Mary's eyes.
"Some of it," Mary answered honestly.
"About the television…"
"Television?" Mary seemed puzzled.
"Wow, you really weren't paying any attention, were you?  I'm almost but not quite offended.  You used to pay pretty good attention to me."

Mary listened to every word this time, having regained her composure.  An acerbic reply along the lines of, "You used to be worth the attention," went through her mind but she remained silent.  Fawn became circumspect as well.  The cell became tomblike for a moment.
"What about the television?" Mary finally asked.
"I was going to tell you to not get your hopes up.  It probably still runs on cathode tubes or some such nonsense.  But it's-"
"The best you could do," Mary finished the sentence.
"Actually, I was going to say that it's a color TV so we'll be needing back those crayons we gave you."
Mary wanted to laugh.  Really, she did.  She wanted to acknowledge Fawn's attempt at silly humor.  But in the back of her mind, she kept hearing the other part of the day's proclamation.
"So, tell me about these delays that we're experiencing."
"They're uncrating the TV as we speak."
"I meant the delays in the court proceedings."
"Ah, those delays," Fawn stated and then hesitated.
It was one of those hesitations that had bad news written all over it.  "Well?"
"The defense has some pretty sharp lawyers"
"And our side doesn't?"
"There's just a jumble of pre-trial motions that the judge is sifting through."
"More than usual?" Mary wouldn't have known usual from unusual where pre-trial motions were concerned, but she still wanted answers.

"Terrorism cases are never usual."

Mary could only nod, not necessarily in agreement as much as acceptance of facts.
"How big?"
"Excuse me?" Fawn said.
"The TV. How big?"
"We are hoping you will be happy with it."
"Is that all you're hoping?"
"I'll be back another day."
And then, she was gone. After two hours of apparent uncrating, a modest-size flat-screen TV appeared in her cell. The remarks about tubes were just kidding around. Mary was mollified if not totally impressed. Unfortunately, all the news channels had been blocked to avoid tainting her testimony, so she had to endure reruns of comedy shows and other fluff to pass the time. It was still better than playing solitaire.

It was taking a lot longer than Lisa had dreamed possible to get comfortable with solitude. Up until now in her life, she had surrounded herself with people. Once she had struck out on her own from her family home, there had been a constant stream of friends and girlfriends. A woman as beautiful as her had never lacked for romantic partners. So even though she felt, as most people do, that a respite from the social world would be welcome from time to time, she soon found discomfort in her quiet surroundings. She had a dreary house, a lumpy twin bed, a decrepit truck and a month's worth of groceries. Honestly, who could ask for anything more!
The first couple of days, she caught up on her sleep. Being on the run, even if you were being driven everywhere, was still tiring. She had read and reread the newspaper that Agent Smith had left behind. News didn't get any newer the second time through.
After a couple of days, Lisa started cooking and baking with all the groceries supplied by her first stipend. It helped her feel a little more at home, but it also made her long for being at Trish's house. Even broccoli sounded good about now, if she could just be sharing it with Max. And Rose. And Trish. They really hadn't even been able to say a proper goodbye before Lisa had been whisked away. All of

27

these thoughts had been kneaded into the bread dough that she was now keeping on the stove until it doubled in size. By the time it was ready to be punched down, Lisa did so with a vengeance. She decided that she would bake these loaves flavored with salt tears and then pack up and leave. Bread and all. She would probably break the record for the shortest duration in WITSEC, but at this point she really didn't care. Smith would be disappointed in her, but it was a risk she was willing to take. Living out here in the middle of nowhere was worse than death.

The charter flight from Kansas to Colorado never took very long, even on a bad day. And this was one of those bad days. Trish's phone call had made it clear that Max wasn't doing well. His vital signs were already in the danger zone and time was ticking. In the intractable nature of the ebb and flow of the human body, the late evening and early morning were times crucial to survival. When the life energy ebbed too low at two a.m., a funeral would inevitably follow.

No one was saying it out loud, but Mitch's supposed healing touch had worked the first time. Just thinking about this was giving her a headache.

"Are you going to be okay?" Reb asked when she saw Mitch rubbing her temples.

"It's just a small headache."

Reb rustled around in her handbag for an aspirin. Mitch took two tablets and closed her eyes. Reb continued to talk. "The flight won't be much longer."

"Uh huh," Mitch agreed without nodding. The less head motion the better.

"In fact, this would always be a short journey."

Mitch tried to think through the pain, wondering if Reb was making general comments about the law of aerodynamics or had traveled to a more specific realm of conversation. It hurt to think, so Mitch hoped that Reb would get to the point before they touched down.

"Colorado and Kansas are real close," Reb got to the point.

"They share a border," Mitch demonstrated that she was keeping up with the conversation, if not the geography lesson.

"And with these really nice fast jets you charter, it hardly takes any time at all to get from point A to point B."

Mitch's headache was clearing quickly. Maybe it was just an altitude issue. She asked, "Do you want to talk about whatever you have on your mind or do you want to wait until after we see Trish?"

"I've been doing a lot of thinking."

"Thinking about what?" Mitch asked, mostly to encourage Reb to continue.

"I've been thinking about something we should've been paying attention to a long time ago."

"Ah," Mitch nodded wisely.

"I want to live in a state that is more tolerant of gay and lesbian people than Kansas. I want to adopt Miranda's baby without any legal problems. And I need to know if you would consider co-adopting the baby?"

"Of course I would."

"Even though it's no blood relation to you?"

The question may have seemed brutal to a passerby, but Mitch heard clearly what was being asked of her. "This baby will be as close to me as if I had given birth myself."

"You know what that means?"

"It means that we're probably going to move back to Colorado."

"We can still build the house in Kansas. You know, have a place to stay when we visit Miranda."

"And we'll need to buy another house in Colorado. Again."

"Too bad we didn't keep the first few you bought."

"Italian marble and baby burps just don't go together."

"I suppose not."

Life's biggest decisions can be made in the most improbable of places. Not everyone decided to adopt and relocate while jetting from state to state, but in the rarified air at ten-thousand feet, it seemed to be the best course of action.


Trish had picked up her phone a dozen times and then put it down a dozen times. The action was not lost on Rose nor Silver. They had sat for long minutes stretching into hours. Any repetitious action would've been noticed eventually.

"Who are you thinking of calling?" Rose asked.

"The rent-a-nanny service to check on Josh," Trish lied.

When Max had been transported to the hospital, Trish had initially stayed behind with Josh. They were still under guard by men and women hired after Mary and Lisa's house had been torched to the ground. But Trish wanted someone without a gun strapped to their body to change and feed the baby. So she called a professional nanny service that she had first looked into when Lisa left town. Trish was grateful to have done the initial research. The nanny would be carefully guarded and assisted as she managed her duties. Trish had felt comfortable enough to head to the hospital. Now she sat, waiting for the courage to call anyone who could get a message to Lisa.

WITSEC had a method where messages were concerned. You contacted WITSEC with your message and then they sent it along through all sorts of proprietary channels to the recipient and then their reply was forwarded to you. In the age of instant communication, this seemed a bit like two empty tomato soup cans tied together with a string.

"Why don't you send a communique to Lisa instead?" Rose asked. Perhaps she had intended for it to sound like one of her famous out-of-the-blue suggestions, but they both knew better.
"I suppose I should do that," Trish tried to sound subdued considering the circumstances, but her voice betrayed her.
She fished around in her wallet for the business card that she was provided when Lisa was taken into protective custody. It was pristine white. She had never used it to make a call. She had wanted to about a hundred times a day, but something had prevented her from doing so. That much hadn't changed. When Lisa was still working for her, Trish had been careful about calling Lisa during her off time. There had been a few calls, but never enough for Trish upon retrospect. She had tried to be respectful of Lisa and Mary's home life, but the truth was that Trish would never have had too many conversations with Lisa. Love did that to a person.

"Are you going to make the call now or now?" Rose asked
Trish came out of her reverie and looked at Rose.
"It's going to take them a while to get the message sent," Rose continued her vocal support.
"I'll go somewhere where my cell phone gets better reception."

"The courtesy phone is on that table in the corner."

Trish nodded agreeably. It wasn't as if she was going to say anything intimate to Federal Agents. No mushy mush stuff. So, she mustered up her courage and walked over to the phone. It didn't take as much effort as Trish thought it would to send a message. Perhaps the wheels were greased to break through the bureaucracy. She went back over and sat next to Rose.

"See. That wasn't so difficult." Rose patted Trish's hand.

With everything that was happening to Max, it was a miracle that Rose stayed as calm and collected as she did. Maybe when you had lived as long as Rose and had survived the most horrific experiences that she had, you would be more prepared for every other shock that life held in store.

They lapsed into silence, each awaiting word about their respective loved ones.


Lisa had put a few things in the battered truck. That's all she had was a few things, including the freshly-baked bread. When she went into WITSEC, she left with the clothes on her back, quite literally. Other items had been provided along the way. A comb and toothbrush the first day, some shampoo and a hair brush the next, and so on. It was all cheap goods gathered from various gas mart shops. Although Lisa had changed her ways to the better this past year or so, she was still used to owning the best of the best where personal items were concerned. It was just the natural consequence of being surrounded by people who had money. The downside of this condition is that any ordinary toothbrush or shampoo was far inferior to the premium products that Lisa used to own. The shopping list of items that the agents had bought in town were mostly groceries and household items. None of that was going to make the trip to freedom with her.

She stowed only the most necessary items in a couple of nondescript plastic bags and tossed it all quite cavalierly into the filthy front cab of her decrepit truck. Her cover story was that she was going to the store to buy mouse traps for the four-legged frequent visitors to her house. It was miles to town over a highway in need of repair. If she traveled too fast, the fillings in her teeth were liable to bounce out.

She was three miles gone from the house before she noticed that another brave driver shared the road with her, a unique circumstance out in the middle of nowhere U.S.A.

People do need to get from place to place and Lisa wasn't the only soul who had to drive to town. She continued to drive at a slower speed than the law allowed. Usually, someone would have passed her by now, but the other vehicle kept pace, neither passing nor falling behind. So she slowed down even more, and so did her follower. It dawned on her that that's exactly what was happening. She was being followed. It would've been logical for Lisa to panic. All the precautions lately had made her a touch jumpy. She was, after all, hiding from the bad guys. Rather than panic, however, she grabbed up her cell phone and dialed Smith. He picked up on the first ring.

"Yes, Ms. Beaumont?"

He obviously had called ID.

"Hello, Smith."

"How may I assist you?"

"I think I'm being followed."

"I know you're being followed."

"How would you know that?"

"Because it's us following you."

"Oh," Lisa was underwhelmed. Maybe she had secretly been spoiling for a good car chase and wanted permission to race the bad guys. "You do know that being followed scares people on the lam."

"So, where are you headed off to?" He asked genially.

Lisa remembered her cover story and blurted out, "I'm getting mouse traps."

"Well, I guess that makes sense since I shot your other one."

"Oh right, the snake," Lisa acknowledged. It wasn't easy to forget snake bits blown all over your bungalow.

"And so, what all is in the bags that you have in the truck?" he asked.

Lisa didn't want to give the impression that she was the least bit irritated by the apparent intense scrutiny that she was under. But honestly! What were they doing? Watching her with a satellite? "It's all that cheap crap that your agents thoughtfully picked out for me at the gas station."

"Sounds like you have a plan?"

"I'm going to toss it in the first dumpster I encounter. Do you have your satellite uplink ready to capture that?"

Smith chuckled. He was good for the game. "Do you have enough money to purchase upgrades?"

"Not really."

"Well, if you'll allow your escort to continue her job, I'll instruct her to help you with the funding."

Lisa's brow had furrowed at the reality of having a female Fed on her tail. There hadn't been a female agent on her detail so far, so it was new blood on the case, so to speak.

"Is that long pause a yes or a no, Ms. Beaumont?"

"Oh sure, it's okay. I hope she doesn't mind shopping at Walgreens."

"All the best Feds shop there. When you get there, let's talk."

"Why?" Lisa asked.

"Because I want to talk to you when you're not driving."

They disconnected the call and Lisa checked her rear view mirror again. The pace was the same so she relaxed into the rest of the drive. It was only twenty more miles anyway. What the heck, she was in no hurry now. Her first attempted escape had been easily thwarted. She would just need to plan better next time. Not be so obvious about bringing things along, even if they were stashed in a plastic garbage bag rather that a Gucci suitcase.

When she pulled into the parking lot of the Walgreens, her escort into town pulled up perpendicular behind her so she wouldn't be able to back up. The vehicles formed a makeshift chunky capital T. Then, only because the Feds apparently had nothing better to do with their time, three other black SUVs surrounded her car. It honest to God looked like a major drug bust. So much for not being obvious. The only good part was that Agent Smith was one of the occupants of the SUV that Lisa was escorted into.

"I didn't know you were in town," Lisa smiled despite the circumstances.

"Normally, I wouldn't be here," he said slowly.

"Things aren't normal?" Lisa fended off that same kind of panic she felt when she had first sensed being followed into town.

"I have a communication to share with you."

"From who?"

"A Ms. Weingarten."

"Trish?"

"Correct."

"What's the message?"

"She wanted to inform you that Mr. Goldstein is in the hospital."

"Max is in the hospital? What happened?"

"He had another heart attack."

"Oh my God. This is not good news at all."

"I imagined not," Smith sounded sympathetic.

Lisa quickly gathered her wits about her. It wouldn't do to go to pieces at this point in time nor would it be wise to tip her hand about her escape plan.

"Can I send a message to her?" Lisa stalled for time to think.

"Of course. That's why I'm here."

"And here I thought you just wanted to see me again," Lisa thought it best to keep him off guard.

Just as he was about to answer, a knock came at the car window, like a prearranged code. Tap tap. Tap tap tap. Tap. He pressed a button to lower the window. "What is it?" he gruffed at the agent standing almost at attention at the window.

"We're ready, Sir."

Smith sent the window back up. He wasn't ready.

"What are we not quite ready for?" Lisa asked. She intensely disliked being kept out of all these official loops.

Smith inhaled like it was going to be a long explanation. "Normally, we would let you send a letter to communicate with loved ones." He paused, most likely to inhale again. Lisa needed the time to absorb all the implications of the words "loved ones."

"Okay," Lisa said into the void.

"But under the circumstances, we're setting up a phone call."

At this prospect, Lisa's heart leapt. She was going to hear Trish's voice and the government was going to pay the charges. She regretted the reason, but having the opportunity to talk to Trish for the first time since they were separated was a thrill she hadn't anticipated when she started her morning. Lisa hadn't fully realized until now just how much she missed her old life. Being on the run had been novel for the first fifteen minutes. But now, she yearned for any contact from Trish or Mary or anyone back home.

Meanwhile, she noticed that the agent outside the window appeared to be shifting from foot to foot like she was lacking patience. Smith appeared oblivious.

"You do realize the logical extension of your escapade, don't you?" he asked solemnly.

Lisa shook her head. She wasn't in a logical frame of mind just now.

"You've blown your cover."

"I'm not the one who showed up with the cavalry."

It was Smith's turn to shake his head. "You were making a getaway."

"I'm innocent until proven guilty."

"It really doesn't matter anyway," Smith answered vaguely.

The female agent was shifting back and forth to the point where Smith finally decided to take action. He rolled down the car window and held out his hand. A device was placed in it and he transferred it to Lisa.

"What's this?" she asked.

"It's a phone call from Trish."

"Pretty fancy headset," Lisa bantered out of pure nervousness.

"It's a secure line."

Lisa put the headset part over her ears and adjusted the mouthpiece so she could be heard.

"Hello?"

A second or two went by, like they were talking long distance and the sound waves were playing catch up.

"Hi Lisa. It's Trish."

"It's good to hear your voice," was all that Lisa could think to say after all the anticipation.

"Same here," Trish answered like she wasn't alone.

"What's the latest news about Max?" Lisa asked the questions that had been nagging at her since this entire encounter had started.

"He's in CCU."

"I'm coming for a visit," Lisa blurted out.

Smith was shaking his head and Lisa noticed it. "How do you put this thing on hold?"

She got simultaneous different answers from Smith and Trish, which consisted of "You can't," and "Huh?"

"Smith and I need to have a talk."

"Smith who?" Trish asked.

"Agent Smith. My guardian angel," Lisa made it sound more fanciful than it felt at the moment.

"We can't put you on hold. This is a secure line and every word you say is recorded. There are no secrets," Smith sounded very official.

"Fine. A family member is dying. Let's have WITSEC hear the whole tragedy firsthand," Lisa replied testily.

Smith grimaced. It made his face look more aged than usual. "We can't change the rules for every family event."

"My cover is already blown. I can travel to Colorado under guard while you fellows set up a new hiding place for me. One that doesn't have snakes this time, preferably."

"We can't just go on and on setting up new covers for you."

"Of course you can, Smith. You can do anything you set your mind to."

Catering to the male ego usually worked for Lisa. Smith wasn't your usual male, but he still had a sense of pride and professionalism.

"The only place I know of that doesn't have snakes is Ireland."

"I'll apply for my passport. Right after I get to Denver."

Smith sighed. He had worked with the most hardened criminals ever to rat on the Mafia. None were quite as wily or determined as this beautiful young blond woman.

"Can you tell me what that sigh means in English?" Lisa asked.

"It means we're heading to Denver."

Lisa had the good grace not to gloat, but her shy smile let Smith know that he had a heart of gold. Trish had been listening to all of this and finally spoke up, "I'll have your room ready."

"Not a good idea," Smith said into the phone.

"Tell him I have more bodyguards on my payroll right now than he has," Trish said.

"She says she can protect me," Lisa loosely translated Trish's message.

Again, Agent Smith sighed. Why did he even bother talking sense to people of the feminine persuasion?

"What does *that* sigh mean?" Lisa asked again.

"It means have the guest room ready."

After a brief goodbye, the connection was terminated. "These calls cost money, you know," Smith groused without malice.

Without delay, the vehicle door opened and the agent who had been guarding the car got in. It was a bit of a squeeze with Smith on her left and Lisa in the middle. But if it meant that they were heading to Denver, then it was all good.

Had Lisa considered herself a single lady, she would've noticed right off the bat how gorgeous this woman was. As it was, it took about a minute for this reality to set in. Was it "hire a model week" at the agency? Lisa looked at Smith. He looked back. Psychic transmissions passed between them.

Lisa awkwardly held out her hand and introduced herself, "Hi, I'm Lisa."

The agent turned her head. Her lip gloss looked like some shade that would've been called Wet as Rain. Wet as Rain lip gloss in the land of sand and snakes and rusty trucks.

"I know," was Agent Lip Gloss's only response.

Sensing that it was going to be a long, silent trip, Lisa leaned closer to Smith and closed her eyes. He held her like a grandfather for the duration of her nap.

Thankfully, when she woke up, it was bathroom break time. Agent Lip Gloss stood guard like it was Buckingham Palace rather than the gas station. Lisa was short on cash, so she borrowed ten dollars from Smith in order to buy snacks. She purchased candy bars and chips and a quart of soda. The look of disapproval on her new guard's face was unmistakable.

"It would be nice to know your name," Lisa tried one more time to be nice.

"Fuck off," was her reply.

"Excuse me?" Lisa replied.

"Do I need to spell it for you?"

"Only if you want to," Lisa came up with as polite a reply as she could offhand.

"V-U-K-O-F-F. Vukoff."

"Oh, Vukoff," Lisa repeated, trying her best not to laugh. "Is that your first or last name?"

"That's not your concern."

Agent Vukoff must have had loads of issues that weren't going to get solved during the rest of their journey together.

"I just like to know who I might be sharing my candy bar with."

"Then you don't need to know because I'm not going to eat your candy bar."

"I can't even begin to count the number of times I've heard that before," Lisa kidded.

They scouted for all kinds of danger before they walked the twenty paces from the store to the car. Lisa was truly glad to have protection and snacks. It was a long, meditative ride the rest of the way.

Life is full of myths, one of which is that hospitals are quiet places. Some parts are quiet, more parts are noisy and the majority is a mix. When Mitch and Reb arrived, the noise level automatically went up proportionately to Reb's ex-Senator status. Relief flooded Trish's face when she saw Mitch walk through the door to the waiting area. They exchanged the briefest of hugs while Reb rolled into the room. Rose stood up to greet company. Even on her worst day, she remembered her manners. Reb maneuvered her wheel chair close to Rose's chair and beckoned for her to sit down so they could be at eye level.

"How are you holding up?" Reb asked Rose.

Most people would've asked about the patient first. Reb wasn't most people.

"We're doing okay. The staff here is doing everything they can for us and Max."

"He's in CCU right now," Trish followed up. This meant that he was still alive and visitors were restricted. He was one very ill man.

"It's his heart again," Rose reported the fact calmly enough, but the fear in her voice betrayed her demeanor.

"They have him hooked up to a lot of equipment," Trish added.

"Will you go in and see him?" Rose asked Mitch.

It was really more of a pleading. At least they were now at the main purpose of the visit. Mitch sat down on the other side of Rose.

"Of course I'll visit Max, but you know I'm not a healer of any kind."

"He will know that you and the Senator came to visit. It would mean the world to him. No matter what else happens."

Mitch nodded. "When's the next visiting time?"

"In twenty minutes. You only get a few minutes to see him."

"I'll make the most of it."

"We'll make the most of it," Reb corrected.

"Right," Mitch nodded. Her stomach started to clench. "I'm going to take a walk."

"Want some company?" Trish asked.

"Sure," Mitch agreed. She knew that Trish probably needed breathing space as much as she did right about now.

"We won't be long," Trish reassured Rose.

Rose nodded. She would be okay with Reb for company.

Mitch and Trish headed down the hallway toward the elevator. As they waited for it, Mitch asked, "When is Lisa going to be here?"

"How did you know she was coming?"

"I could tell just by looking at you."

"Lisa and her entourage are driving up from an undisclosed location. Hopefully, it won't be long now."

"You think that's a good idea?"

"I don't think it's a bad idea."

"Can you keep Lisa safe?"

"I've been able to keep everyone else safe so far," Trish sounded borderline indignant.

The elevator arrived and they got in for the short ride to the lobby. Each was aware that the clock was ticking.

"Let's get a cup of coffee."

"I thought we were going for a walk?"

"We didn't drive down here, did we?"

"Okay. Why don't you get me a coffee to go. I'm going to use the restroom."

"I'll meet you back here."

"Thanks," Trish said as she headed down another series of hallways to find the public restroom. Hospitals always seemed like a maze to her as she walked along. Good thing she wasn't in that much of a hurry. She took an extra minute to wash her face and towel dry before she went back to the lobby. Trish scanned the area to locate Mitch. She was nowhere to be found. If Trish had to find her way to the cafeteria, they would be hard pressed to get back upstairs in time to visit Max. It made sense to Trish that Mitch probably sensed

this and went back upstairs with the coffee. Or maybe Reb had come down to get Mitch for some reason. Why didn't they let her know? Trish fought back her irritation as she took the elevator back upstairs. She walked into the family waiting room to collect her cup of coffee and was met with curious looks from Rose and Reb.
"Where's Mitch?" Trish asked.
"She was with you," Reb answered.
"She didn't come back with two cups of coffee?"
"She didn't come back here at all."
"Maybe she went in to see Max?" Rose was thinking of every possibility.
"Let's go check."

They went as a group to the nurse's station that controlled the CCU to inquire. No one had tried to visit Max. Reb encouraged Rose and Trish to take this turn visiting Max. Mitch could always visit later when she turned up. Reb went back to the waiting room and dialed Mitch's cell phone. There was no response. She asked the hospital personnel to have her paged. There was, again, no response after several minutes. It wasn't unusual for Mitch to need time alone. Maybe they had put too much pressure on her with all this healing business. If Reb were in similar circumstances, she might've readily done the same thing. Except she'd be answering her phone. When Rose and Trish returned from Max's room, Reb was busy formulating a plan.
"Can I ask Silver to help locate Mitch?"
"Sure," Trish replied. "And I'll help. Mitch owes me a cup of coffee."
"And if we don't find her pretty soon on some park bench feeding pigeons, we'll get the police involved."
They set in motion a search of the hospital and grounds using all available resources. Mitch was nowhere to be found.
"I've gone from irritated to concerned," Reb confided to Trish.
"Maybe she's just having a psychic break or something," Trish tried to make it sound medical, but it came out sounding mental instead.
"I'm sure she will have some sort of elaborate explanation when we find her," Reb sounded more confident than she was feeling.
"I'm sure she will," Trish agreed as if it would somehow help to be agreeable.

# Chapter 3

Mitch really couldn't say exactly when she knew things weren't right. Real life isn't like the movies. Scary music doesn't play right before the bad guys show up. One minute she was in line for coffee and the next thing she knew, she was being spirited away in a vehicle of some sorts. Of course she had memories, but they were addled by the adrenalin rush. She was asked by the man behind her in line if she wished her friends to be safe. She nodded assent. Who wouldn't? She was asked very politely to join these fellows on a walk. She went along, never thinking that it would be unsafe. Well, maybe just a little unsafe.

They walked to an SUV and once inside, a hood was placed over her head and the car sped off. This was when Mitch figured out that there might not be a good ending to this event. She tried to be like Nancy Drew or one of the Hardy Boys by trying to mentally document sounds and turns and smells and bumps in the road. Did anyone ever ask why it took two boys to do the work of one girl? Frank and Joe barely kept up with that clever Nancy. Distracted by juvenile literature, Mitch lost track of everything she was trying to remember. It wasn't exactly over the river and through the woods. A GPS couldn't make sense of this route. So she relaxed into the situation. It would do no good to panic. Whoever had taken her needed her alive for a reason.

Agent Smith's phone buzzed. Smith, Lisa and Vukoff were still on the road. Smith answered the phone and didn't say anything after "Hello." Someone on the other end of the line was obviously giving an extensive report. Lisa found herself holding her breath inadvertently. She hoped that it wasn't bad news about Max. Lisa watched Smith's facial expressions for a clue, but he was a poker player at heart. He nodded a couple more times and then disconnected the call.
"What's going on?" Lisa asked, knowing that he wouldn't volunteer information without some sort of request and maybe not even then. His first words were to the driver.

"Pull over at the next available spot."

In this deserted desert, there were plenty of spots from which to choose. They wheeled over to the dirt shoulder and came to a halt. "There's been a change of plans, which involves a change of route."

"What happened?" Lisa asked her question again, just in different words.

"We're going to Las Vegas."

"Las Vegas?" Lisa was stunned. "That's too far out of the way!"

"That's right."

"Why are we going all the way to Nevada?"

"We're not. We're heading to Las Vegas, New Mexico."

"Oh, okay. Honest mistake," Lisa muttered and then asked, "Why?"

"Because right now, we can't be predictable."

"Why not?"

"Because there's been an abduction and my orders are to close ranks and reroute."

"Who's been abducted?" Lisa was afraid to know and afraid not to know.

"Mitch Tanner."

Lisa nodded. Their government car made a U-turn, heading west for the junction that would allow them to head south.

Mitch had no sense of direction. Period. It wouldn't have mattered if she had been able to see where they were going. However, they had now stopped and car doors had opened and closed and opened again. So they were probably at their final destination. She sat still. It seemed the safest thing to do.

"Out of the car!" instructed her handlers.

"Right or left side?" she asked.

She received a poke on her left arm. It wasn't the clearest of directives, but Mitch hoped that right was the correct choice. She scooted that direction until she could easily extract herself from the car. Nobody bothered to help her, but they hadn't hurt her so far, so they were forgiven. Someone took hold of her arm and guided her down an uneven path to some sort of structure. Mitch knew this because it had a door that opened and only structures had doors. They gingerly crossed a threshold and after walking only a few more paces, Mitch was pushed down into a chair. It was neither soft nor hard, along the lines of a 1950's version of a kitchen table chair with vinyl padding. A few moments ticked by. So far, so good. Mitch wasn't one to panic without foundation. She heard another door open and the sounds of someone sitting opposite to her in perhaps another retro chair? By commands that she couldn't see or hear, her hood was removed. After taking a moment to adjust to the lights, Mitch got the first real good look at her kidnapper.

"Jesus Christ," was all Mitch could think of to say.

By now, all wheels had been set in motion to find Mitch. Reb knew exactly what to do. After the preliminary search of the hospital had turned up nothing, except a doctor and nurse making out in a third-floor storage closet, she did what she always did. Go directly to a higher authority. Her phone conversation with the President went well. He didn't have anything else to do but run an entire country and be the leader of the free world. He had lots of staff for that. Finding Mitch jumped way up on the priority list. After all, we can't let the terrorists win. Within moments of her phone call, entire agencies went into action. Of course, Smith was notified, but so were airports, bus stations, squadrons of uniformed officers and even people whom your average American didn't even know about. And then, unfortunately, it all became a waiting game. Mitch could be anywhere in ten-trillion locations. They needed either a call from the kidnappers or a miracle.

Even though she knew that it was all about her safety, Lisa wasn't happy to be heading farther away from Trish.

"How many miles to Las Vegas?" Lisa asked. It was her adult version of, "Are we there yet?"

"Many," Smith answered.

"How many?" Lisa didn't appreciate the vague reply.

"Why don't you just be quiet!" Agent Fuckoff stuck her nose in where it didn't belong.

"Why don't you just shut the hell up!" Lisa countered.

"Ladies!" Smith interjected with a sharpness seldom used, and gave his sternest look toward his agent. He had always made his best effort to treat the innocent victims of crimes with kid gloves, and he expected no less of his agents.

"When we get there, which will be soon, a flight to Denver is arranged. So it really won't be long now."

Lisa was mollified. At least it would be a comfy airplane ride once they got to the airfield. She could use a little first-class coddling after having Fuckoff's elbow in her ribcage. At least, she thought it was her elbow.

Rose felt responsible and, by extension, terrible. "This is all my fault," she confided to Trish.

"This is not your fault. Why would you even think that?"

"Because I was selfish and only wanted what was best for Max and myself."

"You wanted family and friends to be around you. That's a perfectly normal thing to want."

But Rose only shook her head.

"What?" Trish asked.

"I wanted Max to be healed again. I hoped Mitch could do that. I wasn't thinking that I'd be bringing her to a place of danger."

"Mitch came willingly and of her own accord. You couldn't have kept her away."

Rose had ceased shaking her head and now glumly pronounced, "It doesn't bring a good end when you ask for one too many miracles."

Mitch's captor looked at her with some amusement. "I imagine that you are frightened."

"No, not really," Mitch answered honestly.

"But your exclamation?"

"Oh, you mean the Jesus Christ thing? Gee, that's only logical."

"Logical?"

Okay, so Mitch, being a people watcher of the highest order, had seen a lot of interesting folks in her time, but never one who had most closely resembled Jesus. Yeah, the one from Nazareth.

"So, nobody's ever told you that you look like Jesus?"

44

"My name is Herman."

"Herman is a nice name…too," Mitch was acutely aware that she was on the verge of babbling and did her best to keep quiet.

"Do you know why you are here?" he asked.

"Because I'm not anywhere else?" Mitch answered. She was still sorting out this man's appearance. He looked exactly like that quintessential portrait of Jesus that hung in every Catholic Church around the globe. The one with the sacred heart and upheld hand.

"Are you trying to be funny?"

Mitch had to think about this for a split second. "I rarely try to be funny, at least, in the way that other people try to be funny. But things sometimes sound amusing when I don't mean for them to." Mitch trailed off. Herman didn't look very amused.

"So, you have no idea why you are here?"

"Of course I know *why* I'm here. I just don't know why I'm *here*. In this place. I know the why but not the where. Does that make sense?"

Herman was looking very annoyed by now. Mitch couldn't very well help that. After all, he was the one who was asking the obtuse questions.

They sat in silence for a moment. Herman was afraid of something. Mitch could easily sense that much in the energy in the space between them. Gee whiz, she was the one being held captive against her will. Perhaps he was afraid of losing his temper and doing something he would regret before he got what he needed from her. Maybe these verbal sparring matches angered him. It was most likely caused by something in his childhood. Like maybe he could never win an argument with his father or mother. Aren't we all scarred somehow by our upbringing and seeking a soul with a merciful heart to make it all better?

"What can I do to help you?" Mitch asked plainly.

"You can shut the hell up until I tell you to talk!"

Such language, especially from Jesus! Good thing his mother wasn't here for this.


Mary had gotten used to a life of solitude. At first, she had felt inconvenienced verging on martyrdom. She had been uprooted from her life in Colorado and sequestered under the protective wing of the

Feds. The first week or so had found her to be restless and then, once she established a routine, things weren't so unbearable after all. She got three meals a day and she didn't even have to cook them. She couldn't go out to fancy restaurants, but that was probably good news for her arteries. She didn't have to work anymore, no punching a time clock or cramming down lunch in order to get back to her desk. Of course, that's where this entire situation had evolved from: work. Now, she was cooling her heels, waiting to give testimony in one of the biggest terrorism trials of the year. But, as anyone who had been involved in court proceedings knows, the wheels of justice grind at a glacial pace.

Once in a while, just because she felt she owed it to Mary, Fawn paid a visit to the penitentiary. When Mary was busy uncovering criminal activity, Fawn was busy protecting her. Mary didn't know that at the time, and had allowed herself to become emotionally involved. So now, when Fawn stopped by, Mary had to remind herself that Fawn had a husband and kids. Still, every time she was with Fawn, Mary had to remember to exhale. Fawn looked exhausted. Beautiful, but exhausted.
"Hello," Mary greeted with trepidation.
"We have a situation."
That was "Special Agent in Charge" talk for "things have gone to hell in a hand basket."
"Sit down and tell me what's going on."
"I don't have much time."
"You have time to sit. We're not talking until you settle in and relax."
Fawn didn't know why she even thought that she could win an argument with this stubborn woman. So she sat. Perched was actually more like it, but it was enough for Mary.
"There's been an abduction," Fawn went right to the heart of the matter.
Mary's head jerked up. "Is it Lisa?"
"No. She's safe. It's your friend Mitch."
"So what happens now?"
"A plan is being formulated," Fawn answered vaguely.
"Which means that we don't know what to do yet?" Mary translated Fed speak into lay terms.

"We're waiting to be contacted by the kidnappers."

"How long did it take before my mother called the President?"

"About twenty-two minutes."

"That long, huh?"

"They had to search the hospital first."

"The hospital? Who the hell is in the hospital?"

"Max."

"Max is in the hospital and nobody bothered to tell me!"

Fawn couldn't tell if Mary was upset with her or her family.

"It's a recent event."

"Why was Mitch there? Last I heard, she was in Kansas."

"They flew out when they heard about Max."

Mary grew quiet, verging on pouty. There was no excuse for leaving her out of the loop, particularly with news as important as this. Her glowering was not lost on Fawn.

"I'm sorry you had to hear like this."

"Yeah, me too. I want you to tell me the status of every single person involved in this."

"Okay, I owe you that much. As I said, Mitch has been abducted. Max had a heart attack. He and Rose, Trish, Rebecca and Silver are secure in the hospital."

"Where is Lisa?"

"Somewhere in a car being transported to Denver."

"Why?" Mary was puzzled to hear this.

Fawn sighed. Sometimes, telling the truth was so involved.

"She was running away from home."

Mary nodded. Somehow, this did not shock her.

"I'm surprised you caught up to her."

"So were we. She got all the way to the nearest Walgreens before we surrounded her."

Mary scrutinized Fawn's facial expression. She was telling the truth, however absurd it sounded. Had they not had more important things to consider, it would've made for interesting discussion exactly to whom Lisa was running. Lisa was in love with Trish. Mary didn't even try to kid herself about this reality anymore. The fact that she would put her life in jeopardy to be with Trish only sealed the acknowledgement tighter than a tomb. If Fawn was psychically picking up on any of this, she was too kind of a person to say anything. It hadn't been an easy thing for Mary to receive the thanks

47

of a grateful nation only to lose to another the woman she cared about most.

"So, we wait for the kidnappers to call?" Mary reiterated.

"We are waiting to be contacted by whatever means they choose."

"What? You think they are going to post it on the internet?"

"We are hoping that they remain calm and have the capacity to deal with our best negotiators."

"I certainly hope everyone knows what they are doing," was Mary's final comment.


Rose fretted in such a dignified and understated manner that unless you knew her well, you never would've guessed she was terrified. Trish knew her well. She put her arm around Rose's shoulders as they sat in the very heavily guarded waiting room. Rose sighed.

"What?" Trish asked.

"When do you think we'll get some sort of update about Mitch?"

"I'm sure we'll know something when Reb gets word."

Rose sighed. Again.

"What now?" Trish asked, trying to scrub any annoyance from her voice. It was hard to continue to prompt Rose without sounding irritated.

"Why do you think they kidnapped Mitch instead of anybody else?"

"Maybe they are masochists?"

"Maso what?" Rose needed clarification.

"Our mistake is that we are trying to apply the rules of logic and reason to illogical and unreasonable people," Trish spoke quietly.

"As much as you are trying, I am not finding comfort in our discussion," Rose stated bluntly.

"I'm not trying to comfort. I'm preparing for the worst," Trish replied with equal bluntness.

Reb rolled in, not exactly to the rescue, but at least she was a welcome distraction.

"Are you two doing okay?" Reb asked. She wore her senatorial air about her, like a shield. Or maybe more like a buffer.

"No," Rose answered.

"Any news?" Trish was content to forge ahead.

"Not yet, but it's still pretty early in the game."

Reb's choice of words was interesting. Maybe if she categorized this as a "game," it would keep her from true and total panic.

"What do you mean?" Rose asked.

Reb glanced from Rose to Trish. Sensing that she had perhaps interrupted a difficult conversation, she felt no need to exacerbate the situation. "It just takes a while to have first contact in these types of situations."

Reb couldn't help it, she sounded like a Fed.

"You think they are driving around looking for a phone booth?" Rose wanted details.

The modern world had passed Rose by and large. Anyone who had seen a spy movie or read a spy thriller knew that sophisticated kidnappers had access to communication methods far superior to phone booths. But, then again, so did the people who would help apprehend them.

"I'm pretty sure the delay is more psychological than logistical at this point," Reb tried to sound soothing.

"I'm sure you are right," Rose nodded absently. She really couldn't concentrate on more than one crisis at a time anymore. Her thought process needed to stay with Max, lest her mind fracture and then not be able to reconnect later. Mitch hadn't been able to visit him and every minute that ticked by worked against them. In the grand scheme of life, there are those who believe that living is a miracle. There's another contingent that believes that dying is the real miracle. It usually depended on which side of the health spectrum you were on. Some people in nursing homes prayed every day to die. In many cases, it was the kindest deliverance.

Max had been unusually quiet lately. Trish couldn't recall any discussion about his final disposition wishes or medical directives leading up to that. Now didn't seem to be a good time to bring this up with Rose. And yet, it had to be on her mind as well. Anyone who lived to the age of Rose and Max would've had to have thought about these things.

"Max doesn't want to be cremated," Rose said, as if she was reading Trish's mind

"I understand," was all Trish could come up with for a response.

Reb took Rose's hand and gently said, "Max isn't dead yet."

As soon as the words were spoken, the doctor in charge of Max's care walked into the room with a solemn look on his face. Max, indeed, was dead.

Lisa had hoped for, at the very least, a first-class seat for the flight to Denver. It would've made up for riding all over the southwest desert to avoid trouble. It would also give her a little breathing space from Agent Vukoff and her pointy elbows. What Lisa failed to realize was that she was the guest of a chronically underfunded government program. So instead of being on a fancy jet, they were relegated to a prop engine plane that looked like it pre-dated the Wright brothers. Something along the lines of a well-worn commuter plane in need of an overdue inspection.

"I'm sure we're really fooling the bad guys with this one," Lisa muttered as she took care to avoid bumping her head on the low archway of the door to the passenger cabin.
"When I was told to fly under the radar, I took my orders seriously," Smith explained.
Vukoff remained silent but sat across from Lisa so that she could glower at her face to face. As glowers go, it was actually kind of pretty. In a dark and foreboding kind of way. But Lisa didn't have time for this right now. She was going home to see Trish and maybe this time she could stay. Even if she couldn't be with Trish, anything was better than being on the run. With snakes.

Mitch always thought that she would enjoy a life of relaxation. Sitting around. Doing nothing. So many hard working people asked for only this: a chance to just sit down for a spell after a long day at work. So, although being held hostage didn't qualify as relaxing, at least she was sitting. Jesus Herman had left her alone. Mitch had spent the first few minutes pondering over Herman's remarkable resemblance to Christ. Had he always looked that way? She wondered how his early school years had gone. Was he teased on the playground? Of course, he didn't have a beard when he was in elementary school. But did anyone notice the other resemblances? It was at this point in her ruminating that it dawned on Mitch how very soft and feminine the various depictions of Christ really were. The soft eyes. The peaceful expression. The wavy hair. Jesus certainly didn't look like a lumberjack. Unless there was some Gay

Guy Lumberjack calendar in print. Herman could be any month he wanted to be. Mitch was pretty sure that he wouldn't be particularly pleased at the prospect, so she would be sure not to mention it during their next conversation, whenever that was going to happen. It was a good thing that Mitch was a patient person. It came in handy when one found themselves on the hostage end of a situation. Like she said, she was sitting, resting, and not being harassed. At least, not yet.


Things couldn't be going much worse for those who weren't hostages. Death had come to the Goldstein family again. Even though Rose had survived one of the most death-filled wars in history, she hadn't gotten used to it. Good people never do. First a daughter. Now a husband. The grief was crushing her heart and closing in on her soul. The only thing that she had going for her was the incredible support from Rebecca and Trish. They sat on each side of her. Trish held her hand and Reb handed her tissues. Rose had wanted to see Max before they started the process of preparing for the transport to the funeral home, but when Rose had tried to stand up, her knees failed her. She had to sit back down to avoid falling. Reb suggested to the hospital staff that Rose might need a wheelchair to help her down the hallway, but Rose shook her head. "Just give me a moment," she said softly through tears. "I want to stand on my own two feet when I see him."
Reb nodded. Rose suddenly looked at her. "I'm so sorry. I didn't mean to be insensitive to you."
"You don't need to apologize," Reb answered calmly. "I'd feel the same way in your shoes."
Rose took a couple of deep breaths and then stood up. With Trish on one side and Reb on the other, they took the long, slow walk back to Max's room.

When they entered his room, it was quiet. The machines that had previously been beeping were turned off and relegated to one corner of the room. Although it would have sounded trite to say that Max looked peaceful in death, it was the best descriptor of him. He must've accepted death in the same calm way that he dealt with everything else in his life.

Rose approached the bed and leaned over to gently kiss Max one last time. She remained stoic, but both Trish and Reb had tears forming. Trish remembered how this had felt when Robbie had died. Giving someone a final kiss goodbye was one of the most traumatic experiences in one's lifetime. Reb's tears were a function of the uncertainty of the status of Mitch. It felt selfish but still very real. Rose didn't need to know that everyone was crying over their own situations. It would be comfort enough to know that they shared this most dreaded experience of death as a family. They weren't related by blood but it was still as close to family as one could get.

Trish held onto Rose until the man from the mortuary showed up. "Let's wait out in the hall," Reb advised. Although she had never witnessed it personally in other deaths, she surmised that the loading up of Max's dead body would be far too upsetting for Rose.

After Rose squeezed Max's unresponsive hand one last time, she followed Reb to the family waiting room. Silver was there guarding nothing but some trays of food that a liaison with the hospital had provided. Usually, hospital food didn't need to be guarded, as anyone who had been exposed to it could attest. However, this stuff actually looked and smelled edible. Unfortunately, nobody was hungry and their business at the hospital was coming to a close.

Out of respect for Rose, Reb asked as gently as she could, "Do you want Max interred before sundown?"

"I want everyone who wants to attend the funeral to have that opportunity," Rose answered calmly.
Reb silently considered the far-flung condition of the family. Mitch was missing, Mary was in protective custody, and Lisa was in transit between there and here. Getting everyone together would take a miracle. Reb prayed for that as they headed back to the house. When they arrived home, Trish went directly to check on Josh. He was awake and smiled at Trish when she picked him up. Josh was still too young to know how his life was so different from so many other babies. Since he had first been diagnosed in utero with TAR,

Thrombosis Absent Radii, it had been explained to Trish that the condition could literally be a matter of life and death. She preferred to think about the life part first and foremost. Allowing the specter of death to creep into her consciousness was counterproductive. When Lisa had been Josh's nanny, he had the best care any baby could hope for. Trish was a great mom, but having Lisa for help in child rearing had made the entire situation magical. In Lisa's absence, Trish worked hard to make Josh's life remarkable in every way. Right here and now, holding him and softly singing to him comforted both of them. It was as if by holding on to Josh, she was herself being held by invisible comforting arms.

Meanwhile, Rose and Reb and the Feds had settled in the kitchen to plan their next steps. There had been no word yet from Mitch or whoever may have abducted her. Every hour that passed created more anxiety for Reb. Everyone shared the concern, but while Reb hid it well, she was all knotted up on the inside.

"Maybe the kidnappers don't have the right phone number," Rose offered her logical explanation. "They have Mitch's phone. I'm sure they have it all figured out by now," Reb gave her logical reply. "So why don't they call and demand a ransom and get it over with?" Rose asked.

Reb had asked herself that same question numerous times, and every time she disliked the answer more.

"Why don't we talk about funeral plans?" Reb changed the subject as tactfully as possible.
"Again," Rose replied.
Reb looked puzzled.
"A person should only have to plan so many funerals in their lifetime," Rose said quietly.
"I'm here for you every step of the way," Reb assured her.
"And so am I," Silver voiced her support.

Rose then stood up and did what she always did for company. She started a pot of coffee and then began to assemble the ingredients for baking chocolate chip cookies. Reb and Silver exchanged knowing looks. No one would benefit from forcing Rose to discuss funeral plans. It would be so counterproductive at this point that it could delay the conversation indefinitely. So, Silver went to check on security issues, an exercise in futility but a welcome diversion. This left Reb to make small talk with the two agents stationed in the kitchen guarding the larder.

"Do you have a theory about the abduction?" was Reb's idea of small talk.

"Not until we have contact with anyone claiming responsibility," the senior agent in charge answered succinctly. As a group, they had all decided that this was now a kidnapping as opposed to Mitch just wandering away to feed pigeons. Even if she had felt uncomfortable with the idea of being called in to perform another miracle, she was responsible enough to not cause undue anxiety for everyone.

Reb pressed on, "But you must have some idea who's behind this." The agent in charge looked like he was developing a case of heartburn. It wasn't easy dealing with the relatives of a crime victim, and when one of them had a direct line to the President, it made the reflux even more pronounced.

"Our profiling team is working on several scenarios."

"Well, the scenario that needs the highest priority is the one where they have kidnapped Mitch to ransom her life in exchange for quashing my daughter's testimony." If Reb hadn't chosen politics as a career path, she would have had a good job opportunity at the FBI.

"We've been monitoring that possibility," Agent #2 piped up and was the immediate recipient of a withering glare from Agent #1. Agent #2 must've been tired of Agent #1's unwillingness to defend the agency's intelligence. They had thought of this motive right off the bat but weren't allowed to share it with the civilians. Now that Reb had forced the conversation, at least they could have a productive dialogue. Maybe even have a coherent reply ready when they were contacted.

"I want to talk to my daughter," Reb announced.

"We're working on it," Agent #2 said.

"What is there to work on?"

"She's still being debriefed."

"Well, debrief faster. I want her on a secure line in an hour or I'm calling the President. Again."

This remark held so much gravitas that it even caused Rose to stop making cookies in order to hear the next comment. After a brief moment of silence, Agent #1 took out his cell phone and made a call. The necessary arrangements would be made as quickly as possible to satisfy Reb's demand. Agent #1 disconnected the call, Reb nodded her head, and Rose went back to making cookies.

Mary was watching TV. It had been a welcome diversion, even if it was all just syndicated nonsense. Her only real contact with the outside world was Fawn. Mary had been fortunate to have Fawn visit today, so she really hadn't planned on another visit on the same day. Mary stood up and ran her fingers through her hair as Fawn walked in. She looked even more exhausted, if that was even possible. This did not bode well. "I didn't expect to see you again so soon," Mary bantered nervously.
"I have bad news," Fawn got straight to the point.
Mary fought the urge to turn this into a guessing game by asking questions. Fawn took advantage of both the silence and a chair. Mary sat down as well. Nobody should have to take bad news standing up.
"Max died."
Mary was not surprised. In fact, she had expected this outcome when she learned of his heart attack. "Can I send a sympathy card to Rose?"
"You can voice your condolences when we set up the phone call."
"You're setting up a phone call for that?" Mary sounded suspicious.
"Well, we are setting up a call anyway, so..."
"My mother demanded a phone call," Mary interrupted.
"The Senator felt that you and she needed to talk."
"Talk about what?"
"We're not quite sure," Fawn answered. Mary considered this to be a non-answer. She was certain that the agents knew the gist of what Reb intended to discuss but may not know how forcefully she would convey her thoughts. Reb was never good at following someone else's script. "Can you give me a hint so I'm not caught off guard?" Mary intoned.
"We are still waiting to be contacted by Mitch's abductors. We think that the Senator wishes to discuss terms with you and we would advise against that at this point."

"Terms of what?" Mary asked.

"Terms of negotiation."

"So you think that the kidnapping was something other than a simple ransom for money," Mary was putting the pieces all together, and it wasn't a pretty picture.

"That's what we're waiting to find out," Fawn nodded.

"How soon is the phone call?"

"Any minute now."

"That soon?"

"We didn't want to bother the President. *Again.*"

Mary noted the emphasis. "Isn't it comforting to know that you have the easy part of this situation?" she remarked.

"What do you mean?"

"The only person you have to worry about is me."

"You are the most important person in this entire situation. Please keep that in mind when you talk to your mother."

"You think that Mitch was abducted in order to silence my testimony." Mary summed it up succinctly.

"That's the theory."

"It's an impossible choice."

"You need to testify," Fawn said forcefully.

Mary resisted the urge to argue back immediately. She could easily see things from Fawn's point of view. They had all worked too hard and put in too many hours to abandon the trial. And knowing that they were dealing with terrorists made her testimony even more compelling to follow through on. There was a big difference between letting a criminal off the hook versus allowing an entire syndicate to continue without impunity. But it was Mitch they were talking about here. One of the finest human beings that Mary had ever met. Mary knew just how much her mother loved and depended on Mitch. But if the terrorists walked now, it would only be a matter of time before they would lash out again at someone close to Mary. Then, the logic of the entire situation dawned on Mary. It didn't matter whether or not the trial went forward. They would all continue to be in danger. So the impossible decision became easy. She would refuse to testify in exchange for the possibility of Mitch's release. And Fawn would just have to deal with it.

Fawn was well trained.  All she had to do was to watch Mary's facial expressions to know what she was thinking.  "You need to follow through with your testimony," she reiterated.

"What if they had your husband?" Mary asked Fawn.

"What do you mean?"

"What if the person they had kidnapped was your husband or child?  What would you ask me to do?  Would you still be so intent on my going ahead with the trial?"

"It's just standard procedure that we don't negotiate with terrorists."

"That's a handy answer when it's not *your* family that's involved."

Before Fawn could formulate a reply, there was a knock on the cell door.  Fawn went over and consulted with the official.  The phone call was set up and waiting.  Fawn motioned to Mary and they proceeded through the building to what looked like a bare-bones conference room.  The chairs in the room were filled with the team of lawyers that had spent hours preparing her.  They had planned this all out very carefully.  Mary would have to look them all in the eye if she had indeed decided not to continue.  She sat in a chair indicated for her by Fawn and then closed her eyes.  If it was going to be a stare down, she wanted to be rested and ready.

Meanwhile, the chairs around the table in Trish's kitchen were filling up as well.  Rose had baked a batch of cookies and the coffee pot was full.  Although the agents initially balked at the idea of having everyone present for the phone call, they were overruled by Reb.  The compromise was that no one would talk to Mary except her mother.  However, if Reb needed to consult with them, the wisdom was that they would all be on the same page.  When everyone was ready, the call was put through secure channels.

"Hello Mary," Reb said with as little emotion as possible.

"Hi, Mom.  It's really good to hear your voice.  How are you doing?  Have you had any contact with Mitch?  I was so sorry to hear about Max.  Can you give Rose my condolences?" Mary stopped long enough to draw a breath.  It was obvious that she was starved for human interaction.

"Honey, slow down a little.  Let's go through things one at a time.

Rose is here and she appreciates your condolences."

"I didn't know who was there with you. I'm surrounded by agents and lawyers."

"We have a couple of agents here as well. As wonderful as it would be to have a nice, long talk, we really need to stay on track here."

"Of course. I understand. I'm pleased that Rose could hear my words. I wish I could be there in person."

"That's not going to happen anytime soon," Reb stated firmly.

"What do you mean?" Mary asked.

"I mean that no matter what happens, you are going to stay there and do whatever is asked of you to complete the trial."

A moment of silence engulfed everyone. No one had expected Reb to take this stance. Especially Mary.

"I'm not sure that's the best course of action," Mary began making her argument to her mother.

"I'm sure it is," Reb reiterated.

"But what if it's a condition for Mitch's release?" Mary countered.

"Since we haven't heard anything yet, there's no negotiations."

"But what if there is?" Mary began to sound disappointed. She had been certain that her mother was going to demand her noncompliance with the trial proceedings, but quite the opposite was occurring. The small window of opportunity for going home was quickly closing.

"We can always revisit the topic, but even if it's one of their conditions, I don't trust them enough to fulfill their side of the bargain."

"So, you're not going to negotiate at all?"

"I'm hoping for another way out. Meanwhile, I want you to stay put and continue the preparations for the trial."

"And that's it? That's all you have to say?"

"I'm proud of you for doing the right thing, and Mitch would be proud of you, too. And when we get her back unharmed, we'll be at the trial."

"I hope you are right," Mary said unenthusiastically.

Reb nodded silently. She hoped she was right as well. "You'll be able to come home soon," she reassured Mary.

"I miss all of you so much," Mary replied but inwardly wondered to herself what there was to come home to anyway. No one was willing to talk about Lisa and the Feds would've frowned upon it anyway. They chatted for another minute or two about Max's pending funeral. When Rose had stated that she wanted everyone to be at the funeral who wished to attend, no one acknowledged Mary's complication at first. They couldn't wait forever.

"I'll be there in spirit since I can't be there in person," she said quietly.

Then, as quickly as the phone call had been put through, it was disconnected. It was as if there was an unspoken toll and the limit had been reached. Mary sat glumly for a minute. Fawn had no handy words of consolation, but she had the decency to sit with her and wait out the mood.

"At least you know what I'm going through," Mary finally said.

Fawn had expected any number of reactions from Mary. Empathy wasn't even on the list.

"I have a minute understanding," Fawn demurred.

"All that time, all those days when you were shadowing me in Colorado, you must have been missing your family something terrible."

"Yes, but I was able to go home and see them."

"You were?"

"I spent a lot of time on airplanes, but it all worked out."

"Isn't there a way that I could take just one brief trip back for the funeral?"

"The risk is too great. Even if we went out there with a contingent of security, we couldn't guarantee safe passage. Flying is inherently dangerous."

"You're afraid the plane would crash?"

"It's always in the realm of possibility."

"Well, if I can't be there in person, can you set up some sort of webcam or something?"

Fawn studied Mary for so long that it made her self-conscience.

"What?" Mary asked.

"Please forgive me for asking, but why is this funeral so important to you?"

"It's important because it's my family."

Fawn didn't need a genealogical chart to divine that Mary wasn't related to Max, so the answer stumped her.

"I know what you're thinking," Mary said. "Even though I'm not related by blood to Max and Rose, they are still very important to me. When you are gay, you tend to form family ties with people who are supportive of you. Sometimes, it's as close of a bond as you have with your biological family."

"Are you sure it isn't just Lisa who you want to see again?" Fawn probed.

Mary knew that sooner or later this question would crop up. Answering this inquiry would be as challenging as negotiating a mine field.

"I'm pretty sure that Lisa and I no longer have a future together."

"Why do you think that?"

"Because Lisa loves Trish and I love you."

Upon hearing this blunt declaration, Fawn broke off eye contact. They had danced around this issue during her undercover work. It had even been one of the tactical ploys of the operation. Fawn had executed the plan flawlessly and knew that eventually it would all come back to haunt her. It's a high price you pay for toying with someone's emotions.

"I'm sorry for what happened," Fawn said softly.

"I have only one question for you," Mary stated.

"Which is?"

"Why haven't you been reassigned to some other project?"

"This is my case."

"I'm sure they would give you some other secret mission if you let them know how awkward this is for you."

"I do what I'm told to do. I follow orders."

Mary thought this over and then smiled.

"What are you smiling about?"

"I think you stay on this case because you want to be around me."

"I think you're going to need larger living quarters to house your ego," Fawn retorted.

"Prove me wrong. Ask for reassignment."

"Do you really think it's a good idea to pick on the one person who has stuck by your side through this entire ordeal?"

"So, you want to be around me?"

"I like to finish what I start."

"It's been a long day. Go home to your husband and kids."

Fawn stood to go. "I'll be back."

"I'll be here," Mary answered.

Finally! They were on the ground. Lisa had never been so happy to be out of an airplane. Part of the reason was the company. Agent Vukoff had been hostile at best. Most of the reason, however, was that she was one step closer to being reunited with Trish. Due to the sensitive nature of her transport, Lisa was whisked from the plane to a waiting armored car. She had hoped for a limo and champagne, but the bullet-resistant SUV and the sparkling water would do nicely. She was stuck in the back seat with Vukoff while Smith rode shotgun, quite literally. At least they were getting closer to home and the butterflies were fluttering in her stomach.

"When we get there, you need to stay in the vehicle until we can ascertain the situation," Vukoff intoned, sounding more bored than dutiful.

"I'm not a child. I understand the gravity of the situation."

"No one has called you a child."

"It's your condescending tone of voice that gives you away."

"The average citizen does not know all the protocol involved with a security detail."

"I may not know all the protocol, but I've had quite the initiation. I've seen Agent Smith shoot a snake."

"You shot a snake?" Vukoff asked Smith.

"Right between the eyes," he nodded.

"Snake guts all over everywhere," Lisa elaborated happily.

Vukoff didn't have a ready reply.

"Do you think you could shoot a snake?" Lisa asked her.

"I'll shoot anything or anyone that gets between you and safety."

"Smith, you better call ahead and make sure everyone at Trish's house approach me with caution."

"Already done."

Lisa nodded. She didn't need to see agents talking into their shirt cuffs to know that all conceivable precautions were set in place. They zipped through traffic, shielded in the knowledge that there would be no speeding tickets issued and pulled into the driveway of Trish's mansion in record time from the airfield. Before the vehicle had even come to a complete stop, Vukoff was out of the SUV and walking quickly beside it. Agents were approaching from the house, ready to complete the transfer. They were all trained to recognize authentic gear and credentials. It was a delicate balance between taking appropriate time to secure the property versus delivering the package as quickly as possible. So although time seemed to stand still for Lisa, she was whisked inside the house thirty seconds after the SUV had come to a complete stop. Logically, Trish was the first person to greet Lisa. They barely looked at each other as Trish pulled her into an embrace.

"I can't believe you are here," Trish whispered.

"Neither can the Feds," Lisa whispered back.

Trish smiled. There was no time for tears. Everyone else wanted in on the reunion as well. Lisa hugged Rose next and then shook hands with Reb. They had never been on hugging terms.

"Will Mary be here?" Lisa asked.

"*She's* still in protective custody," Reb answered.

"Have you any news about Mitch?" Lisa hoped she was asking questions in the order that Reb would've approved of.

"Nothing yet."

"Well," Lisa exhaled, "Is there anything I can do to help?"

When no one else had a ready suggestion, Rose stepped forward.

"Would you mind checking on Josh to see if he needs anything?"

"I'd love to," Lisa smiled.

"I'll go with you," Trish offered.

Together, they went to Josh's room with Smith and Vukoff in tow. Rose then looked at Reb. "I think we need to start thinking about the funeral."

Reb nodded. They went to the kitchen to begin making phone calls. Silver stood guard over them and the cookies.

Once Trish realized that there would be no privacy with the new protection detail, she relaxed a little. She had been nervous at first about the prospect of seeing Lisa again, particularly with Reb on the premises. Having a chaperone served a helpful purpose rather than being an irritating intrusion.

Josh was awake. His eyes lit up when he saw Lisa. She scooped him up like she had never been away and cooed at him until he giggled. The tears that they hadn't had time for a few minutes ago now flowed freely. Emotional release was governed by its own mysterious timepiece that couldn't be ignored. Under the watchful eyes of Smith and Vukoff, they behaved like any other reunited family on the planet.


Mitch was sure she had dozed off. There wasn't much else to do. She had been left to her own devices in a small locked room with one chair. She had sat until she became weary of that. Then, she had decided to lie down on the cement floor. It was cold and hard, but at least she could stretch out. As a child, she had actually slept on the floor from time to time. Of course, she had a bed, but occasionally the floor seemed to be better for her back. So she would pretend to be camping and would often wake up feeling refreshed. Those were the days. And they were a long, long time ago Mitch mused as she tried to get comfortable on the concrete. It must've worked. She slept until she heard the door open. Not wanting to be caught off guard, she sat up. Standing would take a while due to her stiff leg muscles. Herman walked over to her and pulled her to her feet. It only took two seconds and then Mitch steadied herself against the wall. Her last exchange with Herman had been testy at best, so she waited for him to speak.
"I need your cooperation," he said.
"I need a bathroom break," Mitch countered.
Herman nodded. This request was not unexpected.
"Follow me."
They walked single file out of the room. The hallway was narrow and dimly lit. Even if Mitch had decided to make a run for it, she wouldn't know which way to go. Before they had taken three steps, a second guard came up on Mitch's flank. Thankfully, the bathroom was close. Her escorts were thoughtful enough to leave her alone in the room. Obviously, there was no chance for escape. Due to the condition of the commode, Mitch made quick work of things and reappeared outside of the room to rejoin her escorts. They continued to walk in the opposite direction of her holding cell. Apparently, it was time for her cooperation. They walked into a small room with a table, two chairs and a phone. Not the most sophisticated set up.
"Sit down," Herman directed.
Mitch obeyed.
"We're going to call your loved ones and begin negotiations."
"What are your demands going to be?"
"Just be quiet and talk only when I tell you to talk and say only what

63

I tell you to say."

Herman dialed the phone, knowing that whoever picked up would have homeland security on the tap.

"Hello," a feminine voice came on the line. Mitch recognized Trish's voice.

"I have your friend Mitch. Let me talk to the Senator."

There was a pause and then Reb came on the line, "This is Senator Fairbanks."

"You need to convince your daughter to not testify."

"That's not going to happen."

Herman frowned. He might have thought that this was going to be the easy part.

"You will change your mind," he stated firmly.

"No, I won't," Reb replied forcefully.

Realizing the futility of this discussion, he directed his attention to Mitch. "You are going to get on this phone and beg for your life."

Mitch took a deep breath and then echoed Reb's words. "That's not going to happen either."

"I could force you to do so."

"I imagine you could, but it won't make any difference. They won't negotiate with terrorists."

"We are not terrorists!"

"Well then, the court case should go very well for you."

Herman disconnected the call. Mitch watched him for a sign. She didn't want to trigger his anger, but her curiosity got the best of her. "How did you know that it wasn't Rebecca who answered the phone?"

Herman made eye contact. Mitch could tell he was pondering his answer carefully. "It was a guess."

"No, it wasn't," Mitch said. She was walking a fine line here and didn't want to be too argumentative. Herman gave a signal to the guard standing just outside the door and they all set off down the hall. They weren't going back to the cell so Mitch figured they were heading to some unpleasant place for further interrogation. They reached what appeared to be an outside door. Once again, a hood was placed over her head and she was handcuffed. She heard the door open and she was loaded into some sort of vehicle. She was sitting up, so it was most likely a white panel van. They made sure she was buckled in before they took off for parts unknown. At first, the road was bumpy but then the ride smoothed out. They were on a highway going somewhere fast so Mitch closed her eyes and used her time wisely. She slept.

Chapter 4

When Lisa had overheard the conversation between Rebecca and the kidnappers, it was a testament to her continuing maturity that she didn't have a temper fit then and there. The fact that the call was terminated so quickly unsettled everyone but the Feds. They were used to volatile negotiations.

"They'll call back," the senior agent spoke calmly.

"How can you be so sure?" Lisa asked immediately.

Since she had basically just arrived on scene, she was summarily ignored. Trish gently pulled her into the family room and sat with her on the couch.

"Do they even have a plan for getting Mitch back?"

"I think they are playing hardball."

"They should just do whatever it takes to get Mitch back safe and sound, particularly since it is as easy as pulling Mary from the trial."

"If Mary doesn't testify, they all walk."

"Since some of them are on the loose right now, I don't see the point of the trial at all. Maybe some go to prison, but it won't stop the others."

"I guess they think that prison will be a deterrent."

"Who wants to tell them that they are wrong?"

"I'm not sure it would do any good."

"We have them outnumbered. We don't have to play host to the Feds. I think I can change Rebecca's mind if I can get time alone with her."

"The problem with this idea is that if we kick the Feds out of the process, we'll all be in danger."

"How did Mitch get abducted in the first place?"

"That was my fault. I left her alone for two minutes at the hospital."

"Who would've thought that they would be lying in wait at a hospital?"

"I still should've been more careful."

"That's my point. Whether Mary testifies or not, we're always going to be in the crosshairs of this group. I don't think it's worth sacrificing Mitch's life in exchange for a false sense of security."

Trish thought about everything Lisa said. "Let's give them one more

phone call to make a deal. I think they deserve one more try."
Lisa didn't look happy, but she remained silent. Rose appeared at
the doorway. "I'm ready," she said calmly.
Trish nodded. "Let's have Silver go with us."
"I'll go as well," Lisa offered.
"I'm sure that we're going to have Agents Smith and Vukoff
accompany us as well. Do you think you'll be okay with that?"
"I'll be fine. I don't think I can sit around here and wait for the
phone to ring."

After checking in with everyone and notifying the mortuary of their
impending arrival, they headed out. Normally, any funeral provider
would've asked for more time, but this was a unique circumstance.
It wasn't every day that a service needed a level of security just
below a Presidential visit. Rose didn't care about any of that. She
simply wanted to arrange a funeral befitting her wonderful late
husband.

When Robbie had died, Trish remembered very little of this process.
The crushing grief following Robbie's suicide left everything a blur
for weeks. Although death is always a shock, Rose was a little more
prepared, due to Max's age and prior heart troubles. They had
already discussed funeral plans. Max had insisted on this so that
Rose wouldn't be overwhelmed when the time came.

They pulled up to Kaminsky's, the most renowned Jewish funeral
provider in Denver. Smith had alerted the local police department of
the security precautions. Although separate law enforcement
agencies are often portrayed as oil and water where cooperation is
concerned, between them, they ensured the safety of their charges.
Rose, with Trish on one side and Lisa on the other, walked into the
opulent office of David Meyer, the funeral director. Silver stood by
the doorway with Smith and Vukoff until Rose said, "Please sit with
us."
"Thank you," Silver was doing her best to remain stoic. It wasn't
easy.
David shook hands all around before sitting behind his polished
wood desk.
"I'm so sorry for your loss," he began solemnly. Even though he

must say these words dozens of times a week, he sounded genuine. Rose nodded her thanks. "Max wanted a simple funeral," she said. "Of course," David nodded back.

Usually that translated into a pine box sendoff.

"However, I want it to be a nice funeral," Rose added.

"We will arrange whatever you want," David agreed.

He remembered the last time the Goldstein family had called upon his services. They knew how to plan a nice funeral. Spared no expense, in fact. Funeral planning was both an art and a challenge. If you went out on the Internet and searched for wedding plans, the resources seemed infinite. There were magazines and books dedicated to the subject. There were sections in department stores and indeed entire stores that carried attire for every wedding theme a person could conceive. Wedding consultants were available to tend to every detail. No such thing existed for funerals. It made sense, of course. Marriages were planned for. Death wasn't. Death arrived on its own timetable and everyone had to work around it. And as with every other milestone in life, paperwork was involved. It was tedious but necessary. The main purpose of the meeting was to agree to the general form of the services involved, to arrange for death certificates and then to select a casket. Casket rooms could be very intimidating. They were cleverly designed for the commercial purpose of highlighting the most expensive caskets in the most favorable places in the showroom. Rose, being a wise shopper, wasn't taken in by this tactic. She took her time and looked at every casket in the place.

"Do you have anything in red?" she asked.

"The mahogany casket is red," David answered.

"I was thinking more along the lines of fire engine red."

"We don't have any in stock, but I can order one."

"Can I see a picture of it?"

"I have a catalogue in the office."

They all went back to the office and sat back down.

Trish said to Rose, "Red is an interesting color choice."

"It was Max's favorite," Rose said.

Trish thought about this. She had never seen Max wear anything red or have any household furniture or items that were red. Another more logical idea came to her.

"Rose, don't you think that it's going to take a while for the special order casket?"

"It will ship very quickly," David interjected.

"Did I mention that I also wanted gold hardware on it?" Rose answered them both.

"The hardware is gold," David checked the picture in the catalogue.

"I meant solid gold," Rose explained.

"You want a fire-engine red casket with solid gold hardware?" David checked to make sure he understood.

"Do they make something like that?" Rose asked calmly.

"Not usually, but if that's what you want, I'll make a phone call."

Trish felt compelled to talk to Rose in private. "Can we talk alone for a moment?" she asked the entire group. Everyone but Trish and Rose left the office. It gave them some much-needed breathing room.

"Rose, you know I don't mind at all if you want to buy this red and gold casket. Money is no object."

Rose nodded. She seemed so serene.

"But I just want to know if you are doing this to delay the funeral."

"It's like I said before, I want everyone to be able to attend."

"And so you want to buy some time to make that happen by ordering a special casket?"

"I know it's a lot of money."

"I'd buy a solid gold casket if that's what you want, but wouldn't it be easier if we just delayed the funeral until things settled down a bit?"

"I guess we could do that," Rose agreed.

"It's done all the time."

"I just don't want to disappoint Mr. Meyer by downsizing his profit margin."

"Here's what I would do-let's go ahead and get the red casket without the gold hardware and then make a donation to the funeral home."

"I guess there's no practical value in burying all that money."

"I agree. Let's ask David and the group to come back in and get everything in order."

When they explained their revised decision to David, he looked relieved. Not only was the money going to be used in a better way, but it saved him a lot of time and effort with the ordering process.

He hadn't come up with a plan for explaining everything in a phone call to the casket company and now he didn't need to.

"How long may we postpone the funeral?" Rose got around to asking the question that distressed her the most.

"Usually, a funeral can be delayed ten days to two weeks if the deceased is embalmed. Do you wish to have a viewing?"

"Do you think we want a viewing?" Rose turned the question over to Trish.

Trish didn't know how to tactfully answer the question. She wasn't fond of viewing dead bodies and frankly didn't know anyone who would attend the viewing besides family. And they all knew what he looked like. However, if they put a detailed obituary in the newspaper, who knows who might show up. Rose noticed the long pause. "Perhaps we don't need a viewing," she said thoughtfully.

"How many people are we expecting at the funeral?" Trish asked delicately.

"Not many, I suppose..." Rose trailed off. Outliving one's friends was a painful consequence of growing older.

"Let's put a proper obituary in the paper and plan to have the funeral in two weeks."

This course of action met with approval all around. David gave them a list of things to do and decide upon. They left the mortuary under the same umbrella of protection and had a somber ride home.


Reb was never good at waiting patiently. When the phone call had been abruptly terminated, she was angry that she hadn't been able to talk with Mitch.

"We can't be certain that they even have her," she had stated to the agents at the table.

"That will be our top priority when he calls back, but we need to be very cautious how we approach the demand."

"What do you mean?" Reb asked warily.

The agent masked a sigh. His job wasn't nearly as glamorous as it was portrayed on TV. There was always reams of paperwork to complete and only once in a while a plum assignment came along. This assignment had all the ear markings of an advancement possibility if he could just get through it without perturbing the Ex-Senator. So, how to put this succinctly?

"I wouldn't want to receive a special delivery box containing severed fingers for fingerprint analysis."

Reb didn't flinch. She knew what they were up against.

"All I would need to do is to hear her voice over the phone. Let's not get to the digit-severing phase by being stubborn."

"That is why we are trained negotiators. We do our best to keep personalities and emotions out of the process."

"So all we need now is for the phone to ring."

As if on command, Reb's phone lit up and buzzed. It was a different number than the one they had used to call Trish's home phone, which was no surprise. They had assumed from the start that several cell phones would be used and discarded during the ordeal. It seemed also that the abductors had decided to go directly through Reb this time. Maybe they were going to try every number in Mitch's cell phone until they got what they wanted? Foregoing all pleasantries, Reb went directly to the point. "I want to talk to Mitch Tanner."

There was a bit of hesitation on the line. Finally, the caller said, "So do I."

This remark irritated Reb. If they were going to play games, then things could go downhill fast.

"And Rebecca Fairbanks," the caller added.

"You are talking to Rebecca Fairbanks."

"Oh good. We are trying to reach Rebecca Fairbanks and Mitch Tanner."

"Who is this?" Reb was confused.

"This is Kansas Central Hospital."

"And why are you calling?"

"We wanted you to have an update on your niece, Miranda Knight."

Reb switched emotional gears instantly. In all the confusion of Max's death and Mitch's abduction, she had neglected to keep in close touch with Miranda and the upcoming birth of the baby. Reb knew that the timing wasn't right. The baby wasn't due yet. Something was wrong and this was the official notice. She steeled herself for bad news.

"Do you need me to come to the hospital?" Reb got to the point quickly.

"That would be best."

"What has transpired?"

"There's been a complication."

"What kind of complication?"

"How soon can you get here?"

Although Reb was normally irked when someone answered a question with another question, she held her temper in check. She looked at the agents watching her intently. They had only heard her side of the remarks and would have no clue what was transpiring.

"I can be on a flight within the hour."

"Let us know when you have arrived. We can arrange for transportation to the hospital."

"That won't be necessary," Reb assured them. She knew that the Feds would take care of that.

She disconnected the call and took a deep breath. This explanation was going to take a lot of oxygen.

"I'm going to need a flight to Kansas to visit my niece, Miranda." The agents looked at each other.

"Within the hour," Reb added.

It was their turn to take a deep breath. But instead of arguing with her, something that Reb truly expected, they simply nodded.

"We'll arrange for the flight and ground transportation. And, of course, a protection detail. But first we are going to contact the hospital to make sure it was they who called you in the first place." Reb nodded. As much as she wanted to trust people, it would be foolish to walk right into a trap. The agent in charge started making phone calls. Whatever was going on a Kansas Central Hospital would be verified or disproved in a matter of minutes. Agents were dispatched to the facility in order to investigate the situation and secure the premises. When their first report came through, the agent took action. He now knew more than Reb did about the circumstances. A private flight was arranged and Reb prepared for the trip. Rose was concerned that she was going alone.

"One of us should go with you," she said.

Reb thought this over. In fact, she pondered it for so long that Lisa finally volunteered herself.

"I'll go grab what little I packed," she said.

Reb opened her mouth to object and then closed it. There was no other logical alternative. Trish, Rose and Silver needed to stay in Colorado to plan the funeral and take care of Josh. Lisa was expendable. So although Reb would've preferred to go by herself, she acquiesced to Rose's suggestion.

"Hurry up then," Reb said to Lisa.

Lisa had such few scant items that everything fit into her small handbag. "I'm ready when you are."

Rose smiled. Trish frowned. Silver just shook her head back and forth. Before they headed out, Trish gave Lisa a quick hug. "You take care of yourself," she whispered in her ear.

"I will," Lisa whispered back.

And then, they were gone. Whisked out the door by Smith and Vukoff and still another security detail. They were in the back seats of an SUV and halfway to the airport before they exchanged words.

"I suppose you are going to need to go clothes shopping when we get there," Reb groused.

"A change of underwear might come in handy when we settle in," Lisa answered. She seemed content, almost happy, to be making this journey. Reb felt sheepish.

"I'm sorry I snapped at you."

"It's okay. You are under a lot of pressure right now. If I were you, I'd be screaming into a pillow about now."

"As soon as I get my hands on one, I may just start doing precisely that."

"If the pillows at the hotel aren't suitable, we can go pillow shopping as well," Lisa suggested kindly.

Reb nodded. If she said much more, she knew she would start to cry and she didn't want to do that in front of Lisa. And the Feds.


Mitch was once again in a locked room. She had no idea how far they had traveled from the previous location since she had slept through the trip. This room was a slight upgrade from her previous holding cell. It had a thin mattress on a slab of concrete. It was like the cell she had been in during her Paris detention.

This made Mitch feel retrospective. She was neither young nor old, yet she had been in jails and cells enough for one lifetime. She had never been in jail until she had won the lottery and met Reb. Hence her retrospection. If she had remained poor and unknown, she might never have ended up this way. She would've worked day in and day out and stayed out of trouble. Of course, money had opened up so many new vistas for her, but at what price? If she were to die at the hands of terrorists due to her stubbornness, then so be it. Perhaps their plan was to starve her to death. There had been no sustenance offered so far and no promise of such. She had worried that Reb would be anxious about all that had transpired until she heard that she wasn't willing to negotiate. This actually heartened Mitch. It reassured her that Reb was staying strong and expecting Mitch to figure a way out of her predicament by herself. Mitch was actually smiling when Herman returned.

"You seem amused," he said flatly.

"I'm just trying to make the best of a bad situation," she replied calmly.

"I have a feeling that you are going to be here awhile."

"You don't seem to be a man who has a lot of feelings," Mitch remarked bravely, "so you must have some facts to back up your statement."

"There has been another development."

Mitch had been kept in the dark about all developments so far. She assumed that developments were just piling up at this point. One on top of another.

"Would it help you to let me know what's going on?" Mitch framed her question cleverly.

"Mr. Goldstein is dead," he answered.

Mitch nodded. She had assumed as much. "I'm sorry to hear that. I had gone to the hospital to see him. People hoped that I could help him, but I never got a chance to visit his room."

"You are not a doctor."

"No."

"Then why did people think you could help?"

Mitch sighed. Why did she even bring this up? She didn't enjoy talking about it so it must be happening for a reason.

"Some people think that I can heal people just by touching them or a piece of their clothing or just by being in close proximity to them." Herman was taking all this in with rapt attention. It was quite eerie, really.

"Is that true?" he asked.

"I don't think I'm a healer. I can't help what other people believe about me."

74

"There's been another development as well," Herman changed subjects abruptly.

Mitch hoped that one of these developments would sooner or later involve a dinner tray.

"The Senator has completely walked out of the negotiations for your release."

"That doesn't surprise me. She doesn't much like not being in total control of every situation."

Herman studied Mitch as if his eyes were lie detectors and he could ferret out any fib just by staring at her. Mitch just sat there, following a strong intuition to remain silent. Then he took a step toward the door. "You must be hungry," he remarked.

"That's what happens when you sign up for the Continental Plan." Herman left without further comment. Two minutes later, there was a knock at the door. It was another minion delivering what looked suspiciously like an MRE. Beef stew ala military cuisine. At this point, cardboard would have tasted good. She ate slowly, resisting the urge to wolf down her food. It wasn't bad for rations. The water they provided in a paper cup tasted like something out of a tap, but she drank it down as well. Then she propped herself up on her bunk and kept her mind busy wondering how things were really going for Reb, Trish and Rose. If indeed Reb had removed herself from the negotiations, Mitch knew there had to be a good reason. And then it dawned on her what could possibly be the reason for that. Miranda. If anyone could handle three crises at once, it would be Reb. Mitch only hoped that she had some support that wasn't wearing a badge.


Lisa could be good company when she wanted to be. And now seemed as good a time as any to be pleasant if it killed her. Why should it make any difference that they had both slept with Mitch?

"So, tell me anything that you think would be important for me to know about this situation with Miranda?" Lisa asked her carefully-thought-out inquiry. Lawyers asked less intricate questions in court.

"The hospital staff wasn't very forthcoming during their phone call," Reb offered little in the way of an answer.

"Give me the history then," Lisa pursued.

"What exactly do you want to know?" Reb played for time. She felt that just because Lisa had volunteered to come along, it didn't entitle her to know everything.

"Math never was my strong suit, but isn't it a little early for the baby's birth."

Reb, too, had done the math and it was early. Uncomfortably early. It wasn't that long ago that Mitch and Rebecca had gone baby-furniture shopping in France with nothing to show for it but a lot of problems with the French police. Although they had tracked Miranda's pregnancy, they had done little more to plan for the big day. Mostly because they weren't assured that when all was said and done, that they would be granted custody. Their biggest unspoken fear was that Miranda would change her mind and attempt to raise the baby in prison. Lost in thought, Reb didn't speak again until they boarded the private jet bound for Kansas.

"Yes, it is early," Reb finally said to Lisa once they were off the ground.

"Did the hospital say that the baby had been born?"

"No."

"So we really don't know anything for sure."

"We will know soon enough. This is a short flight," Reb remarked. It was one thing to be thankful for. She didn't feel like engaging Lisa in small talk for hours on end. Reb closed her eyes and pretended to sleep. Fatigue caught up with her and pretend became reality. It was only when the plane landed that Reb woke up. Her sleep had been so deep that it felt jarring to come back to reality. She felt cranky and awkward.

"Did I snore?"

"Not at all," Lisa lied. No use telling the truth in this regard. No one wants to hear that they sound like a wood chipper when they are getting their beauty sleep.

"When we get inside the airport, can you take me to the ladies room?"

"Of course. I was planning to make a visit myself," Lisa smiled.

"I suppose the Feds are going to clear the place out just for us."

"I hope no one will be terribly inconvenienced."

Once off the plane, they were whisked like rock stars to the restroom and guarded like royalty until they had finished freshening up. Reb took time to splash water on her face and run a brush through her hair. Despite the stress, she looked beautiful. Lisa took note of this and remarked as much, "You look great."

Reb thought of several snarky replies, of which Lisa deserved none. "So do you," she said kindly.

Anyone who would lie to your face about snoring deserved a break.

People stared at them as they and their entourage walked through the terminal to their awaiting vehicles. They were soon speeding, sirens and all, to the hospital faster than any ambulance dared.

"You're probably used to this, being an ex-Senator and all, but I'm feeling a little discombobulated," Lisa confessed to Reb.

Internally, Reb always bristled when she heard the term "ex-Senator." Lisa probably didn't know this or do it on purpose, so Reb gave her a pass.

"I was rarely driven around Washington D.C. at breakneck speeds. I'm a bit rattled as well."

"Hopefully, things will calm down once we get to the hospital."

Reb didn't say it out loud, but she seriously doubted it. Things rarely improved in a hospital setting.

Once they arrived, they were shown to the administrator's office. The gentleman came forward from behind his desk to greet them. His desk nameplate read Paul Seibert.

"Senator Fairbanks, it's an honor to meet you," he extended his thick, meaty hand. Reb took it gingerly. He looked like a man who didn't know his own strength where handshakes were concerned.

"Allow me to introduce my chief of staff, Dr. Bagley."

Dr. Bagley had the more typical hand structure of a surgeon: long fingers and a smooth palm.

"Hello Senator," he said through a tight-lipped smile.

Reb took his hand politely but then quickly shifted her attention back to Mr. Seibert.

"What can you tell me?" Reb launched into her questions. No one bothered to introduce Lisa to anyone so she sat down to listen. Normally, she would've been petulant, but these weren't normal circumstances.

"Your niece, Miranda Knight, has given premature birth to her baby."

"What is her condition?"

Administrator Seibert looked at Dr. Bagley. They must have rehearsed this presentation in anticipation of Reb's reputation as a tough questioner.

77

"Ms. Knight is on life support," the doctor answered quickly, like he had other more important things to be doing than standing around this office. Reb heard his attitude loud and clear.

"How did that happen?" Reb now focused her laser-like attention on the doctor.

Dr. Bagley looked at his boss. This wasn't going to go nearly as well as they had hoped.

"She went into cardiac arrest," Seibert answered.

"How does a healthy young woman go into cardiac arrest?" Reb interjected quickly, before they could start up with a lot of medical mumbo jumbo.

The silence stretched like taffy.

"Ms. Knight wasn't healthy," Dr. Bagley answered after the long pause. It was like testimony. The less said the better.

"I realize that prison life doesn't provide for the healthiest of existences, but maybe you could narrow down the possibilities for me," Reb honed her line of questioning.

"She was underweight," the doctor said cautiously.

"How underweight?" Reb's anger was just under the surface. Part of her anger was with these two men, but part of it was with herself as well.

"She was anorexic," Seibert answered.

"So, let me understand this correctly," Reb was ready to sum up the problem, "You had an anorexic, pregnant woman go into cardiac arrest after giving birth to a premature baby?"

"Actually, it was the other way around. She went into cardiac arrest first. We were lucky to have saved the baby."

Reb became quiet. Very quiet. Everyone waited out of respect for her to speak again. Either that or they knew that a lawsuit was *this* close to being filed.

"I'd like to see both of them," Reb finally said.

"Of course," Mr. Seibert agreed. He rose from his over-padded executive chair and held the door for everyone. Reb was wondering why the hospital lawyer wasn't in on this meeting and tour.

The first stop on the sojourn was Miranda's room. Apparently they wanted to get the worst of it over first. As Reb approached the bed, it was obvious to anyone with two working eyes in their head that Miranda was pathetically thin. Her facial features were sunken and the machines that surrounded her dwarfed her body. She was literally skin and bones.

"What is her prognosis?" Reb asked.

"She is in critical condition," the doctor answered bluntly.

Reb only nodded. After a somber moment, they headed down a hallway to the critical care unit for infants. Until they could stabilize the baby's condition, it would need to stay in isolation. As they peered through the glass divider, Reb and Lisa allowed themselves a smile. For such a small being, he was handsome. A baby boy all wrapped up in a blue blanket.

"He has your strong chin," Lisa said to Reb.

Reb didn't say it, but she appreciated Lisa's observation.

"Let's go," Reb directed everyone.

"Where to?" Lisa asked.

"We will need a hotel room close by. Who wants to make the arrangements?"

Their protection detail started talking into their shirt cuffs again. In twelve minutes, they were back in the car and heading for a hotel known for its exclusive suites. If Reb, Lisa and their entourage wanted to set up camp, they would need a lot of breathing space. Breathing space translated into absolute luxury. They were driven into a back garage entrance of the hotel and taken to an elevator that went up to an entire floor of suites. Too bad they had packed light. There were closets and bureaus and dressers enough to hold more clothes than Lisa had owned in her entire life. And that was saying something!

"I suppose you'll really want to go shopping now," Reb said to Lisa as they toured their rooms.

"If it's going to be a long stay, I may need a few incidentals."

Reb didn't want to know if that was a code word for a budget-busting shopping spree, but if Lisa needed anything, she would try and be patient with her.

Meanwhile, the agents in charge, including Smith and Vukoff, were settling in as well. They rarely had the opportunity to bask in this level of luxury. However, they were ready for business as usual within minutes. It was still a waiting game as far as further communications with Mitch or her abductors. But if you had to wait, this was a great place to do so.

"At the risk of tying up the phone, I'm contemplating calling the lawyer," Reb said to Lisa.

Lisa tried to look thoughtful, mostly to hide her surprise that Reb was actually confiding in her.

"You have something to say?" Reb asked pointedly.

"You've become a mother today and all you can think about is calling your lawyer?" Lisa spoke her mind.

This comment brought Reb up short. "First of all, technically I haven't become a mother again."

"We're going to argue technicalities? Is that what you're going to hide behind?"

"What do you think I'm hiding?"

"A lot of emotions for starters."

"That's pretty rich for someone who specializes in a vast amount of glib in the majority of her conversations."

"I'll own up to being glib if you'll admit that you are stonewalling just a bit concerning what you are going through right now."

"I'm going through so much right now that I'm going to need a lawyer to sort it all out. It isn't going to do anybody any good for me to fall to pieces right now."

"You think that if you show any emotion, that you will fall apart?"

"It's a distinct possibility."

Lisa studied Reb for a brief moment. "Okay. Give your lawyer a call, but by all means, feel free to talk to me about anything at all. Right after I take the hottest bath in the history of hot baths."

"Save some hot water for the rest of us," Reb made it sound like they were back on the farm with an undersized water heater. Lisa only smiled and left the room.

Reb turned to the agents, all of whom were watching the retreating Lisa.

"If anyone has a moment, could one of you bring me my phone?" Reluctantly, the junior member of the agent group fetched the phone for Reb. She could have easily gotten it for herself, but that wasn't the point. Not everyone had their lawyer on speed dial. Reb wasn't everyone.

It took a few minutes to explain everything that had transpired in the last couple of days to the family lawyer. He agreed to catch a chartered flight to meet with her. This was going to be pricey, but Reb figured that where the newest addition to the family was concerned, no expense was too great. And maybe he could weigh in on Mitch's situation as well.

Mitch had rested for as long as it suited her. She was grateful that she had a bunk off the floor and one meal under her belt. Although kidnapping stories weren't the usual genre that Mitch read, she still had a working knowledge of how things like this worked. Victims were usually terrified after physical or emotional abuse. There were tearful pleadings over the phone or on some closed-circuit hookup. Mitch hadn't been exposed to any of this so far. It hadn't bothered Mitch at all that Reb refused to negotiate with Herman. Most other people might have felt betrayed, but Mitch trusted Reb's instinct. Her main concern right now was how to get more information about Miranda from Herman without appearing too anxious about it. She didn't want to accidently give him any more leverage over the latest development. Unexpectedly, there was a knock on the door.

"Come in," Mitch said.

Herman hulked into her cell. Mitch waited to be spoken to lest she irritate him.

"What would you offer for your safe release?"

The question so surprised Mitch that she inadvertently found herself shaking her head. This signaled to him that she was unwilling to negotiate with him as well.

"You aren't willing to save yourself?" he asked for confirmation.

"I suppose I could give you some cash. Goodness knows it seems to bring me nothing but trouble. But aren't you giving up a little too soon on your main objective?" Mitch simply couldn't keep quiet. This wasn't going at all like in the movies and for some reason, it irked her.

"How much cash?"

"I'm not naming a figure until you tell me what's really going on," Mitch forged ahead with her plan. If he wanted money, he would need to offer more than her release in return right this minute.

"My offer is off the table," he retorted.

"Then so is mine," Mitch remarked back.

They sounded more like a bickering married couple than a hostage situation.

"You are forgetting who you are dealing with," he said curtly.

"I really don't think so," Mitch assured him, albeit cautiously.

"You are becoming less useful every minute."

81

"That's not the case. Otherwise, I would be dead by now. You need me alive for a reason. I just haven't figured it all out yet. But I will," Mitch decided to speak her mind now, while she had the opportunity.

Herman stood there for so long that they both wished he would've brought a chair with him.

"It is my understanding that you were planning on adopting a child," he finally got to the point.

Mitch nodded. They were communicating in fits and starts, but it was better than nothing. Her strategy was beginning to pay off.

"You wouldn't want any circumstance to endanger that process." When Herman spoke this way, it sounded more like a statement than a question.

"What are you proposing?" Mitch asked.

"I'm simply suggesting that negotiating your release just became more important for your side."

"You think that they require my physical presence at the adoption agency?"

"I think it will improve the Senator's chances of gaining custody," Herman stated his point clearly.

"I don't think it matters one way or the other. If you kill me, the Senator would most likely get the sympathy vote."

"Not if she refuses to negotiate for your release. She will appear ruthless and hard hearted. And if you don't negotiate for your own release, then you just look stupid and foolish."

Mitch thought this over for so long that Herman began to shift his weight from foot to foot. It was a cue that he was quickly approaching the end of his patience.

"I know only one thing," Mitch finally spoke. "I know that no matter what happens, people will realize that I was brave and you were a terrorist. Unless you are willing to alter that reality."

This wasn't the answer that Herman had hoped to hear. A lesser terrorist would've snapped, but Herman was a professional.

"I'm going to allow you the opportunity to give this more consideration," Herman announced as he walked over to the door.

Mitch watched him leave without further comment. Admire would have been too strong a word, but Mitch marveled at how Herman was comporting himself. Whatever was going on, it must be important to keep her healthy and unhurt. In return for this cautious treatment, Mitch decided to follow his advice and do some more thinking. After all, there was nothing else to do.


Lisa was grateful for the luxury of not only having a wonderful bath, but also for the bathrobe furnished by the hotel. It wasn't like she hadn't had a shower or bath in forever, but this opportunity to settle in felt good. The robe provided ample coverage just in case the agents were guarding the bathroom door. The only person waiting for her was Rebecca.

"Is there any news?" Lisa asked.

"The lawyer is in the air. I was hoping to freshen up before he arrives."

"Will you need help with that?" Lisa heard the hesitation in her voice and knew she hadn't been successful in masking it.

"I'm able to take a shower all by myself," Reb sounded matter-of-fact.

"Can I bring you some clothes?" Lisa struggled to find ways to be helpful. She wanted Mitch to be proud of her efforts. It all seemed a little ridiculous. If everything worked out as planned, and Mitch was brought home to a hero's welcome, probably the last thing she would want to hear was how Lisa helped out like some ill-prepared valet. Nobody gets accolades for bringing towels to the freshly-bathed celebrities.

"That would be nice," Reb broke through Lisa's reverie.

"What?"

"I have put out on the bed what I plan to wear."

"Of course," Lisa nodded.

This was just one of the many differences between Reb and Lisa. Reb was always prepared and polished. Lisa wondered what it would be like to live with someone like that. She also wondered how Mitch felt about it. When she and Lisa were together, having everything just so didn't seem to matter all that much to either of them. They were young and in love and even though she had absconded with Mitch's life savings when she left, Lisa had still loved Mitch very deeply. And it hadn't depended on money or status or having your wardrobe all laid out on the bed. They had made much better use of a bed with their raw yet tender affair of the heart. It was boisterous and buoyant, feeling like they were the only two people in love in the entire universe.

"Is there another robe?" Reb's voice interrupted Lisa's mental stroll down memory lane.

"Another robe?" Lisa stalled for time to avoid seeming distracted by sensual recollections of Mitch.

"Are there two robes or will we need to share the one you are currently wearing?" Reb asked pointedly.

"Let me check," Lisa offered.

Sure enough, there were spare robes. These fancy hotels thought of everything.

"You're all set," Lisa said, a bit too happily. All this pleasantry was beginning to wear on her.

"Are you going to be like this the entire time we are here?" Reb asked out of the blue.

"Be like what?"

"Be like *fake*."

"I'm a nice person. I'm trying to be nice to you."

"What were you thinking about a moment ago?"

"I was thinking how happy I am that you and I don't need to share a robe."

"Before that," Reb pushed.

Lisa hesitated. It was enough of a pause for Reb. "No more glib answers. What's really on your mind?"

"I was remembering how happy Mitch and I used to be together," Lisa answered honestly.

"Oh really?" Reb shot back. It was her way of deflecting the topic.

"Yes, really."

"Before you took off with her life savings and broke her heart."

"Everyone thinks that that's the defining element of the entire relationship," Lisa shot back.

"It is for Mitch," Reb answered smoothly.

"Well, if I was Mitch, I wouldn't be telling you anything else either," Lisa said.

"Are you suggesting that Mitch hasn't been forthcoming with me?"

"I'm practically guaranteeing it," Lisa responded.

Reb was now seriously beginning to question the wisdom of allowing Lisa to tag along.

"If you wish to rewrite the history of your relationship with Mitch, please do so in your own mind."

"I bet you haven't told Mitch all about your marriage to Jeff."

"I really need to freshen up before the lawyer arrives."

Lisa chuckled. "I'm sure that's more important than having an honest discussion with me about relationships."

"It's not more important. It's just all about the timing."

"A convenient excuse at best."

Reb looked at Lisa. It may have turned into a staring contest had they not been interrupted by the agent in charge.

"There's something you need to know."

"It can't wait until I've had a shower?" Reb asked the agent pointedly.

He truly didn't know how to answer the question, so he just stood there.


When Herman had left Mitch with the admonishment to continue to think things over, he had no real intention of checking back in with her to see if she had changed her mind. Instead, he took the opportunity to forge ahead. He placed another call on a different cell phone to Trish's residence.

"Hello?" Trish answered with the Feds listening in.

"I want money," he stated succinctly.

Trish had been schooled to attempt to stall the negotiations, just like in the movies. She held out little hope that this was going to be at all relevant in this modern world of disposable phones. Burners? Isn't that what the criminals called them? So, out of sheer habit from her normal everyday experiences of being the chief funder of everything, she asked, "How much money?"

Herman must've been taken aback because there was a brief silence on the line. It was like he had expected resistance that wasn't there. Almost like steeling oneself to pick up a seemingly heavy object only to discover that it weighed less than one expected, catching one temporarily off balance.

"One-hundred million dollars," Herman finally stated.

Trish couldn't help it. She laughed. Guffawed would be a better description. A hundred-million dollars was outrageous.

"You think this is funny?" Herman asked like a lawyer cross examining a jovial witness.

"I think it's absurd," Trish snapped back, much to the consternation of the Feds.

"Your friend isn't worth a hundred million?"

"Not the last time I checked her bank balance!" Trish shot back. The Feds were, by this time, frantically signaling Trish to tone it down. She wasn't having any of it. Terrorist or not, Trish wasn't willing to agree to his demands.

"I'm certain that among all of you *lesbians*, you can come up with the money."

Trish was already irritated by this man, so when he phrased things this way, she got downright angry.

"I want to talk to Mitch," she demanded.

"Your friend is not available."

"Then don't call back until she is," Trish said curtly and then disconnected the call.

The Feds looked like they were going into apoplexy.

"That's not how to handle these types of negotiations!" the senior agent said angrily.

"Until I can talk to Mitch, it's exactly how to handle these negotiations," Trish argued back.

"You could be causing harm or even death to her if you anger him."

"He is intimidated by women. That gives me and Mitch and Reb the upper hand in this situation."

The agents exchanged a look. Trish didn't care. She was a people person who had spent years in real estate. She knew all about negotiating and sizing people up and calling people's bluffs.

"We're going to handle negotiations from here on out," senior agent said.

"No, you're not. In fact, you are going to pack your gear and get the hell out of my house!"

There was a brief moment of silence while all parties took a deep breath. Then, Rose stepped forward to address the situation. In her usual motherly tone, she inquired of the agents, "Do you need help packing?"

"You ladies really can't do this on your own."

"We will do our best to carry on without your help."

The agents seemed resigned to the fact that they were losing an argument with a diminutive senior citizen. Legally, Rose and Trish had every right to take this action. Reluctantly, the agents retrieved all their gadgets and left the premises.

"I'm thinking that they might still guard the perimeter of the house," Silver said to Rose.

"Then they will need to jockey for position with the media," Rose replied calmly. At first, it had bothered her that so many events in their lives had garnered such attention. She was now used to it. The seemingly insatiable appetite of the media was feasting on their misery and trauma. A sad fact of modern life.

Reb was used to having her questions answered immediately. So, the longer the agent hesitated, the more irritated she became. She was already plenty irritable after her conversation with Lisa, so this agent was on thin ice indeed.

"Just tell me what you think I need to know," she huffed.

"The protection detail at the Denver residence has been *excused*," he spoke like a school boy trying to impress a stern professor.

"What do you mean by *excused*?" Reb asked.

"Ms. Weingarten threw them out."

"I'm surprised it took this long," Reb remarked.

"How do you wish to proceed?"

"Are you asking if I'm going to throw you out as well?"

"The thought had crossed our minds."

Reb looked at Lisa. The thought of getting through this ordeal with only her for company was unappealing in the extreme.

"No."

"No?"

"I want all the protection I can get," Reb answered definitively.

"We will proceed as planned."

"Thank you."

The agent was so surprised that Reb had used the words "thank you" that he simply nodded and left the room.

"That's one way to stun him into silence," Lisa observed wryly.

"What do you mean by that?"

"Politeness goes a long way in these situations."

"I'm always polite," Reb snapped.

"I'm sure you think so," Lisa remarked.

"You don't think so?"

"Go take your shower. Please."

Reb threw up her hands in frustration and then wheeled herself into the bathroom. She thought she was dealing rather well with what was on her plate right now and didn't need any more pointed remarks from Lisa. The shower felt wonderful. It wasn't as easy to take a shower without Mitch's help. Or as much fun. Reb couldn't help but consider for a brief moment what her life would be like without her. Life would be unbearable without Mitch. Not only was it unpleasant to consider this possibility, but another ugly truth also surfaced. She was troubled by the thought that she had always taken Mitch for granted. Reb's ego had created this reality. Reb had been a governor and a senator. Somebody important. Somebody who did what she wanted to do and expected everyone else to dance attendance. And that "everyone else" often included Mitch. And she never really complained. She didn't fuss or fume. Mostly, she just asked how she could be more helpful. Reb was feeling overwhelmed by a mixture of fear, guilt and dread. And if this continued, she knew that she would seriously snap at any benign remark from Lisa or anyone else in her path. So she took an inordinate amount of time showering and then toweling dry. Maybe by the time she was finished, the lawyer would be here. Then, they could move forward in a constructive manner. Having some sense of purpose and control would allay her nerves.

The lawyer had indeed arrived and had a drink in his hand when Reb emerged from the bedroom. She was impeccably dressed and coifed. She looked like she was going to a State of the Union speech instead of a meeting with the family litigator. Hopefully, he would be sober enough to help. The look on Lisa's face gave Reb the distinct impression that they were going to need a lot of help.
"What's going on?" Reb asked Lisa point blank.
Lisa took a deep breath. "It's Miranda."
"What about her?"
"She died about an hour ago."
Reb bowed her head as a short but meaningful prayer went through her mind. No one spoke until Reb said quietly, "I guess we should go to the hospital."
Lisa opened her mouth to make a remark but then thought better of

it. Her mouth closed, but not before Reb took notice.

"You have something else to say?"

"Maybe we should call Trish first."

"Good idea," Reb nodded.

"And I have another idea as well," Lisa added.

Reb waited just a tad before she asked, "Another idea?" It was like Reb didn't think Lisa capable of having two good ideas in a row and her tone of voice indicated as much. Lisa ignored the inflection.

"I imagine that Trish kicked the Feds out because they were being too heavy handed."

Reb sensed that Lisa wanted verbal encouragement to continue, but she just sat and waited. The silence was too much of a void for Lisa.

"I think we should ask Smith to go and help them. We have a lot of bodyguards for just the two of us. And Smith will be a soothing influence."

"What about Vukoff?"

"I suggest we let Smith figure that out."

Reb gave the impression that this idea was going to require a lot of scrutiny when, in fact, she realized it was brilliant. She wished she had come up with it first. She nodded assent.

"When we call Trish, why don't you present your idea?"

This was a huge concession on Reb's part. She gave Lisa two major considerations. She would make sure that Lisa had full credit for her ideas and also have an opportunity to talk with Trish. The latter was the real challenge. It had been difficult to accept the reality that Lisa and Mary were no longer a couple. Reb hadn't exactly been thrilled when they had gotten together in the first place. Now that they had split up, Reb was annoyed on behalf of her daughter. Knowing that Lisa had chosen Trish over Mary lowered her opinion of the both of them. Reb fought the temptation to be sanctimonious. She had left her husband and in short order had taken up with Mitch. It hadn't been easy on Mary at the time, but Reb had to follow her heart. So how could she find fault when others did the same?

When Lisa presented her idea to Smith, he readily agreed.

"If she'll have us, we'll assist however we are able."

It sure sounded like he would take Vukoff with him.

"Do you think Vukoff can be low key enough?"

"You just leave that to me."

Trish picked up on the second ring. "Hello!" She sounded tense.

"Hi Trish, it's me."

Only people very familiar with each other used this type of salutation.

"Oh, hi."

Normally, Trish was more voluble on the phone with Lisa. These weren't normal circumstances.

"I heard you threw the Feds out of the house," Lisa kick-started the conversation.

"News travels fast."

"I have a proposition for you," Lisa phrased things interestingly. It was a habit of hers.

"Really?" Trish sounded guarded.

"What if you had a Fed who was nice and mellow?"

"Does such a person exist?"

"You did briefly meet Smith, my gentleman friend."

"Are we on speaker phone?"

"No. Why?"

"He's a bit old for you, isn't he?" Trish sounded edgy.

"I'm not throwing you over for him, if that's what you're wondering."

At this exchange, Reb rolled her eyes. Lisa took note. For all they knew, the kidnapper was trying to get through on the line. They didn't have time for this nonsense. So before Reb got the notion to take the phone away from her, Lisa got to the point.

"Smith has agreed to help you. We are going to be here a while. Miranda died about an hour ago."

"Oh Dear Lord. Did she die intestate?"

"I have no idea, but the lawyer is here."

"That was fast."

"He was already en route."

"Why?"

"Reb doesn't want us tying up the phone line. We'll tell you all about it later."

"Don't hang up yet. It's just, you know, really good to hear your voice."

"Yeah," Lisa said noncommittally. It was difficult to have an intimate conversation with Reb and the Feds listening in.

"Why don't you come back and leave Smith there?" Trish asked for a miracle.

"Because I'm not a Fed. I have no experience in these matters."

"Reb is falling apart, isn't she?"

"There's no indication of that yet."

Reb had had enough of this. She reached up and wrestled the phone away from Lisa, who didn't put up much of a fight.

"Are the two of you finished chatting away!"

"Apparently we are now."

"Good! We are sending Smith back to Denver. Lisa is staying here to help." Reb couldn't believe she was saying this with a straight face.

"I'm sorry about Miranda."

The condolence caused Reb to pause and take a breath.

Remembering her earlier discussion with Lisa about politeness, she answered, "Thank you."

"It seems as though we are all planning a funeral."

"The good news is that the baby survived."

"Was that ever in question?"

"That's what we are going to find out."

"Is that why the lawyer is there?"

"That's right. Do you want to say goodbye to Lisa before we hang up?"

"It's up to you."

Reb handed the phone back to Lisa with an admonishment to "make it quick!"

Lisa wanted to ignore the request but knew it was in everyone's best interest to comply.

"I'm sure we'll all be able to talk again soon," Lisa said wistfully.

"When this is all over," Trish set the intention.

"Bye for now."

Lisa put on a brave face but it was all pretend. She would've given anything to be going back with Smith and chided herself for volunteering for this thankless mission in the first place. Reb wasn't so absorbed with her own situation that she didn't sense Lisa's mood.

"I appreciate your support," Reb said to Lisa.

Although it sounded an awful lot like an excerpt from a campaign speech, Lisa acknowledged Reb's words with a simple, "Thank you."

When it was evident that they were all out of small talk, Smith vocalized his plan of action.

"We'll be leaving soon. Is there anything I need to know before we head out?"

Reb looked at Lisa like she expected her to come up with all the answers.

"Trish is usually pretty mellow, so whatever happened between her and the Feds must have been pretty intense."

"These situations are often conducive to a lot of tension."

"And Trish is pretty territorial about her house and family," Lisa continued, hoping to somehow convey as tactfully as possible that Smith really needed to keep a watchful eye on Vukoff. The best part of this deal was that Smith was a genius in this regard. After all, his soothing manner had kept Lisa and Vukoff from exchanging fisticuffs so far. As long as he didn't change his mind about taking Vukoff with him, things should go swimmingly.

"And what do you need before I go?"

Lisa figured it would be awkward to ask for a hug, so instead she said, "A change of clothes?"

"Well, we probably don't have time for a shopping spree at the local mall, but maybe we could arrange for something to be delivered. If you ladies give your sizes and preferences to your security detail, I'm sure they will be most helpful."

Smith had been around long enough to know the ins and outs of witness protection. Mostly it was about protection, but enough was also about the day-to-day issues of livability that could make or break the success of the mission. These ladies weren't the first to ask for a change of clothing and certainly wouldn't be the last. Had he tried a little harder to make Lisa's life more pleasant at her safe house, they wouldn't even be in this situation. At least, that was the lie he told himself. Lisa was going to run sooner or later. She was just that headstrong.

"Okay," Lisa nodded.

It wouldn't have been obvious to anyone else that Lisa was upset, but Smith wasn't just anyone. He was a trained professional and a compassionate human being.

"This isn't the last you'll see of me, young lady. And you too, Senator." Smith assured them.

If Reb was offended by not being included in the classification of "young lady" she had the good grace to not raise a fuss. "Thank you, Agent Smith," she answered pleasantly.

And then Smith and Vukoff were gone, leaving Reb and Lisa to manage the crisis at hand.

Meanwhile, the lawyer was on his third scotch and water, long on scotch, short on water, before Reb decided it was time to have a serious conversation with him as well.

"I'm going to sue the hospital, the prison, and every doctor who has had contact with Miranda," Reb stated flatly, like she litigated all day every day.

The lawyer poured himself another scotch, this time without the water and drank it before the ice cubes had a chance to dilute it. If things went well, he could afford some very expensive scotch. The kind of scotch that sold at auction instead of at the corner liquor store. To hell with his liver. He could afford a transplant as well and it would probably be cheaper than the scotch.

Reb was watching his reaction like a cat. She knew instinctively what was going through his alcohol-addled brain.

"We will need a team of lawyers," he slurred. "Of course, I'll be head counsel."

"Can you handle the case?"

"Isn't that why you called me in the first place?"

"I did call you for advice, that much is true. However, I didn't realize that stockpiling the liquor cabinet was going to be the priority. Even if you did want the case, I wouldn't hire you. I need someone with a clear mind."

He stood to leave. "I'm billing you for my time."

"I'll gladly pay the bill to be rid of you," Reb assured him.

He stalked out and slammed the door behind him. The field of people for Reb to pick on was narrowing. Lisa looked around. It was her and two Feds. Everyone had better steel themselves for the next round of demands. Reb noted the gaping silence.

"We need to find another lawyer. A competent sober one this time."

When Lisa realized that the comment was directed to her, she said, "Sounds like it's time to crank up the old computer."

Having run out of options, Reb simply nodded. There had to be a sober, pro-gay family lawyer somewhere in Kansas, didn't there?


Mitch had once again scooched down far enough on her cot to fall asleep. There was really nothing else to do. And although it wasn't a complaint, to date this was one of the most boring experiences of her life. Almost as bad as high school algebra. The initial rush of adrenalin had long since worn off and there was nothing to take its place. For whatever reason, Mitch wasn't holding on to any fear or trepidation. Other than Herman's occasional sour moods and snappish behavior, he had been quite decent to her. If she was feeling anything, the closest she could come to describing it was suspicion. Like something was going on that she would soon be made aware of and they had just been biding their time until now. There was a knock at her cell door. Seriously, who knocks on a cell door?

"Come in," Mitch called out.

It was Herman. "Follow me," he said brusquely.

Mitch didn't want to grumble, but she had gotten used to this room and cot and didn't feel like moving.

"Where are we going?"

"To another safe house."

"We're not safe enough here?"

"Every time I make contact with the other side, we need to relocate."

It sounded almost spiritual, all this talk about "the other side."

"You called to demand a ransom?" Mitch asked.

"Apparently, no one wants you back," Herman did his best to be sarcastic.

Rather than rise to the bait, she calmly said, "They all drive a hard bargain. I'm glad it's you and not me who's doing the negotiating."

"You think you could do a better job?"

"Oh Heavens no!" Mitch used one of her own standard spiritual terms just for good measure.

"You must use the restroom before we leave. It's going to be a long drive."

"Do I have to wear the hood again? It tends to make me car sick."

"We can't allow you to know your location."

"Unless we're driving through New York City or Los Angeles, I probably won't have a clue where I am."

"You are not impressing me by trying to act stupid. Follow me. Now!"

Mitch reluctantly got up and walked behind Herman to the bathroom. She was still under heavy guard, but it was all beginning to feel different. Almost as if she was being protected instead of threatened. Like she was precious cargo instead of ransom bait.

However, much to her chagrin, she was once again hooded for the next leg of the journey. Fortunately, there was nothing on her stomach to upchuck. It was a long and uneventful drive. If the earth was flat, they would've surely driven off the edge by now. Mitch was stiff and sore by the time she was instructed to disembark. Her knees were shaky and she was dizzy from hunger. There had better be some nutrition at this location. She was supported on each side and guided, still blindfolded, to a doorway. It creaked open and then they stepped over a threshold. The door creaked shut and Mitch's hood was removed. She had expected to see another dark dank cell but instead, they were in a wooden farmhouse. It was beautiful compared to where she had been before. She looked at Herman, thoroughly confused by now. What came out of his mouth next was unbelievable.

"I've brought you home to meet my mother."

Mitch was tempted to reply, "I'm not your type," but held her tongue. It was neither the time nor the place to be making clever comments.

"Why am I here to meet your mother?" was her next best attempt at dialogue.

Herman didn't reply. He seemed reticent. It puzzled Mitch. He, above everyone, should know why they were here. His silence was baffling. Mitch waited for a long moment for an answer.

"Do you want to meet my mother or do you want to get back in the car and go to another holding cell?"

"I never said that I wouldn't want to meet your mother. I just don't understand why I should. Is she the mastermind behind this entire scheme?"

At the word "mastermind", Herman bristled. It appeared that they

95

were getting to the crux of the matter.

"If I were you, I'd be very careful how you talk about my mother."

"To you or to her?"

"To me. It doesn't make any difference what you say to her."

Mitch couldn't be more stymied. It always mattered what you said to someone's mother. That social norm was inculcated practically from birth. Whatever was going on here wasn't even close to any usual situation. Nevertheless, Mitch announced firmly, "I'm ready when you are."

Together, they walked into a cozy bedroom softly decorated for its female occupant. The lights were dim, so it took a moment for Mitch's eyes to adjust. When they did, all she could think of to say was, "Holy Mother of God."


Mary was restless. She didn't have the luxury of running away from the Witness Protection Program like Lisa had. She had awakened from a dream about sitting in a coffee shop where she had dreamily been enjoying a delicious gourmet cup of coffee and sumptuous pastry. It was amazing how hungry she was for even the smallest of pleasures. Just being able to sit at a window and watch traffic roll by would've been grand entertainment at this point. As her thoughts drifted to the predicament Mitch was in, Mary felt a twinge of guilt. For all she knew, Mitch was being tortured or worse. At the very least, Mitch was trapped in similar circumstances. Mary imagined, rightly or wrongly, that Mitch was handling her situation in the same even-tempered way that she handled everything else. For a moment, Mary envied Mitch. Mitch was as close to being a pillar of the community as anyone else Mary had ever known. She was the one you went to with your troubles and she always knew the right thing to do to support you. She was stoic yet approachable. All these thoughts started to sound like an obituary. Mary remembered reading somewhere once that obituaries for famous people were already pre-written by news outlets. Just in case anyone ever wondered how it was possible that obituaries appeared almost instantly after the death of actors and rock stars and the like. All the media needed was a sentence or two to update the latest developments. Just add that part about the last movie or tour or trip to rehab and they all look like geniuses. So, if you were really somebody in this world, there was a prepared obituary just waiting for you to die. Mary was certain that her mother had one. She was a political figure and media sensation. Mitch probably had one as well with all her notoriety. However, Mary wasn't so sure if she had one. Would it be possible to find out? Imagine what that phone call would sound like?

"Thank you for calling media outlet XYZ. How can I help?"

"I was wondering if there's an obituary written for me?"

Click.

That would probably be the most favorable response. She'd be lucky to avoid being reported to the authorities as a nut case. Of course, she would actually need to have access to a phone to make this a reality.

A knock on the door stirred her from her reverie.

"Who is it?" Mary asked.

"Who else would it be," the familiar voice answered.

Mary opened the door and motioned Fawn to enter her spacious cell. Fawn, a profiling expert, made note of Mary's mood.

"What's troubling you?" Fawn asked right out of the gate.

"Do you think I have an obituary already written about me?"

"That's a morbid topic to be thinking about so early in the day."

"I hadn't noticed."

"You hadn't noticed whether it's morbid or early?"

"Both, I guess."

Fawn sat down opposite Mary. She seemed to be settling in for a spell. This wasn't usual. Usually, Fawn gave the impression that she wished to impart news and then leave as soon as possible. Mary didn't know quite how to react.

"If you want some coffee or tea, I can make some."

"Which would you prefer?"

"I'd prefer steak and lobster."

"Sounds more like a final meal request."

"What kind of dumbass remark is that?"

"You're the one who brought up obituaries."

"You think I'm suicidal?"

"It's in our best interests to keep you in the best frame of mind possible."

"I imagine it's a daunting challenge here in the likes of Sing Sing."

97

"Well, we can't offer you a ride in a blimp to allay your boredom, but there are other options."

"You're not talking about conjugal visits, are you?"

"I was thinking more along the lines of counselling."

"Therapy?"

"That's right."

"No, thanks," Mary refused abruptly.

"It might be more helpful than you think."

"Are you seriously suggesting that I need therapy?" Mary was getting snappish.

All of a sudden, she realized that she was beginning to sound like her mother. Something she had promised herself she would never do. It had to be the inherited stress reaction. Whether it was genetic or environmental didn't matter at this point. What mattered was making the right choice without appearing to give in to Fawn.

"Well…" Fawn had started her next sentence with a neutral tact in mind when Mary interrupted, "Okay! Fine! You don't need to browbeat me into this!"

"But-" Fawn tried again to get a word in edgewise without success. "Just do what you have to do. Bring any paperwork you need me to sign so we can get this over with."

Fawn sat in silence for so long that Mary finally asked, "What?"

"Those acorns don't fall too far from those oak trees, do they?"

"What's that supposed to mean?"

"I'm sure you'll find out in therapy," was Fawn's parting reply.


After Trish had asked the Feds to leave the premises, she had been hesitant to agree to yet another intrusion into her household. Had anyone other than Lisa suggested the arrangement, Trish would've said no. But Trish couldn't say no to Lisa. Trish couldn't remember ever saying no to Lisa. In fact, she wished more than anything that they could have a more conventional relationship. Trish used to judge men harshly for remarrying so soon after the death of their wives, but now she understood. Still, the guilt hung over her. Robbie's death had been a shock and a tragedy and while it was happening, Trish had been wooing Lisa in a snowbound cabin in the woods. It was an ugly truth that haunted her. Trish had taken refuge for now in Josh's room. He was asleep after his feeding and Trish had kindly but firmly shooed Silver back to her primary protection detail, namely, Rose in the kitchen. She felt herself nodding off and was awakened by a voice that said softly, "It's okay."

Trish awoke irritable. She had wanted to be left alone and didn't appreciate someone trying to reassure her. She stood up and went to the doorway. There was no one there. Now she was really irritated. Apparently someone spoke words of encouragement only to scamper away. Josh was still sleeping, so Trish went to the kitchen to find the culprit. Everyone was gathered around the table, as usual.

"Who came to check on me?" Trish asked.

"What do you mean?" Rose asked.

"Someone came to Josh's room and told me that things would be okay."

"Someone?" Rose asked.

"I heard a voice."

"You didn't see anybody?" Silver sounded concerned.

"I was asleep."

"Maybe it was a dream?" Rose suggested.

"It was loud enough to wake me up."

"Maybe it was a talking dream?"

"A talking dream?"

"You know, when your subconscious mind talks to you in your sleep."

"You think I'm psychotic?"

"Of course not. Sometimes normal people hear voices. It's all in our primitive brains."

Trish shook her head. The voice had been external. She was sure, almost certain.

"Why don't you try and get some sleep. Go and rest in your own room and we'll keep an eye on Josh," Rose said.

Trish didn't appreciate being sent back to bed like a child, which indicated that she really did need sleep.

"Okay, I'll go and rest, but let me know if anything happens."

"Of course we will," Rose nodded.

Trish went in to check on Josh and then retreated to her bedroom. After settling in under the covers, she listened for any stray voices parceling out advice. Hearing nothing, she slipped into a deep sleep.

Chapter 5

Mitch was speechless. She was looking at a woman who resembled the Virgin Mary if the Virgin Mary was about sixty years old. As Mitch looked from mother to son and back, she saw not only a family resemblance, but also a distinct softening of Herman's features in her presence.

"Hello," Mitch said.

"Hello. Who are you?" the woman said quietly, in that somewhat shaky voice that is endearing if you are elderly but creepy otherwise. Her countenance was one of peace and contentment.

"My name is Mitch."

"That's an interesting name for a woman."

"My parents were interesting people."

"Are they here?" the woman looked vaguely around the room.

"No, Ma'am," Mitch stated and then looked at Herman.

"Are you going to stand there all day?" Herman's mother asked Mitch.

With that remark, Herman went to fetch a chair. Apparently, looming over Mitch was now the least of his concerns. The chair he brought was actually comfortable and Mitch settled in to continue their chat.

"What's your name?" Mitch asked, sensing that Herman was having issues with introductions.

Things got very quiet for a brief moment and then she answered, "Mom is my name."

Mitch looked with puzzlement at Herman. He was obviously still under the influence of the Angel Dumbstruck.

"What was your name before you became a mother?" Mitch attempted logic to glean the answer.

"It's been so long ago, but people used to call me...Martha. That's right. Isn't it? Isn't my name Martha?"

"It's a nice name," Mitch said. She heard herself talking to the woman as if she were a child instead of an adult, but no one seemed annoyed by it. Except Mitch.

"What's your name?" Martha asked Mitch.

It was beginning to dawn on Mitch what was going on here.

"My name is Mitch."

"That's a nice name."

"Thank you."

"Do I know you?"

"No. We've just met."

"What's your name again?"

"My name is Mitch."

From out of the corner of her eye, Mitch had noticed that Herman had begun to shift from one foot to the other. She surmised that he was unconsciously betraying his impatience with this exchange. When she made eye contact with him, he silently signaled for her to leave the room with him. Mitch patted Martha's arm and said, "I'll be back."

"Thank you, Mitch", Martha replied with a smile.

Herman paused long enough to take note of his mother's words and then led Mitch out of the room. They went to the kitchen area where someone had prepared a simple meal.

"Sit," Herman instructed monosyllabically.

Mitch did as she was told. He placed a plate of food in front of her. "Eat."

Again another one word order.

"Aren't you going to have something as well?"

"I can't eat and guard you at the same time."

"You think you still need to guard me?"

"You might run."

"I wouldn't know where to go."

"That wouldn't stop you."

"You've given me no real reason to run. And now, I'm too curious to give it a second thought."

"Eat your food before it gets cold."

"My mother used to say the same thing to me."

Herman turned away. It served to hide any show of emotion from Mitch. She shrugged it off and picked up her fork. When someone tells you twice to eat your food, they mean business. The fare was simple yet tasty. Meatloaf, mashed potatoes and peas. Protein, starch and a vegetable. Except for the food purists who would've considered peas a starchy vegetable, this was a square meal. That's what they called it when Mitch was growing up. They had a lot of these kinds of meals. Chicken, rice and broccoli. Turkey, noodles and green beans.  The variations went on and on.  It was like a food version of a three-reel slot machine.  You pulled the handle and a meal plan popped up.  Then, when Mitch left home, this all went out the proverbial window and Mitch's diet went to hell in a handbasket.  She would eat potato chips for breakfast, fast food for lunch and bar food (mostly liquid) for dinner.  And she had seen no real reason to change all this until she met Reb.  Reb had also been one of those mothers who put good, nutritious food on the table.  Now that they were going to be parents very soon, those dietary guidelines would become even stricter.  Mitch would want to be a good example to their child, but it would be difficult to change her ways overnight.

While Mitch was reliving her history with food, Herman had fixed a plate for himself and sat opposite her at the table.  Even though Mitch had suggested not two minutes ago that he do so, things now felt terribly awkward.  They ate in silence for the first half of the meal, all of about five minutes.
"This is good," Mitch finally ventured into small talk.
Herman didn't say anything.  Obviously he hadn't prepared the meal since they had only just arrived.
"Who did the cooking?"
"We follow Mom's recipes."
"I've done that as well," Mitch tried to be convivial despite the fact that preparing a meal like this didn't require much culinary skill.  The more important part of the statement, however, was the pronoun "we."  They weren't alone here.  Someone must always be here doing the cooking and caring.  And guarding.  Mitch could inquire about that or she could instead ask the burning question.  She opted for the latter.
"So, tell me more about your mom."
"She's ill and you're going to fix her."
At last Herman finally arrived at the heart of the matter.
"Is that why you kidnapped me instead of someone else?" Mitch asked the question she already knew the answer to.
"We did our research.  You were the logical choice."
"And everything else was just a ruse?"
"We would still prefer that the court case would go our way and ransom money is always welcome.  But first and foremost, you are required to heal my mother."

"What's wrong with her?"

"Does that matter?"

"I suppose not, but you do realize that I'm not a healer. We've had this discussion."

"Our research indicates otherwise. You have healed people. Right on national TV."

"Those are all coincidences."

"And just now, when you touched my mother, she remembered your name."

"She heard it three times."

"There are days when she hears things thirty times and still can't remember them."

"So, it's something like dementia?"

"That's right."

"And there's no medical cure."

"So you are here to do what you do."

Mitch was beginning to have her usual sinking feeling when she was called upon to perform impossible tasks.

"What if it doesn't work?"

"You don't want to know the consequences."

"Fair enough. But before I attempt anything, I want to contact my loved ones and tell them to sit tight and not worry. You wouldn't want a rescue attempt to interfere with the process."

It was Herman's turn to think things over.

"Okay," he agreed, much to Mitch's surprise.

He produced a cell phone and handed it to Mitch with the caveat to not say anything stupid. It took a moment for her to remember Reb's number, but when she dialed it, Reb picked up on the first ring.

"I don't know who you are, but you had better be ready to negotiate," Reb spoke forcefully into the phone.

"It's me," Mitch answered calmly.

"Are you okay?" Reb was caught off guard.

"I'm doing well. I'm being treated well."

"Where are you?"

"I have no idea where I am," Mitch maintained eye contact with Herman as she spoke. So far, so good.

"Is our conversation being monitored?"

"Yes, and I have no clever clues or code words to pass along. I just wanted to call and tell you that everything is going to be okay."

"Can I help in any way?"

"No. Just take care of things on your end and I'll be home soon. Do not try to rescue me. I'll be fine."

Mitch heard Reb sigh. She was being so brave through it all.

"I love you."

"Love you, too."

Mitch disconnected the call before they ran the risk of getting any more emotional and a trace could be put on the call. She wanted to stay on Herman's good side.

"Thank you," she said to him.

He tried to not acknowledge her gratitude, but his head nodded involuntarily.

"Let's get to work," he said as he stood up and motioned for Mitch to follow him back to his mother's room.


"You couldn't keep her on the line any longer?" Lisa said to Reb when she hung up.

"We ran out of things to talk about!" Reb snapped at Lisa.

"It was important to trace the call."

"She hung up on me, not the other way around!" Reb cleared up Lisa's misconception.

"What did she say?"

"She's fine. She has things under control. I'm going to call Trish to pass along the news."

"Okay. What should I do in the meantime?"

"Find me a good lawyer!"


"Honey."

"Hmmm," Trish answered sleepily.

"Are you awake?"

Trish thought she was awake but couldn't get her eyes to open. It must still be a dream and now she really was hearing dream voices in her head. This time, they were calling her "Honey". Like a disembodied spirit since there was no person in the dream. Just this voice asking questions.

"Did you want to take this phone call?" it was asking.

Trish had had a lot of dreams in her life, but never one that asked if she wanted to talk on the phone.

"Trish!" the voice sounded insistent.

She jolted awake to find Rose hovering over her.

"What? What's going on?"

"The Senator is on the phone."

"Huh?" Trish tried to shake herself out of her sleep stupor.

"Senator Rebecca is on the phone. You said you wanted to know if anything happened."

While the words sounded ominous, Rose's facial expression conveyed otherwise. Trish took the phone from Rose's outstretched hand.

"Hi," was Trish's truncated greeting. Her cautious brain couldn't come up with anything more cogent.

"You sound tired," Reb stated her opinion right off.

"I was sleeping."

"That explains it."

"You have news?"

"Mitch called. She says she is fine and not to worry."

"Did they talk about a ransom amount?"

"There was no *they*. It was just Mitch and there was no mention of a ransom."

"I don't understand."

"Neither do we. She sounded calm and in control."

"No pleading for money or anything?"

"Not a word."

"So she's still being held and there's no demands and we don't need to worry?" Trish summed it all up.

"That's the news so far."

"Do you have any idea what's going on?"

"Not at this point."

"Well, whatever Mitch is doing, I hope it works."

Reb hadn't exactly looked forward to this phone call and was now on the verge of getting testy. She took a deep breath to calm her nerves. She really wished that she and Trish were on better terms, mostly due to the fact that she was one of Mitch's closest friends.

"I'm not sure what you are saying?"

Trish was now wide awake and thinking clearly. "Well, it the kidnappers aren't asking for money or making any other demands, then they obviously think that Mitch will be useful for some other purpose."

Reb thought this over. It was interesting to her that living with Mitch day in and day out had blinded her to the overall special qualities that were the essence of Mitch. In some respects, Mitch was famous in her own way and yet Reb took it all for granted, or worse, ignored it entirely. This was the second instance in the past few hours where Reb acknowledged her own overblown ego that had always taken center stage in their relationship. She had been a *governor* and a *senator* and yet it was Mitch who had been deemed valuable enough to be abducted. It almost bordered on envy, which was absurd.

"Are you still there?" Trish spoke into the silence.

"Yes. I'm still just trying to sort it all out."

"There's nothing to sort out. I think the answer is pretty obvious."

Reb felt her testiness return stronger than before. It irked her that someone else thought they knew the answer that had eluded Reb's logical intellect.

"I'll get back to you," Reb abruptly ended the phone call.

"That was short," Lisa remarked after Reb had hung up.

"I wasn't rude."

"That's not what I meant."

"Aren't you supposed to be finding me another lawyer?"

"What I meant was that you didn't stay on the phone very long."

"It's a habit of mine. Besides, I didn't have anything else to say."

"It seems like Trish had something to say."

"Gee, I'm sorry I didn't put it on speaker phone so you could listen in," Reb was millimeters away from sarcasm.

"Whatever Trish said has really set you off, hasn't it?"

"I have a right to be upset," Reb was now full-blown defensive.

"Of course you do, for all the right reasons," Lisa remarked obliquely.

This caught Reb off guard. "And?"

"What did Trish say?"

Any answer that Reb would come up with would be paraphrasing overlaid with her own theories.

"We could call her back?" Lisa suggested,

"She's trying to get some rest," Reb answered honestly.

Lisa only nodded, hoping that Reb would continue.

"If Mitch wasn't abducted for the purpose of altering the trial or for money, why else do you think she was abducted?"

"Are you asking me?"

"I'm doing both. I'm giving you the gist of my conversation with Trish and asking for your opinion."

"You think there's a third scenario?"

"Trish thinks so and I tend to agree with her."

It didn't take Lisa long to put two and two together.


Mary was caught off guard. When Fawn had put out the idea that therapy would be a viable option, Mary had no idea things could and would be arranged so quickly. Here she was, sitting in an ugly, uncomfortable chair across from a woman who was prison's version of an appointed therapist. Along the lines of the kind of attorney who was court appointed for indigent people. The woman had spent the first ten minutes reading through Mary's file like it had been handed to her as she had walked through the door. There had been no greeting. No eye contact. No offer of coffee or tea or water.

"Your file indicates that you are suicidal," she finally broke the silence.

"I'm not suicidal," Mary answered flatly.

The therapist leveled a glance in her direction over glasses perched precariously on the end of her nose.

"So, you're not suicidal?"

"No."

"Well, I think we're done here," she closed the file and made motions as if she was going to lift her considerable girth out of what looked to be a much more comfortable chair than was afforded to Mary.

"And that's it?" Mary chided.

The therapist paused. She hadn't made much headway in her attempt to extract herself from her chair but was still poised to stand if necessary.

"Well, are you or are you not thinking about your own obituary?"

"I was musing about it."

"And you think that's normal behavior?"

107

At the word "normal," Mary felt her temper kick in. It must've been evident to the therapist because she glacially slid back in her chair like they were in session for the long haul.

"Tell me, what is "normal" behavior for someone in solitary confinement?" Mary asked.

"Well, first off, it's normal to come up with any excuse to get out of one's cell."

"Do you think that's my objective?"

"It's a common strategy of the inmates around here."

"I'm not suicidal so you can go and tend to the rest of the flock."

"Before I go and put on my shepherd disguise, I'd still like to have it on the record as to why you were musing about your obituary."

"Famous people have pre-written obituaries and now I'm sorry that I ever brought it up with Fawn."

"Fawn?"

"Fawn. O'Neal."

"Special Agent O'Neal?" the therapist reopened the file folder for reference.

"Right."

"You're on a first-name basis with your Special Agent?"

"Isn't everybody?"

Things got real quiet again, like the kind of silence a recalcitrant student experiences in the principal's office. Mary imagined that they had encroached on the prickly territory of divulging doctor-patient confidentiality issues. Or in this case, doctor-inmate confidentiality issues.

"So, the two of you are chummy?"

"I bought her a real expensive necklace when she was undercover," Mary boasted.

"I see that," the therapist nodded as she continued to scan the file.

"Do you have a name?" Mary asked.

"Everyone has a name," she answered, almost poetically.

"Only because someone gave us one," Mary opined.

"My given name is Anna."

"Please don't tell me that your last name is Lyze?"

"Has anyone ever told you that you are very intelligent and extremely clever?"

It was Mary's turn to be thoughtfully silent. She had excelled in school, mostly to subconsciously make up for the fact that she was gay.  And, yes, teachers had told her along the way that she was smart.  However, there had been a dearth of accolades recently.  "Sure," was her best answer.

"So, how does such an intelligent woman make such a mess out of her personal life?" Anna was peering steadily at Mary.  It felt like her eyes were boring right through her and that the Universe had decided that Mary needed a good ass-kicking and had sent this individual to administer the deed.

"Can I read my file?"

"No."

"Why not?"

"It contains sensitive information."

"And from that you have gleaned that I've made a mess out of my life?  I'm a national hero!"

"I said personal life."

"Are you referencing the fact that I'm a lesbian?"

"No.  I'm referencing the fact that you bought, in your words, *a real expensive necklace* for a woman who you thought was a prostitute while you were in a relationship with another woman."

"I bought her a necklace, too."

"And so you think that excuses your behavior?"

"The woman I was in a relationship with was interested in someone else."

"Why?"

"I don't know.  How am I supposed to know?"

"You didn't ask?"

"No."

"So, you went around buying necklaces for women without knowing all the facts?"

"I didn't have much of a fighting chance with Agent O'Neal."

"What about with Lisa?"

Mary paused for a moment and then the truth came out.  "I was afraid to know the answer."

"That's the most honest thing you've said so far.  Now, explain to me about the obituary remark."

"I said that famous people have pre-written obituaries.  It was simply a statement of fact."

"Except that you didn't mention the *famous people* part to Agent O'Neal."

"Is that important."

"It would've helped."

"Helped what?"

"Helped her understand the origin of the remark."

"What does that mean?"

"It's most likely the reason we are here today."

Mary began to get impatient. She thought therapy was supposed to be helpful, or at least straightforward. Guessing games weren't her favorite pastime.

"I'm not following."

Anna studied the file for a moment before continuing. "You were involved in a prior abusive relationship."

"Apparently you know everything about me."

"The goal is to know more about you than you do."

"Is that the goal of therapy or the government?"

"In your case, both."

Mary finally smiled. Despite her best efforts not to, she was beginning to warm up to this whole concept of therapy.

"I didn't stay long in the abusive relationship."

"But you did remain in contact with her."

"Very briefly."

"However brief, it's not what healthy people do."

"She is healing and I wanted to encourage her."

"That's commendable."

"But I didn't get back together with her."

"Did you want to?"

"No. She just happened to be around when Lisa was in the hospital."

"Do you want to elaborate on that?"

"We only have fifty minutes."

"Is that a 'no' disguised as an elusive answer?"

"I was hoping you would instead explain what you said a moment ago about the origin of my obituary remark."

"Well, as you so eloquently stated, we only have fifty minutes."

"It can't possibly be that complicated. Famous people have pre-written obituaries."

"How famous do you need to be?" Anna asked quietly.

Mary thought this over. Usually, the question was, "How famous do you want to be?" The difference between the words "want" and "need" were vast in this context.

"I don't know the answer," Mary hedged.

"Oh, I'm sure that on some level, you do know the answer."

"You think I *need* to be famous?"

"You referred to yourself as a national hero."

"I'm pretty sure I saved the nation, if not the world."

"And was it everything you had hoped for?"

"Right this minute, it sucks."

"That happens a lot. There are people who live enormously satisfying lives and die in virtual anonymity."

"Being famous doesn't necessarily make someone happy," Mary understood.

"Is your mother happy?"

The question took Mary aback. Anna had a knack for changing the subject abruptly, but this shift seemed huge.

"Does every therapy session always end up with a discussion of mothers?"

"You've heard the old therapy joke? How many therapists does it take to change a light bulb?"

"How many?"

"Two. One to screw in the lightbulb and one to hold your mother…I mean, ladder."

"Ah. A Freudian slip without a penis. Very clever."

"It gets a chuckle at otherwise boring conventions."

"I imagine so," Mary was trying to be agreeable just to get to whatever point Anna was driving at.

"In my professional opinion, we'll make more progress talking about your mother rather than penises."

Mary nodded. As reluctant as she felt about discussing her mother, it was far better than the alternative.

"So, do you think your mother has one of those pre-written obituaries?"

"I think all Senators have one."

"What do you think your mother's obituary says?"

"I'm sure it goes on and on."

"And by comparison, yours would be brief?"

"'Saved the world' doesn't take up too many column inches in the newspaper."

"So, you have no issues about how your life compares with your

111

mother's accomplishments?"

"I haven't given it much thought."

"Seriously?"

"Seriously."

"I think it's time that you do."

"How do you suggest I do that?"

"I'm giving you an assignment to complete before our next meeting. I want you to write two obituaries. One for yourself and one for your mother."

"That's the worst idea I've ever heard."

"If newspapers do it, how bad of an idea can it really be? If it disturbs you so much, think of them as resumes with a personal touch."

Mary shrugged her shoulders. She could handle that. It would be like one of those letters you send to unsuspecting relatives every Christmas. The letters that you use to brag rather than engage in further correspondence.

"When is our next session?"

"That all depends on you and Fawn."

"Please don't talk about us like we're a couple."

Anna made a note like she was already preparing the agenda for their next session. Then, she notified the guards that it was time to take Mary back to her cell with enough paper and pens to write obituaries for the entire cell block. Once she was back in her cell, Mary's thoughts shifted to Rose. While she would be completing a simple assignment, Rose would be facing one of life's toughest tests. Mary wished she could just pick up a phone and call Rose and ask her how she was coping. And then, she would want to just start making other phone calls just to see what it was like on the outside. It was so easy to take life for granted. So easy to bury yourself in the day to day existence that people called life but was so devoid of living. It was this difference between the noun and the verb that Mary was contemplating when there was a knock at her door. It was Fawn. Again.

"How did it go?" she asked.

"We're talking about you and me next session," Mary embellished.

"That will be a short appointment."

"You think so?"

"There's nothing to talk about."

"Anna was quite interested by the fact that I gave you a necklace."

"Which is being held in an evidence locker and will be returned to you when this is all over."

"I really don't want it back."

"Don't we have better things to talk about?" Fawn showed a flash of irritation.

"I'm so glad I don't have to go home with you every night," Mary remarked out of the blue.

"I was hoping therapy would be more helpful."

"Thanks to you, I now have to write my obituary," Mary tossed the paper and pens onto her makeshift kitchen table.

"Why?"

"It's a homework assignment."

"Do you want some help?"

"I think I know my own life story well enough."

An awkward silence grew between them. It was as if Fawn wanted to stay and keep Mary company. Maybe her new assignment was to watch her like a hawk so that she wouldn't do harm to herself.

"I guess I should let you get to your assignment."

"You want a cup of coffee?" Mary blurted out. She was truly conflicted. She wanted to be alone and yet she wanted company. She wanted Fawn to stay and yet she wanted to hold her in a place of disdain. Fawn had brought out the worst of Mary's nature and Mary wanted to both act on it and reject it. Maybe she should've been in therapy a long time ago. Her life was a holy mess and she had been solely and completely responsible for making it so.

"Is it made?" Fawn asked.

"What?" Mary jolted out of her self-recrimination.

"The coffee?"

"Not yet. I just got here."

"Can I help?"

"I've been making coffee all by myself since I was eight."

"You've been self-sufficient from an early age?"

"I had to be."

"Really? Why?" Fawn asked.

"I cooked my first dinner when I was nine and baked my first pie when I was ten. I started mowing the lawn when I was twelve and I had a paper route after I learned to ride a bicycle."

"An admirable childhood."

"I didn't come from a privileged background, contrary to popular belief."

"So, do I get my cup of coffee or what?"

Mary exhaled. She had just spent time and energy defending herself to Anna and now to Fawn and only now allowed herself to relax. "Coming right up."

Mary enjoyed puttering around her miniscule kitchen preparing coffee. "I have some stale muffins if you really want to taste my baking expertise."

"Sounds yummy."

One of the perks of being in protective custody, as opposed to being in plain old custody, was an oven, a fridge and a modest pantry. And a coffee pot. In return for her cooperation, she was trusted to not burn the place down. Once they were seated across from one another at the wobbly kitchen table, Mary continued, "I'm sorry if I worried you with the obituary talk. When you spend enough time alone, you have a lot of thoughts go through your mind that you normally wouldn't."

"So, you're okay?"

"Probably not. At least, according to my therapist."

"What do you mean?"

"Apparently, I've made quite a mess out of my life."

"I'm not convinced that's the case."

"You don't know the whole story."

"Actually, I do."

Mary felt disconcerted at the fact that she had been investigated in depth.

"Tell me, did you have an official in-person visit with Hilary?"

"I didn't."

"But someone did?"

"I'm not at liberty to discuss it."

"So, that's an affirmative."

"We wouldn't be doing our jobs otherwise."

"How would you like it if one day somebody pried into every corner of your life?"

"That's part of the process of being hired in my line of work."

"And I bet you've never made mistakes."

"Everyone makes mistakes."

"Just not great big ones like me."

114

"You seem to want to be measured by your mistakes."

"I think it's more of an issue of needing to understand why I do what I do."

"You make it sound like you're one of the biggest criminals in history when in fact you are a decent, upstanding citizen."

"How many decent, upstanding citizens consort with someone who they think is a prostitute?"

"In your defense, you didn't actually 'consort'".

"I ran out of time," Mary said dryly.

"I think you ran. Period."

"You think I wouldn't have slept with you given the right circumstances?"

"You had plenty of opportunity and never took advantage."

"I've wanted to know for a while, would you have slept with me if I hadn't run? Would you have fulfilled that part of your assignment?"

Fawn didn't answer. She remained silent for so long that Mary said, "You don't have to answer."

"If I couldn't have possibly avoided it, I would've slept with you."

"Despite your wedding vows?"

"The nation was at risk. Besides, you were drinking so heavily that my first plan was to get you too drunk to do anything."

"It's a good thing I wasn't a mean drunk."

"Yes, well, I should be going," Fawn said abruptly.

"Had enough bad coffee and worse muffins?"

"I just have things to do."

After Fawn left, Mary cleaned up the dishes. Then, with every good intention, she sat down to work on her therapy assignment. However, she found herself distracted by Fawn's sudden departure. They were getting along so well until the subject of sleeping together had come up. Mary chided herself for beginning the dialogue. She couldn't be convinced that there was enough alcohol on the planet to keep her from sleeping with Fawn had the opportunity presented itself. Maybe the comment about being a mean drunk made the interview with Hilary a touchy topic. Or maybe everyone had a mean drunk in their lives to contend with. Mary shrugged it all off and decided to scuttle her homework in exchange for a nap.

Herman's mother was asleep when he and Mitch went back to her room.

"Does she need to be awake for this to work?" he asked.

Mitch sighed. She knew instinctively that this was not going to be smooth sailing.

"Are you sure that you want your mother to get better?"

"Why wouldn't I?"

"Some people don't want to remember things. Does she know what you do for a living, so to speak?"

At this remark, he bristled noticeably.

"My mother understands my philosophy."

"Does she approve?"

Herman was beginning to glower. Mitch didn't seem bothered by it. Rightly or wrongly, she felt in control of the situation.

"My relationship with my mother is none of your business."

"Are you sure?" Mitch asked.

"You are not here to analyze. You are here to perform a miracle!"

"Herman! For goodness sake! Mind your manners and get a chair for our guest," Martha had stirred from her slumber.

Herman acted like a chastened child as he did what he was told.

"I remember you," Martha nodded toward Mitch.

"That's good," Mitch smiled as she sat down.

"And it's been too long since you've visited, Shane."

Mitch looked at Herman. He had gone from ruddy red to ghastly white in a matter of seconds. If anyone needed a chair, it would be him. Mitch stood up and scooted her chair in his direction. He sat down without comment. Mitch allowed a polite moment to elapse before she asked him, "Who is Shane?"

He shook his head slowly, more to reveal disbelief instead of recalcitrance.

"We don't talk about Shane."

"I'm sorry to know that. Who is he?"

"She. Shane is a she. Shane is my sister."

"You have a sister?"

"We don't talk about it!"

"Apparently your mother wants to talk about it."

"That's not a good idea."

116

"Let's find out," Mitch said as she turned to Martha and said, "Do you remember me?"

"Of course I remember you, Shane. A mother doesn't forget her children."

"How many children do you have?" Mitch asked.

Before she could answer, Herman was up out of his chair and forcibly escorting Mitch out of the room. It was the most force he had used on her during her entire captivity. There's nothing like a discussion of family to bring out the best and worst in people.

"You are not to talk about my sister or pretend to be her or discuss any other family members with my mother!"

"She's the one who started it."

"Family is off limits!"

"I heal people on my own terms," Mitch grew testy. "So, if you're not going to allow me the latitude I need, then shoot me now!"

"Herman...Herman!" Martha's voice carried from the other room.

"Now look what you've done," Herman said angrily.

"At least she's still remembering your name," Mitch defended herself.

They were at a standoff. The choices were to continue to argue or to go back in to check on mom. Herman led the way begrudgingly.

"It's okay, Mom," he said as they approached the bed.

"Hello, Mitch!" Martha brightened at her presence.

"Hello, Martha. You remembered my name."

"Of course I did. I remember a lot of things."

Mitch looked at Herman. He looked like someone had hit him on the back of the head with a frying pan.

"What's wrong, Herman?" Mitch asked cautiously.

He shook his head quickly, as if to clear his mind. "How has she gone from remembering nothing to remembering lots of things?"

"I have a theory and it's not what you are thinking in terms of me being a healer."

"What then?"

"I think your mother is reacting to outside stimulus. Much the same way many people in nursing homes perk up when they have guests. Laying around day in and day out tends to make elderly people dull and unresponsive."

117

Herman only nodded, so Mitch felt safe to continue, "How long has your mom been cooped up here?"

"That's none of your business."

"That long, huh?" Mitch nodded like a know-it-all. It was a risk to be impudent, but it was designed to cajole Herman into being more communicative.

"Shut your mouth," Herman barked at Mitch.

"Herman Thomas!" Martha showed her first flash of true anger with her son.

He jolted at the reprimand. Mothers meant business when they used your first and middle name.

"Apologize to our guest!"

He shifted from foot to foot.

"Apologize now!"

Herman turned to Mitch and quietly said, "I'm sorry."

Before Mitch could respond, Martha said, "Sorry for what."

Herman sighed like a child. "I'm sorry I told you to shut your mouth."

"It's okay," Mitch hurriedly said. "I accept your apology."

This interaction appeased Martha. She appeared ready and willing to talk more to Mitch.

"I'm not sure how long I've been cooped up here, but it's been a long time. I wish I could go somewhere, just for a change of scenery."

"I think that's a great idea," Mitch nodded her agreement. She immediately felt the strong clamp of Herman's hand on her elbow. He was in no mood for a field trip, but Mitch forged ahead.

"If you could go anywhere, where would you go?"

Without hesitation, Martha answered, "Alabama!"

"Why Alabama?" Mitch asked as Herman continued to squeeze her elbow. It was painful but not yet excruciating.

"It's where I was born," she said wistfully.

"I understand why you would want to go back," Mitch nodded.

"And it's where Herman's father is buried."

Mitch sensed that they were getting into extremely sensitive territory. Birth places and burial plots were emotional landmines unless you had led a charmed life. Herman had loosened his grip on Mitch's elbow, a miracle unto itself. She chanced a look in his direction. He seemed distracted by this notion of going back to the homestead.

"Were you raised in Alabama?" she asked him.

"Mostly," he answered vaguely and then turned pensive.

Sensing a lull in the conversation, Martha piped up. "Herman, why don't you go put some gas in the car while we pack a picnic."

"Why don't you just stay here and rest while we make some plans," Herman said to his mother.

"Alright, but don't take too long. I'm not getting any younger." She closed her eyes but a smile lingered on her lips.

Herman led the way back to the kitchen and motioned for Mitch to sit.

"You think you're pretty clever, don't you!" his voice was low but ominous.

Mitch wasn't about to be bullied by him, but she kept herself in control.

"I think we should do whatever we can for your mom."

"You're just trying to escape and you're using her to accomplish your goal."

"I don't have an escape plan. I'm just trying to help out any way that I can."

"Why can't you heal her here?"

"Why can't you grant her a last request?"

"You make it sound like she's dying."

"It's like she said, Herman. She's not getting any younger."

Herman glowered again. His standard response when he was losing an argument with a woman.

"We'll drive all night and get there as soon as possible."

"That's not going to work."

"Why not?"

"Your mother doesn't have that much stamina. She will need to stay overnight when she tires from the travel."

"One night."

"She may need several. We won't know until we actually get on the road. And we're also going to need to plan for some healthy food. She can't eat cheese and crackers all the way there and back."

Herman sat for so long in silence that if Mitch didn't know better, she would've thought he was pouting. He must be feeling overruled at every turn and that wasn't easy for a man who was used to being

119

in total command and control of the situation.

"You're going to be guarded at all times."

"I live with an ex-politician. I'm used to that."

"There will be no chance for escape."

"I'm not under any illusions that this is going to be a vacation," Mitch replied steadily.

Herman was quiet for another few moments. He was going through all the combinations of how this trip could go wrong and weighing it against the alternative. Finally, he went over to the outside door and conferred with the foot soldier on guard. Then, he returned to the table with one sheet of paper and a pen.

"Make a list," he instructed.

"What kind of list?"

"A list of everything my mother will need for the trip."

"A packing list or a shopping list?"

"Whatever you think she will need."

Mitch thought this over. "How soon are we leaving?"

"Why would that matter?"

Mitch sighed, almost exasperated. "It matters because if we're going to prepare food, we'll need to buy groceries for cooking. However, if we're leaving right away, we won't have time to cook so we'll have to buy prepared food."

Herman looked like he was getting a migraine. Mitch knew what that felt like although she hadn't had one herself in a long time. "Plan for both," he decided.

"Okay," Mitch didn't want to argue about it anymore either. If they wanted a list, she'd provide one. A very detailed one. "I'm not sure if one piece of paper is going to be enough."

"Write small," he growled.

Good thing his mother wasn't listening in.

Mitch detached from all the distractions as she concentrated on her project. She imagined that she was making a shopping list with Reb. The task was easier that way. Chicken was always a good choice. Potato salad could be a crowd pleaser as well.

"How many of us are making this trip?" she broke her vow of silence long enough to get a clarification.

"That's none of your business."

"It is if I'm planning a menu."

"You just prepare the template and we'll handle the rest."

"Okay," Mitch shrugged. If they ran out of food, it would be on them and not her. She logically just started going through daily meals in her mind and wrote down the items that would be easy to prepare. Cold cereal was easier than bacon and eggs. Sandwiches were practical. Snack foods would fill in the gaps. After ten minutes of writing, Mitch handed her list to Herman.

"There's no red meat on this list."

"We could switch to roast beef sandwiches."

"That's not good enough."

"Well, other than packing up the leftover meatloaf, we could put steak on the list, but how are we going to prepare it?"

"Over a campfire."

"We're not taking your mother on some survivalist camping trip."

"I understand that. It doesn't mean that we can't stop at a campground long enough to cook a steak."

"We better add firewood to the shopping list, then."

"Why in the hell would we do that?"

"Because we don't want to get in trouble for gathering wood illegally in a state or national forest. I mean, that would be so ironic."

Herman scribbled on the paper. He looked like his headache was getting worse. Maybe they should add aspirin to the list as well?

"Besides," Mitch added, "We'll probably be driving through Kansas and there's no better place to get a steak, right?"

Herman stood up so forcefully that his chair tipped over backwards. He was at a loss for words, but his facial expression spoke volumes.

"Have you had a bad steak in Kansas?" Mitch asked like she was a travel writer preparing a column.

"Do not concern yourself with the route."

"That's not my focus. I just know that you can't get from Colorado to Alabama without going through steak and barbeque country."

"This isn't a luxury excursion," he barked.

"It is for your mother. I suggest we respect her wishes and comfort level."

"It's enough that we're taking her to Alabama."

"No, it's not. It needs to be an enjoyable trip for her and if that means staying in decent hotels and eating at fine restaurants, then that's how we should be planning this trip. Tear up the shopping list, gas up the van and let's get this show on the road!"

Herman may have been physically standing strong, but he was wavering mentally. Every hotel and restaurant would have surveillance cameras. Mitch's photo would be on every TV station and police report throughout the nation.

"You'll need a disguise."

"You mean, like Halloween?"

"I said disguise, not costume."

"What do you have in mind?"

"You're going to become a redhead."

"Then, I'm going to need a new wardrobe. One of these days…"

Herman shot her a warning look. Mitch took the hint, for about thirty seconds. "So are we stopping at the first beauty parlor we see?"

"Not exactly." Herman retrieved the shopping list. He crossed out everything with one big X and then wrote down one item. He crossed the room and opened the door where the guard was standing. "Get this." He handed the list over.

Then he came back and sat down to wait.

"I hope they get a nice shade of red."

"Shut up!"

It was a good thing mom was asleep or he'd have to apologize again.


Rose fretted. Trish knew enough about Rose's habits to pick up on her troubled mood. After all, she had every reason to fret and Trish would have frankly been concerned if Rose hadn't shown emotion.

"Can you tell me what you are feeling?" Trish asked gently.

"I'm feeling lost," Rose answered quietly.

Trish nodded. She knew what it felt like to lose someone you loved.

"It's like you've lost your anchor," Rose continued, "but that's a strange way to describe Max."

"How so?"

"He never weighed me down, but he was always there for me. He was stability. I guess that's why we call people anchors."

"I guess so…" Trish's voice trailed off.

"Can I ask you something?"

"Of course."

"Is it too soon to think about clearing out Max's things?" Rose had a troubled look on her face as she inquired.

"I don't think there's any right or wrong timing for these kinds of things."

"It won't seem hardhearted?"

"It needs to be done at some point."

"And it will help to keep me busy while we wait."

Trish nodded. It would be a good use of everyone's time.

Rose began slowly. It was easier to box up the clothing and shoes that Max hadn't worn in a while. They didn't carry with them the sentimental value that the well-worn clothing did. Before they knew it, they had several boxes lined up for donation.

"I'll take these downstairs for the time being," Trish volunteered. She picked up two of the lighter boxes and headed downstairs to the storage rooms, also known as the haunted section. It had been a while since she had been down here. The house was so big that they really didn't need to store items. Still, it would be handy to have these boxes out of sight for now. Trish went to the far corner of one of the rooms and placed the boxes in a stack. When she turned to leave, the door to the room was shut. Trish went over to open it but it wouldn't budge. She breathed the words, "Not again." It would do no good to yell, so she simply sat on the floor to wait for a rescue team to arrive.

Chapter 6

Reb was impatiently waiting for Lisa. This was becoming a pattern with them. Lisa dawdled like a child, at least as far as Reb was concerned.
"Have you always been this slow?" Reb asked.
"I've never had any complaints," Lisa demurred as she exited their vehicle at the hospital. She had helped Reb and then took a moment to make sure they had everything they came with.
Purses? Check. Sweaters? Check. Newly-hired lawyer? Check. Security detail? Check. Lisa had performed the miracle of finding an attorney available immediately to take on what she assumed would be a very lucrative wrongful-death lawsuit. They had conferred about the case during the ride to the hospital and a retainer had already changed hands. A famous person's relative was dead and there were deep pockets to sue.

"What was your name again?" Reb asked the lawyer as they entered the building.
Lisa shook her head almost inconspicuously. Not inconspicuously enough for Reb not to take notice.
"What's your problem?" Reb shot the question toward Lisa before the lawyer could answer.
"You just made out a check for a huge amount of money to someone and you've already forgotten her name."
"I remember how much the check was for and that it ended in Y." Reb countered.
"Which means that money means more to you than people," Lisa rendered her judgment.
"Which is still better than having issues with my memory."
"Not for the people who have to put up with you."
By now, they had all arrived at the information desk. The volunteer peered at them, surmising that they were there to cause trouble. No offer of help was forthcoming.
"We would like to speak to the hospital administrator Mr. Paul Seibert."

"You can't do that without an appointment," came the clipped reply.
"Well," Reb announced calmly, "We are going to check up on my deceased niece's newborn baby and then we're going to decide how many millions of dollars we are going to sue his hospital and the doctors for. If you think that the head of the hospital would want advance notice of that, by all means let him know just in case he wants to talk to us personally."

With that pronouncement, Reb deftly turned her wheelchair around and headed to the elevators. On the ride up to the maternity ward, Lisa said quietly, "Mandie."
"What?" Reb asked.
"Your new lawyer's name is Mandie."
"Reb nodded. "I knew it ended in a Y."
"Actually, it's an I E," Mandie corrected.
"But it's still a Y sound," Lisa pointed out.
"As long as the check doesn't bounce, you can call me anything you want."
"Don't give her any ideas," Lisa mumbled as the door to the elevator opened.
They exited the elevator and headed down the hallway to the nursery. Times had changed since Reb had given birth to Mary. In the olden days, maternity wards were large with rows and rows of cribs lined up at the visitors' window area. That was back when mothers were still allowed to have a few hours of peace and quiet to recover from the birthing process. Nowadays, in order to form a more perfect bond between mother and child, babies usually slept in the same room as their mothers.

The good news was that the viewing area was practically empty most days. The bad news today was that the nursery area was completely empty. Miranda's baby was nowhere in sight. As Reb glanced around to find some assistance, Mr. Seibert was walking toward them.
"How nice of you to meet with us today," Reb began cordially.
"I heard you were in the building."
"I imagine so. Speaking of which, I'm looking for Miranda's baby."
"Baby Knight has been transferred."
"To another floor?"

"To another hospital."

"And what have you done with Miranda?"

"Ms. Knight's remains have been sent to the county morgue."

"You really are cleaning house, aren't you?" Reb felt her anger rise.

"We have made the best possible decisions-"

"Shut up, you bastard," Reb interrupted angrily.

"Senator Fairbanks," Mandie decided to chime in early to earn her retainer.

"You shut up, too," Reb turned her full fury on her as well.

Mandie was shocked into silence. Lisa had had the good sense to have already staked her claim on that high ground. Mandie turned toward Lisa and asked, "Did she just tell me to shut up?"

Lisa could never quite understand why she always ended up explaining things to people who were supposed to be so much smarter than her.

"I'm pretty sure that's what she told you to do."

Meanwhile, Reb turned back to the hospital administrator. "Where have you transferred the baby?"

"Unfortunately, I'm not at liberty to divulge that information."

"Why not?"

"Patient confidentiality."

"I'm the nearest blood relation."

"That has yet to be established."

"What's that supposed to mean?"

"The baby has a father."

"The baby has a rapist for a father."

"That has yet to be adjudicated."

"So, meanwhile, we're playing hide the baby?"

"May I have security escort you from the building?"

"No thank you," Reb answered politely. "We can find our way out."

Reb looked directly at Lisa and nodded. Their silent interaction gave Lisa her marching orders. She took the lead and they proceeded without further incident to the elevators. It wasn't until they got into their vehicle that Mandie ceremoniously tore up the check that Reb had written a scant few hours ago.

"Nobody tells me to shut up in front of the person we plan on suing."

"I'm going to give you two choices. We can leave you off at your law office or I can double your retainer. However, if you decide to stay on the case, I reserve the right to always tell you to shut up

126

when you are interfering with my handling of this matter. Are we clear?"

Mandie thought it over. "You'll need to triple my retainer."

"Okay."

Now that Mandie was mollified, Lisa started the van. "We need to find the baby," Lisa said all business like.

"You think you can do that?" Reb challenged her.

"I found a lawyer who will put up with your bullshit. Finding a baby should be easy by comparison."

Trish didn't have to wait too long for the search party to rescue her. Ever since the abduction of Mitch, there had been a heightened sense of security and keeping track of everyone. This mostly consisted of Silver asking Rose where Trish had gotten off to.

"She took some boxes downstairs about five minutes ago," Rose reported.

Silver took the lead as they headed down to the haunted room. The door was closed but easily yielded to a push from Silver. Trish was just sitting quietly.

"Are you okay?" Rose asked.

"It's a quiet room. I'm just thinking and waiting for the next logical thing to happen," she said as she stared at the wall.

"Are you sure you're okay? Is she okay, Silver?"

Silver stepped forward. It seemed as if Trish was in a trance.

Maybe she had meditated too hard or waited too long.

"Let's go, Miss Trish," Silver reached out and gently lifted Trish to her feet.

"Are you sure it's going to be okay to leave everything here?" Trish asked.

"Why wouldn't it be okay?" Rose asked back.

"It's just so lonely down here."

"I'm sure the clothes will be fine," Rose reassured Trish as they took a couple of hesitant steps toward the door.

"Let's go," Silver once again took the lead. They walked Trish up the stairs and took her to the fireplace room. After settling her on the couch, they covered her with a blanket when they noticed the

127

goosebumps on her arms.

"There's no reason she should be cold, is there?" Rose asked Silver.

"Maybe she caught a chill downstairs."

"It's not cold downstairs either."

"There's more than one way to catch a chill," Silver said quietly.

"What do you think happened?"

"My best guess is something paranormal."

"But we don't have our ghost anymore," Rose said.

Silver didn't say it, but she knew better than to put limits on the spirit world. Rose sensed an answer in Silver's long pause.

"You think Max is haunting the house now? Or maybe Robbie?"

Silver remained silent. Naming ghosts was never a fruitful endeavor.

"But why?" Rose's question seemed to be directed more toward the universe now than Silver.

"I'm warm," Trish interjected into the silence. "Why am I covered with a blanket?"

"You were chilled," Rose replied soothingly.

"I'm warm now."

Trish removed the blanket. Her arms were bright pink as if she had sustained a mild sunburn.

"Was this an electric blanket? Was it turned too high?"

"No, it isn't."

"Why am I burned?"

"Maybe you are running a fever or having an allergic reaction," Rose was casting around for any earthly explanation.

"I'll call the doctor," Silver offered.

"No! Don't do that!" Trish was adamant.

"Why not?"

"Because. Just because. No doctors! I'm fine. I'll be fine. Just let me get some sleep. I'll be okay if I can just get some good rest."

"Okay. Let's get you to your bedroom."

Rose and Silver got Trish on her feet and guided her to her room.

"Would you just check up on me every couple of hours?"

"Of course, Dear," Rose nodded.

"I just need sleep."

"Of course you do."

Trish rested her head on her pillow and prayed that her mind would rest as well.

128

Finding a newborn baby wasn't as easy as it first had sounded. Lisa had gone about the problem logically. There was a finite number of hospitals in the area and the subset of facilities with maternity or pediatric wards was even smaller. The roadblock was medical privacy. To their credit, hospitals had clamped down on any information getting into the hands of the wrong person. And right now, Reb and Lisa were considered the wrong persons.

"Couldn't we get some sort of court order or cooperation from the Feds to force the hospitals to give us this information?" Lisa asked Mandie.

"We could try, but it may take a while and by then the baby could be transferred. Then, we would be forced to start all over again."

Lisa thought this over. The prospect of the baby being hospitalized indefinitely and transferred occasionally would create a huge burden on the facilities. And at some point, the baby would be discharged.

"If we can't find the baby, let's try to find the father," Lisa suggested.

"Stop calling him that!" Reb yelled herself right into the conversation.

It startled Mandie but Lisa was used to it.

"What term would you prefer?" Lisa asked.

"Anything but 'father'."

"Do you know his name?"

"No. But the prison system will."

"Do you want me to arrange a visitation?"

Reb thought it over. She had never actually met the bastard who had raped her niece in prison. It would be to his advantage that there would be glass separating them lest she give him a shot in his jaw.

"Let's do that. We can find out how much he knows about the current situation."

"That might be risky," Mandie opined.

"Life is inherently risky," Reb answered back.

"What would the risk be?" Lisa asked as she searched the internet for prison contact information.

"We could inadvertently tip our hand and give him more leverage," Mandie said.

"Except we're too smart for that," Reb followed up.

"Well, nothing is going to happen if we can't find him in the system," Lisa muttered.

"If you get stonewalled, I'll call the president."

"You mean Warden," Mandie said.

"No. I mean President of the United States."

"Oh," Mandie demurred.

"Maybe you won't need to call anyone. I think I found our man," Lisa stated.

"How did you do that so quickly?"

"Well, while the two of you were discussing who you were going to call for help, I did some cross checking on recent court case loads and news media coverage. We hit a lucky break. He's in a prison nearby. Do you want to make the phone call?" Lisa had the contact information at the ready.

"Hand me my phone," Reb nodded.

Mandie crossed her arms to silently denote her displeasure with the plan. It was all happening too fast with no real focus. Reb ignored the gesture. They didn't have time to waste having a meeting to set an agenda about how to proceed. Reb did her best thinking on her feet anyway, so to speak. As Reb arranged the prison visit, Mandie sidled up next to Lisa.

"Have you ever thought about working in a law office?"

"Is that a general inquiry or a job offer?"

"That's what I'm talking about! You have such a quick mind."

"And pretty decent research skills, too."

"You should give it serious consideration."

"Give what consideration?" Reb was off the phone and ready to interrupt.

"Nothing," Lisa said.

"What did you find out?" Mandie asked.

"I have an appointment set up. Let's go."

"So soon?"

"I don't waste time. Get the keys to the van."

At this directive, the security detail sprang into action. They coordinated the route to the men's prison with their higher ups and then escorted the group to the van. The route would add miles to the trip, a necessary tradeoff for security.

Mitch looked ridiculous, at least to herself. The guard in charge of picking out the hair dye had selected a particularly hideous shade of red. She looked like she was wearing a gigantic tomato on her head. Not that it mattered, but Herman seemed unfazed by the change. Martha, however, was confused at first. It seemed cruel to force her to accept this new look, but after Mitch sat with her for a few minutes, she settled down. Then, it was time to go. Martha surprised everyone by getting out of her bed as gracefully as any senior citizen could and walked to the door. She had dressed herself with a little help from Herman as Mitch had been altering her hair color. The transportation plan was for Herman to drive, Martha would be in the passenger seat and Mitch and her guard would ride in the back of the panel van. Someone had packed two suitcases full of essentials for Martha, Herman and the guard. Mitch would have to make do with what she was wearing, which was already becoming unwearable. Maybe there would be a washing machine at their first destination. As with any long journey, the first few miles were okay. And then, as more and more miles passed, the less okay it all became. This was magnified by the added boredom factor of being locked in the enclosed van with nothing to do but twiddle her thumbs. This had seemed like a good idea at the time. Most road trips do. Reality was now setting in and there were miles to go before the next meal. Mitch smelled so bad that they would never allow her in a restaurant, so they would probably just toss the food in the back of the van like they were feeding hungry hounds. It was getting downright depressing. Mitch closed her eyes and either fell asleep or passed out from hair dye fumes.

"Wake up, Sweetheart!"
"Huh?" Trish was sleepy and didn't want to be disturbed.
"Wake up," the voice was insistent.
Trish vaguely remembered Rose's promise to check up on her every couple of hours, but it couldn't possibly have been that long. She had just dozed off.
"Has it been two hours?" Trish asked groggily.
"It's been months. Come with me!"
Trish opened her eyes. No one was there. No Rose. No Silver.

131

Nobody. Whatever was going on was another one of those talking dreams that Rose believed in. Trish was becoming a believer as well. What had the talking dream said? She was being asked to go somewhere. Trish got out of bed and just started walking, trusting that she would instinctively follow the correct path. She wandered through the fireplace room where she had been wrapped up in the blanket earlier. No one was there. She felt compelled to keep walking. The kitchen was empty as well. That was strange. The kitchen was rarely empty. Rose was usually baking and Silver was usually drinking coffee. Trish kept wandering, almost in a daze, to the notorious haunted basement room. There was no one here either, but it felt like the correct destination. She went over to the boxes of Max's belongings and sat down next to them. It felt restful. Comforting. She didn't care if the door was open or stuck shut. It was warm and dry and peaceful. She would get better sleep down here than she was getting in her bedroom.

Someone was kicking Mitch's foot. Thump. Thump. Thump. It was beyond annoying. She resisted the urge to kick back because as she woke up, she remembered where she was.
"Mom needs to use the restroom," Herman announced.
Mitch was headachy from hunger and the smell of hair dye. Cranky was just the beginning of how she was feeling.
"You woke me up to tell me that?"
"You're taking her."
"Me?"
"Yes. You. Get up."
"How long have we been on the road?"
"Not long," Herman sounded exasperated.
Mitch stood up slowly. Sleeping on a hard surface was beginning to take its toll.
"Hurry up. She has an old bladder!"
Mitch was actually relieved at the prospect of getting out of the van for a breath of fresh air and a walkabout. Instead, she discovered that the van had been pulled up right next to a decrepit restroom attached to the back of a dilapidated gas station.
"You've got to be kidding," Mitch exclaimed.

"Please hurry," Herman asked nicely. It caught Mitch so off guard that she complied.

Martha had by now disembarked from the front seat of the van and was walking toward them with the help of the guard. Herman handed the restroom key to Mitch.

"There had better be some serious sustenance after this. And I don't mean candy and soda!"

"I'll see what I can do."

"Do good," Mitch intoned as she guided Martha to the bathroom.

This facility was the epitome of a gas station ladies' room that was rarely, if ever, cleaned by the male staff. Mitch checked quickly to see if there was even toilet paper. About one-fourth of a role was on the toilet tank due to the fact that the holder was missing, broken off no doubt by some miscreant for who knows what reason. The floor was gritty dirty and the toilet seat was yellowed and rickety. Mitch hoped it would be steady enough for Martha.

"How much help do you need?" Mitch asked.

"For what?"

"For going to the bathroom."

"I'm pretty sure I can get myself settled, but I might need help getting back up on my feet."

Martha settled in to take care of business and Mitch did her best to preoccupy herself to ease the awkwardness on the situation. It didn't seem to matter. Apparently, people had been watching Martha pee for quite some time. One of the humiliations of growing older was the tremendous loss of personal privacy. She managed to take care of her personal hygiene and needed only a steadying hand to stand up. Mitch was relieved beyond words. She turned the handle on the sink faucet only to have a trickle of rusty water dribble out.

"Let's wash our hands with bottled water," Mitch suggested.

"Do you need to use the potty?" Martha asked.

"Sure," Mitch nodded.

"I'll stand guard," Martha sounded almost gleeful with her newfound responsibility. They were beginning to bond at that unique place where women stick together: Bathroom Use.

Mitch was now relieved in more ways than one as they exited the restroom.

"Can I tell you something?" Martha asked Mitch.

"Of course," Mitch hoped that whatever this was would be okay for Herman to hear.

"And I don't want you to take it the wrong way, but you don't smell very good."

"I agree," Mitch nodded, hoping indeed that Herman had overheard this exchange.

He was standing right by the back of the van. He had a prepackaged mystery meat sandwich in one hand and a tiny bag of chips in the other.

"Here's your food."

Mitch inspected it. "The sandwich is expired."

"Only two days."

"Just give me the chips and something to drink."

Herman began to glower. "You said no soda."

"Is soda all they had? Really?" Mitch sounded skeptical.

The exchange was interrupted by Martha, who added her editorial comments. "She smells bad. She needs a shower and a change of clothes."

"Did she tell you to say that?" Herman was constraining his irritation, but just barely.

"She didn't need to! She stunk up the entire ladies' room!"

"Everyone in the van. Let's go!" Herman barked.

Mitch shrugged her shoulders and prepared to hop back in the van, but Martha was still insisting, "Not until you promise showers and clean clothes!"

Herman sighed. "Alright! I promise. Now will you please get in the front of the van?"

"What kind of drink do you want?" Martha asked Mitch as if Herman didn't even exist on planet Earth at the moment. The more Martha was out and about, the livelier she became.

"Iced tea would be nice."

Martha now turned to Herman, once again acknowledging his earthly presence. "Get us both a supersize serving of iced sweet tea and two much bigger bags of chips than this pathetic excuse for a snack," Martha took the tiny bag of chips and placed it forcefully in Herman's hand. Herman said nothing, but slowly turned to Mitch's guard and nodded his head. The guard headed back into the gas station store.

"Now can we get back in the van?" Herman asked very quietly. Almost too quietly.

Mitch got in the back on the van and waited for everyone else to get settled in as well. Her guard soon delivered a sickeningly sweet large cup of tea and a family-size bag of chips. It would hold off the hunger pangs for now. And if Martha drank her share of tea, it wouldn't be long before their next bathroom break.


After far too many miles on the road, Reb and her entourage finally arrived at the prison. It was a grim, bleak, forbidding structure. Reb's first thought was about Mary, who was residing in a similar place. It had to be a soul-killing experience. She made a vow to stay in better communication and visit at the earliest opportunity. But for now, there was critically important business to attend to. The prison administrator met them at the entrance. Despite Reb's senatorial connections, certain protocol needed to be adhered to. Metal detectors, confiscation of personal items such as driver's licenses, and a double-door locked entry system that led into the bowels of the building. Which, frankly, was what the inner sanctum smelled like. Reb had lived the majority of her life in the rarified air of wealth and cleanliness. She didn't tolerate this well. They were led to a holding room that was cramped and stuffy. Only two visitors at a time were allowed in the high security area to visit prisoners. Reb was reluctant to have Mandie at the meeting, but she inherently understood the wisdom.

Reb and Mandie were then escorted to a partitioned room with a phone in place to converse with the prisoner. Reb hadn't paid much attention to the court case and incarceration of this man, so she really didn't know what to expect. In her mind, she had imagined him to be large and ugly. A typical "bad man" visage. Unfortunately, in an age that idolizes thin, pretty people, large and ugly was easy to discount and hate.

Minutes ticked by. Reb was losing patience and ready to call everything off when a door opened on the other side of the partition and a prison guard walked in followed by the prisoner. He was shackled and shuffled like an old man despite his youth. He looked like a kid. Reb was old enough to be irritatingly reminded from time to time how many young people there actually were in the world. And maybe she was being a curmudgeon, but why couldn't these young people act decently. The prisoner sat down and the guard left the room. Everyone looked at each other for a moment before Reb picked up the phone. He followed suit.

"What's your name?" Reb asked.

He pointed to his uniform that had his last name, Fox, patched on it.

"Your first name?" Reb asked curtly.

"Steven."

"Okay, Mr. Steven Fox. You and I need to have a very serious talk."

"Who are you?" he asked without any trace of emotion.

Reb paused. It dawned on her that he may not have been updated on the latest turn of events.

"My name is Senator Fairbanks. You raped my niece."

"No, I didn't."

"If I were you, I wouldn't make me angry."

He shrugged his shoulders like it didn't much matter to him whether or not Reb got angry.

"You raped her and got her pregnant."

"We had an affair. It was her idea."

"That's a lie."

"You weren't there. In fact, you were hardly ever there at all. You never visited her. None of her family ever visited her. Do you know what that does to someone in prison when the other prisoners are always getting visitors and no one ever comes to visit you?"

"Miranda told us what happened."

"Her self-esteem was so low that I imagine she would have told you anything to hide her behavior."

Reb hadn't expected this turn in the conversation. She struggled to hide her irritation at being reminded by this criminal of her own neglect of Miranda. Reb also knew enough about criminal law to find his story believable. Even if the sex was consensual, since Miranda was a prisoner, it was considered rape. She wished Mitch was here. Mitch had kept closer tabs on the court case. As if he was reading her mind, Steven said, "I pled guilty. I didn't want to make Miranda go through the trauma of testifying."

Once again, silence descended. There are times in life where silence seems to be the one true reaction. This was one of those moments.

"I have bad news," she finally said.

Steven, who had to this point been stoic, showed his first sign of emotion. "What's wrong? Did something happen to the baby?" Reb bowed her head, trying instinctively to hide the tears that were stinging her eyes.
"Please tell me what's going on?"
"Miranda died after giving birth."
Steven went pale so quickly that Reb, fearing he would pass out, called for a guard. No one showed up and Steven waved off the offer of help.
"I'll be okay. Just give me a minute," he assured.
"I'm sorry," Reb said, "But I didn't know any better way to break the news to you."
"Is the baby okay?" he followed up.
"I can't honestly tell you. That's why I'm here. I need your help."
"I'm confused. No one tells me anything in prison. So I don't know how to help."
"The hospital administrators have transferred the baby so we don't know what's going on either."
"Is it a boy or a girl?"
"It's a boy. He was in the critical care unit when we last visited."
"So, he's not okay?" Steven was turning pale again.
"It was a rough birth."
"What happened?"

Reb sighed. She was frustrated. She needed somewhere to put her anger down for a while. She had been so very prepared to take all her anger out on this man. And now, it wasn't working out at all like she had planned.

"Miranda was anorexic. She was too underweight at the birth to survive. The malnourishment affected the baby."
"Is that why the hospital transferred the baby?"
"We don't know. No one is telling us anything because we don't

have any legal standing. The hospital administrators feel that you are the closest blood relative. Has anyone tried to contact you about the baby?"

"I haven't heard any of this. How can I help you?"

"I want you to call the hospital administrator, Mr. Paul Seibert, and demand information on the whereabouts of the baby."

"My phone privileges are extremely limited."

"Let me worry about that. Just please work with me and I promise to keep you in the loop."

"I'd appreciate that. I haven't had a visitor since I was sent here."

"No one has come to visit?"

"You can check the records."

"I'm not doubting you."

"It's just that I'm all alone in the world. Now more than ever."

Reb couldn't believe it, but she was beginning to feel sorry for this man. Of course, she would still check his prison standing with the warden while she was arranging for phone privileges. If he was telling the truth, she would try and find other ways to help as well. It was the least she could do for his cooperation.

Sensing that the visit was coming to a close, Steven asked, "Can you tell me anything about the baby?"

This request gave Reb pause. She had barely seen the baby through a window and hadn't even had the chance to hold him.

"He's amazing," was all that Reb could come up with.

Even at this vague description, Steven smiled. Reb now understood why Miranda had been attracted to him. When he smiled, he came alive. The kind of aliveness that would be so rare in a dead-dreary institution.

"This won't be my last visit," Reb promised as she left the visitation room.

Reb, Lisa and Mandie went back with the warden to his office. When he had initially balked at a meeting, citing prior schedule conflicts, Reb had offered to have him explain himself to the president. His schedule had cleared quickly.

"Mr. Fox is going to require extensive phone privileges."

"He can make phone calls directly from my office."

Reb gave this serious consideration. She wasn't sure if it would give Steven the privacy he might need.

"It will be less problematic for prisoner Fox," the warden explained.

"Problematic?"

"If other prisoners see him getting extra time on the common use phones, it might be detrimental to him."

"And being called to your office won't have that same effect?"

"No one is jealous of a fellow prisoner's visit to my office."

"I imagine not. Has Mr. Fox been a model prisoner?"

"One of the best."

"Here's the information that he will need to complete his task," Reb handed over the paperwork with contact information.

"I'll have him start today."

"The sooner, the better," Reb admonished as she, Lisa and Mandie took their leave.


This time, there was no fooling around. When Silver and Rose found Trish in the basement again, they called an ambulance. Trish couldn't talk them out of it. Literally. She was unable to form a sentence. She couldn't answer Rose as to why she was once again in the basement next to Max's boxes of clothing. She had tried to talk, but nothing coherent was coming out.

When the paramedics arrived on scene, they treated Trish with the same level of care as if she had fallen out of a tree. After checking her vitals, they loaded her in an ambulance and headed for the hospital. Rose was showing signs of shock as well as she faced the reality of one more relative going to the same hospital as her dearly departed daughter and husband. Silver, God bless her, was keenly aware of the reality.

"Do you want to stay here, Miss Rose, while I follow the ambulance?"

"I don't know," Rose hesitated.

"If you will stay and look after Josh, I'll go with Miss Trish and call you with updates."

"Okay," Rose nodded. She felt guilty and relieved all at the same time.

Silver took off for the hospital secure in the knowledge that Agents Smith and Vukoff would soon be at the house to offer support. By the time Silver had parked and entered the hospital, Trish had already been assigned a room in the emergency ward. Silver passed many rooms that had people in them with very serious physical injuries on her way to find Trish. It was easy to see what was wrong with them, but Trish was damaged in a different way. Her mind was fracturing and they needed to act fast before it came apart completely. It was a whole different kind of medicine than setting a broken leg. It had taken a few minutes to cut the red tape preventing Silver from being allowed in the ward to visit. She wasn't family and being the family bodyguard wasn't enough to bypass regulations. Actually, it was Trish who had extended the permission, which was a promising sign. Silver went into Trish's room quietly. It appeared that Trish was sleeping. It was a ruse, however, because as Silver drew near, Trish's eyes came wide open. Startled, Silver jumped back.

"It was her," Trish whispered to Silver like she was fearful of being overheard. By whom was unclear. They were alone in the room.

"What did you say, Miss Trish?" Silver moved closer.

"Shhhh!" Trish held a finger to her lips.

"What?" Silver was puzzled.

"We can't talk too loud," Trish said.

"Okay. Whatever you say, Miss Trish."

"It was her," Trish enunciated slowly and carefully, emphasizing each word.

"Who?" Silver asked.

"It was Robbie," Trish was whispering again.

"Robbie?"

"She was there."

"Where?"

"In the house. In the room."

Further conversation was interrupted by the doctor on call.

"Hello. I'm Doctor Jensen."

"Hello, Doctor. I'm Silver," she greeted as Trish broke off eye contact and drew the blanket up close around her chin. It was evident that Trish wanted no contact with this man.

"So, you are the family bodyguard," the doctor noted.

"That's right," Silver pulled herself up out of her slouch. It added another inch to her already imposing stature.

"Well, thank you for being here for Ms. Weingarten."

"You're welcome," Silver practically stammered. It was the first time she had been thanked by a doctor for anything.

"How are you feeling, Ms. Weingarten?"

Trish remained fearful and wouldn't respond. The doctor turned to Silver.

"She might answer if you ask her," he said.

Silver felt compromised. She didn't want to reveal the notion that Trish was seeing ghosts, but she wanted to be helpful.

"Miss Trish has a therapist. Maybe she can help?"

"Do you have the contact information?"

"Not with me, but I can get it for you."

"Okay. Please give the information to the front desk and we'll proceed from there."

"Will she be assigned a room?"

"I want to go home," Trish finally found something to comment on.

"We can't discharge you quite yet."

"I can discharge myself!"

"You're correct, of course. We can't legally hold you unless we have good reason."

"Is seeing a ghost a good enough reason?" Silver chose her betrayal carefully.

Dr. Jensen studied Silver. "What sort of ghost?"

"Dead girlfriend ghost."

"Does her therapist know about this?"

"There was an earlier incident that involved a cemetery. I don't know if it included a ghost."

Dr. Jensen nodded and then turned to Trish. "Would you do me a favor?"

"What?"

"Would you please stay here long enough to have a visit with your therapist?"

"What if she's too busy to come here?"

"You can talk to her on the phone."

Although he wasn't an expert on mental health, he could tell that Trish was giving this serious consideration. It was a promising sign

141

that her rational mind was still functioning.

"Okay. But I want a private room. I have enough money to pay for it. I don't want anyone listening in when I talk to Dr. Carlson."

"I'll see what I can do," Dr. Jensen nodded.

Within half an hour, Trish had been transferred to the area of the hospital that looked more like a hotel suite than a hospital room. She was enough of a dignitary to be extended access to this swanky luxury. Silver had also completed her homework by calling Rose with both an update and questions. Thankfully, two things had gone her way. Rose had the contact information for Dr. Carlson, Trish's therapist, and Smith had arrived with Vukoff in tow. Everyone was on edge about Trish, but Silver did her best to calm them down.

"She's in the best room with the best care. I'm sure we'll be home soon."

Rose knew all about the chasm between fact and intention. She would believe it when she saw Trish home again.

Therapy was hard. In fact, it was kicking Mary's ass. She hadn't completed her assignment to the satisfaction of Anna and was now embroiled in an argument with her.

"This is a sorry excuse for an obituary," Anna had remarked after reading the all-too-brief summary of Mary's attempt to write a memorial for her mother.

"I listed the highlights," Mary was indignant in her response.

"Indeed. It's all very forensic in its description," Anna made it sound like an autopsy.

"Obituaries tend to be that way," Mary remarked.

"How many obituaries have you read lately?" Anna asked.

"I haven't had access to a newspaper lately."

"Have you ever read an obituary?"

Mary scanned her memory. "I don't recall."

"Well, then, let me fill you in on what a typical obituary might entail. It often includes the listing of the surviving relatives of the deceased as well as deeply felt emotions of the deceased by said surviving relatives. It can, in fact, be a moving tribute to the deceased."

There was a moment of silence as Mary pondered this. Then, she said, "But it doesn't have to be. There's no set rules for obituaries."

Anna nodded. "That's correct. Obituaries can also be pretty cold and unfeeling. Almost like a eulogy written by a complete stranger. Is that how you feel about your mother? Is she a stranger to you?"

"I've known my mother my whole life. How can she be a stranger to me?"

"It's just not coming across in your assignment. As the younger generation would say, I'm not feeling the love."

"My mother and I have a complicated relationship," Mary finally told the truth.

"Do you want to expand on that?"

"We only have thirty minutes."

"You start and I'll watch the clock," Anna said kindly but firmly.

"Have you ever had to deal with someone who was almost like two different people?"

"All the time," Anna nodded.

"It's hard to feel close to someone like that. You never know which person they are going to be on any given day."

"Tell me more about your mother's different personalities."

"It feels like a betrayal."

Anna nodded again. "That's a good feeling to be experiencing."

"It is?"

"It's a vast improvement over a ten-line obituary."

Mary began slowly. "My mother was a very conservative person during my childhood."

"Okay," Anna encouraged.

Mary suddenly realized that this woman had no clue about her family. Anna had been far enough removed from Colorado for any familiarity.

"My mother was a right-wing politician who became a lesbian practically overnight."

"That's quite a transformation."

"It was a shock."

"But you are a lesbian as well."

"What's that got to do with it?"

"Did it bother you at all that suddenly you weren't the only lesbian in the family?"

143

"You ask a lot of leading question for a therapist."

"Well, that's what happens when a therapist is also a public servant instead of being in private practice."

"Why?"

"If I were in private practice, we could just let this go on session after session and I could be charging hundreds of dollars an hour just to sit here and listen and then after a while I could retire to the Cayman Islands."

"And yet, here you are."

"People in prison don't always get the level of care they need."

Mary got the inkling that this conversation was somehow personal for Anna. She felt that it wasn't the proper time to ask follow-up questions. So she continued with her story. "It was okay that my mom came out. Really it was. But it would have been a lot easier growing up if she had told me earlier."

"Maybe she didn't know she was a lesbian?"

"Maybe she did?"

"Did you ask her about it?"

"No. Not really. We haven't talked much about it."

"You are two of the most famous lesbians in Colorado and you haven't talked about it?"

"We don't talk about a lot of stuff."

"Is that your pattern?"

"Pretty much."

"Who did you feel closest to growing up?"

"My dad."

"Do you keep in touch?"

"Not really."

"Who do you feel close to now?"

"Nobody really."

"Does your dad know you are here?"

"I'm sure he does."

"But has he heard it from you?"

"No."

"Why?"

"I'm not sure it would serve any purpose."

"Well, he could visit you."

"And what would we talk about?"

"At least you've given it some thought."

"Not much."

"But some."

"A little."

"And you envision sitting across a table from him saying nothing?"

"I wouldn't know what to say."

"Imagine I'm your dad. Talk to me."

Mary looked away and started to shut down.

"It would be that difficult to talk to him?"

"I couldn't even look him in the eye."

"Why not?"

"Because I'm so ashamed of myself."

"You've spent years helping other people and saved the world. Why are you feeling the way you do?"

"Because of Fawn."

"You think you are the only person who was ever attracted to someone outside of your primary relationship?"

"I'm the only one who has to explain it to my dad."

"So, let's get him on the phone."

"Right now?" Mary sounded alarmed.

"I think I could arrange it."

"I, I don't have his phone number."

"I do. It's in your file."

"I really wouldn't know what to say."

"Let's reverse the situation. Suppose that you are your dad and your daughter is in prison. How does that affect you?"

"I would've called as soon as I found out," Mary blurted.

"Talk more about that."

"I'm his only child and I'm in protective custody and he hasn't bothered to pick up the phone and contact me. I may not be perfect, but I deserve a call."

"I agree."

"So, I guess I'm just really angry about it."

"Why do you think he hasn't called?"

"We've just lost touch. We used to be close but now, after the divorce, I've just been closer to my mother. Not that we are very close either. But at least she calls, only if it's to tell me what to do."

"Well, we have two choices. We can either keep talking about your childhood, or we can get your dad on the phone. It's up to you."

145

"Let's make the call."

Anna nodded and then fished her cell phone out of her jacket pocket. She entered the number and then handed the phone to Mary. Her dad picked up on the third ring.

"Hello?"

"Hi, Dad. It's me."

"Hi, Honey. How are you?"

"I'm in a prison."

There was a pause, neither long nor short. Just a moment of reflection.

"Why?" he finally asked.

"You didn't know I was in a prison, did you?"

"No, I didn't. What happened? Are you okay? How can I help?"

Mary felt badly about making him feel for a short minute that she had done something wrong. It was childish behavior stemming from feeling neglected. She went on to explain, "I'm not really in a prison because I committed a crime. I'm in protective custody and it was the only safe place they could come up with."

"So you didn't break the law?"

"Well, not yet."

"Why are you being protected?"

"I'm going to be a witness for the prosecution."

"Just like in the movies, huh?"

"Right. It's that domestic terrorism case you've probably heard about on the news."

"I don't watch the news. It's too depressing."

"I understand. I'm sorry I didn't call you sooner."

"It's okay. I'll fly right out and visit you. Just give me the name of where you are."

"I will need to let my contact person make the arrangements."

"Okay. I'll wait to hear from them. I love you."

"Love you too, Dad."

Mary disconnected the call. Anna nodded. "We should let Agent Fawn know about this so she can set up the visit."

"Okay," Mary answered, still distracted by the phone call.

"What are you thinking?"

"I'm thinking that I had forgotten that my dad doesn't watch the news. I need to stay in better touch with my loved ones once I am out of here."

"Staying in touch with loved ones is always a good idea," Anna nodded sagely.

As if on cue, there was a knock on the door. Anna didn't seem at all surprised. Their time was about up for the day.

"Come in," Anna said without looking up from her notes.

It was Fawn. Just the person they needed to talk to. Mary might have chalked up Fawn's timely arrival to coincidence, but the expression on her face gave her away. If only she played poker.

"There's been a development I thought you might want to know about. You had mentioned that it was important for you to get updates."

"What's happened now?" Mary braced for the worst.

"Trish is in the hospital."

"What did she do? Trip over one of her piles of cash?"

Things got really quiet. Anna made a note in Mary's chart.

"Was that inappropriate?" Mary asked no one in particular.

"About Trish," Fawn went back to her original news. "She's been admitted for a psychiatric exam."

Anna's focus switched from Mary's chart to Fawn's face instantly.

"What happened to warrant that?"

Fawn paused. There were rules about patient confidentiality that had already been violated once.

"She is hearing voices."

"I'm hearing voices right now," Anna said with a twinge of sarcasm.

"The voice Trish is hearing is her dead partner."

"She's hearing Robbie?" Mary asked.

"That's the issue."

"Sounds like unresolved grief to me," Mary stated like she was now the expert.

"Why do you say that?" Anna asked, now fully engaged in the discussion,

"It's all pretty simple. Trish was carrying on with my girlfriend when Robbie killed herself. My only surprise is that it took so long for her to finally crack."

Anna and Fawn exchanged a look. It was a rare thing when someone put too fine a point on such a complex issue.

147

"What?" Mary asked them both when the silence begged for a break.

"You could be right," Anna nodded.

"Next thing you know, she'll be seeing the ghost of Robbie. Meanwhile, I want to arrange for my dad to visit. Can you help me with that?" Mary directed the inquiry to Fawn.

"I'll see what I can do."


As predicted, everyone needed another bathroom break soon after drinking all that sweet tea. Too soon for Herman. Once again, Mitch helped Martha with her bathroom visit in another grimy dump of an ageing gas station. The real miracle would be that neither one of them would contract some sort of bacterial infection by the end of the trip.

"Maybe we need more salt?" Mitch couldn't believe that the chips they had ingested hadn't helped in this regard.

"That wouldn't be the best thing. Mother has already had too much salt as it is. I don't need her to be retaining fluid. She has an issue with edema."

"Now you tell me!" Mitch groused. She was cranky from traveling too many miles and they didn't even have a good start yet.

"Stop complaining! Every time she gets out of the van, you get out of the van!"

"Then could we at least stop at a better grade of gas station?"

"There are security cameras at those places."

"No one is looking for us on this cross-country trip! Everyone probably still thinks we're in Colorado."

"I'll think about it," he muttered as he slammed the van door.

Mitch took her seat across from her armed guard. The van was uncomfortably warm. It reminded her of the vacations she went on when she was a child. They weren't a rich family by any stretch of the imagination. There weren't any jet trips to New York or cruises to the Bahamas. What there was were a lot of clunky car trips through the southwest desert sightseeing a lot of dry, dusty landscapes. You were lucky if you saw a coyote. Still, in all these opportunities, Mitch had never traveled to the South. The land of heat and humidity. Her thoughts were interrupted by the opening of the van door. It was Herman, bearing snacks. The kind that you buy out of a machine that you sometimes had to rock back and forth until it gave up the goods. The offering was pathetic, worse than the last stop. A can of grape soda and a likely-rancid candy bar.

"Wouldn't want to spoil dinner," was his parting comment.

As soon as Mitch heard the driver's side door slam shut, the van lurched forward. It would be miles again before their next stop, so she parceled out her candy bar into several pieces to make it last. If they were intending to starve her into complacency, they would have a fight on their hands.

The mileage from Colorado to Alabama is roughly 1500 miles. If they traveled non-stop, a highly unlikely scenario, it would take twenty hours. Mitch gave herself a silent pep talk. She could endure anything for twenty hours. It would be no more difficult than say, staying awake through New Year's Eve, right? She ignored the fact that she hadn't actually accomplished that feat in a few years, but then again, she hadn't been riding cross country in a van, either. It was during this reverie that Mitch realized that she had eaten the rest of her candy bar. The human appetite for food was a powerful drive when left to its own devices. She drank her soda to kill the taste in her mouth and then closed her eyes. Maybe, just maybe they could get a few miles more down the road before the next gas station visit.

Reb understood the fact that things take time, but it was difficult for her to accept the concept that important things take more time. She should've been used to it from her political career, but when it came to personal matters, she was chronically impatient. How long could it possibly take to make one phone call? Just one call to a hospital administrator to get information on the whereabouts of the baby? Maybe it was taking more than one phone call? Reb looked pensive. So much so that Lisa took notice.

"It's hard waiting, isn't it?" Lisa said.

"I'm fine."

"Of course you are," Lisa replied, singling each word out for emphasis.

"You have a problem with me being okay?"

"Fine."

"What?"

"You said you were fine."

"I know what I said."

"Okay."

"Why are you picking a fight with me?"

"Probably to distract you from everything that's going on."

"It isn't helping."

"What would help?"

"Silence."

"I tried that. It didn't work."

"Try again."

"It won't work now that you're aware of it."

Reb sighed.

"Now what?" Lisa asked.

"I wish I had left you home."

"You couldn't really do that. I don't have a home."

"Not anymore. You blew your cover and now everyone is paying the price."

"Don't worry about me. When this is all over, I'm not going back to WITSEC. I'll find a job somewhere and take my chances. I'll buy a gun and take care of myself."

The phone rang, bringing a sudden and merciful halt to Lisa's narrative. Reb answered the call, expecting to get an update on the baby. Instead, it was Agent Smith.

"Is Lisa there?" he asked kindly.

"Why?" Reb asked, annoyed that he was tying up the line.

"Because I wish to speak to her," he replied evenly.

"Why?" Reb wasn't ready to hand over the phone.

"I have information to impart to her. Please do not make me get on a plane and fly all the way back out there for the privilege of speaking to her."

Reb, for all her stubbornness, appreciated a person who stood their ground as well. She handed the phone to Lisa. "It's for you."

Lisa took the phone, skeptical of any chance that this was good news.

"Hello?"

"It's Smith."

"Hi, Smith. What's new?"

"I thought you would want to know that Trish is in the hospital."

"What happened?"

"You didn't hear it from me, but it appears that she's having a nervous breakdown."

Lisa's quick mind raced. It didn't make sense. Trish was one of the strongest people she knew and the least likely to crack under pressure.

"Why?" Lisa asked tentatively.

"I'm not sure. It's above my paygrade."

"What do you think I should do?"

"Follow your instincts."

"Thanks," Lisa said and then disconnected the call.

"So what did Smith need to tell you that he couldn't possibly tell me?" Reb asked with just a hint of annoyance.

Lisa slowly shook her head. "I need a few minutes to myself," she said and the stood up to leave the room.

Reb was suspicious of this reflective behavior and ruffled at being left out of whatever was going on.

"Well, don't take too long! I might need your help any minute!"

Without comment, Lisa walked away.


Dr. Carlson arrived at the hospital and was granted access to Trish's private room. Silver was still serving as bodyguard and had been joined by Smith. Vukoff was guarding Rose. Oddly enough, they had hit it off after Rose offered her cookies.

"Hi, Trish," Dr. Carlson said cheerily.

"Oh, hi, Dr. Carlson," Trish sounded almost happy to see her. This was a good sign.

"You remember me?"

"Of course. I'm not psychotic."

"You never were," Dr. Carlson smiled and then said to Silver and Smith, "Would you let us have some private time?"

Both of them tamped down their primal urge to stay and guard, but the strain showed on their faces.

"I'll be fine," Trish said, mostly to Silver, less to Smith.

Once they were alone, Dr. Carlson pulled up a chair.

"So, tell me what's going on."

"Don't laugh, okay?"

"Okay."

"I'm having visits from Robbie."

"How do these visits happen?"

"I hear her voice. I feel her presence."

"What does she say?"

"It's hard to remember."

"Why?"

"Because, it's elusive, like a vague dream that doesn't stay with you."

"How does it feel?"

"What do you mean?"

"Is it positive or negative?"

"It's unnerving."

"Right. But the things that Robbie says, are they good or bad?"

"It's always good. Like things are going to be okay."

"So, it isn't angry messages or negative feelings?"

"No. It's actually kind of comforting."

"That's good."

"But it's not normal."

"It may be more normal than you realize."

"It's normal to hear voices?"

"Yes, and a lot of it is due to the vestiges of our bicameral brain evolution."

"Our what?"

"There's a theory that our brain used to talk to itself before it developed better ways to communicate."

"That sounds pretty far-fetched."

"Maybe so. And it's a lot more complex theory than I've just explained to you. But I think it's a better theory than just labeling people as crazy."

"So, does that mean I can go home now?"

"If you promise to make an appointment with me, I will recommend that you be discharged."

Chapter 7

Mitch was really hungry by now. Which was both good and bad. It was never pleasant to be hungry, but it also meant that they had traveled for a longer distance between rest stops. As Mitch was contemplating just how long, the van slowed to a stop. It was ages before Herman opened the door.

"Do exactly what I say and you will get something good to eat," he said through clenched teeth.

"Whatever," Mitch answered, not feeling terribly defiant.

"Put on this hat," he handed her a baseball cap with a golf logo on the front. Mitch followed orders.

"Now, you are going to get out of the van and follow me to your room."

At the word "room," Mitch brightened up. It would feel great to be at rest, if only for a little while.

Herman took the lead with Mitch and her guard following at a steady pace. As Mitch looked at her surroundings, this was one of those motels that had absolutely no amenities. She would be lucky to have a pillow, let alone a pillow-top mattress. They were at room number 13 very quickly and when Herman unlocked the door, Martha was already resting in the only bed in the room.

"I thought we were going to my room?"

"This is your room."

"But there's nowhere to sleep."

"You'll have a rollaway cot."

"I'd prefer the floor."

"As you wish."

"You mentioned something about a meal?"

"I'm working on it."

"And I'll need some clean clothes. I plan on taking a shower soon so you'll need to get working on that shopping as well."

Herman began to glower again. It was his knee-jerk reaction to being bossed around by a female.

"We will wash your clothes at a laundromat."

"And what am I supposed to wear in the meantime? I didn't get to pack a bag because, remember, I was kidnapped!"

"You can borrow one of my mother's house dresses."

Mitch didn't really look at all stylish in flowery frocks, but maybe it would take her mind off of her stomach. Martha had been asleep throughout much of this exchange and only stirred awake when Herman began rummaging through her spare clothing.

"What are you doing?"

"I'm finding something for her to wear."

Martha looked at Mitch and said, "The purple one."

"Purple?"

"She will look good in purple."

Herman found the correct one and handed it over to Mitch. "Wrap up your clothes in a towel and leave them outside the bathroom door."

The towels, all two of them, were barely big enough to wrap up her clothing. She discreetly opened the bathroom door and left the bundle for the laundry fairy. It took a while for the water to get warm enough to shower without getting a chill. The only thing she had to wash her newly-dyed hair with was the same tiny bar of soap that only the cheapest of motels provided. She watched as the rinse water turned a rusty color and drained down her body. Even in the disguise department, Herman had been cheap. Mitch got herself as clean as tepid water and bad soap allowed and then toweled herself completely dry before putting on the purple duster Martha had so kindly picked out. She felt ridiculous as she stepped out of the bathroom. Martha was asleep and the front door was being guarded, so Mitch sat in the only chair if the room to await further developments.


The phone rang. Reb reached for it immediately. It was the warden.

"It's certainly taken you long enough! When can we see the baby?"

"We've encountered a difficulty," he began a well-rehearsed response.

"Where is the baby?" Reb interrupted.

"That's the problem. We don't know yet."

"Yet?"

"We are still making phone calls."

"I don't understand," Reb said.

"Neither do I. Prisoner Fox and I have talked to every hospital in the state and no one has the baby."

"Why did you need to make all those calls? Obviously, Mr. Seibert knew where he transferred the baby."

"That was the first call we made. The baby never got to the hospital."

"He must have known that to be the case."

"Apparently the paperwork fell through the cracks. That's why we started to make all the other phone calls."

"It's time to alert the police."

"We wanted to call you first, but that's our next step."

"And I will alert everyone on this end of the developments. Thank you for calling," Reb hung up.

The agents exchanged a glance.

"They have managed to lose the baby."

As the agents started making phone calls of their own to their hierarchy, Reb went to find Lisa. She was propped up in bed, hugging a pillow.

"What's wrong with you?"

"I'm trying to figure out what to do next."

"What did Smith say to you?"

"Trish is having some sort of breakdown."

Reb didn't know what to say.

"I don't expect your sympathy," Lisa expounded.

"So, what are you going to do?"

"Smith told me to follow my instincts. It's harder than it seems."

"I want to let you know of the latest development before you make up your mind."

"What's happened?"

"Miranda's baby has gone missing."

Lisa didn't seem at all shocked. In fact, she guessed correctly. "He never even got to the second hospital, am I right?"

"How do you know that?"

"What else could it be?" Lisa answered knowingly.

"So, what are we going to do now?" Reb was at a loss.

"We're going to do the right thing. You and I are going to arrange a Christian burial for Miranda."

155

"Herman. Herman!"

Mitch opened her eyes. She had drifted off to sleep waiting for dinner and was startled awake by Martha's outcry. She stood up and went over to the bed.

"Are you okay?"

"Who are you?" Martha looked upset.

"I'm Mitch. Remember me? We are going to Alabama together."

"Oh, I need to use the bathroom."

"Let me help."

Mitch practically hoisted Martha out of bed and guided her to the toilet. Once she was settled, she remarked, "You look nice in that dress."

"Thank you," Mitch was gracious even though she looked like her grandmother in it.

"I used to have one just like it."

Mitch couldn't bring herself to remind Martha that it was her dress. There was already enough confusion to go around.

"And you smell better, too," Martha commented matter-of-factly.

Just about the time that Mitch had gotten Martha settled back into bed, there was a knock at the door. It was Herman with food. Even though Mitch was practically starving, she made sure Martha was set up with her dinner before Mitch pulled her chair over to join her. Apparently, wherever they were was a town big enough for a fried chicken fast food outlet. It wasn't exactly gourmet, but it was far better than a stale candy bar.

Martha ate slowly. Methodically. Maybe she had been granted more snacks during the day. Mitch slowed down her eating as well, trying to be polite.

"Aren't you hungry, Dear?" Martha asked.

"I just want to make sure you get enough to eat."

"If you need more food, we will send Herman for another meal." Having Martha for a roommate might very well turn out to have benefits that outweighed sleeping on the floor in a purple duster. Herman returned shortly.

"I need more food," Martha demanded immediately.

This order took him aback. "You had a whole chicken dinner!"

"I need dessert,"

"You don't eat dessert."

"Young man, do not tell me what I do and don't do. Starting today, I'm eating dessert. Life is short."

Herman looked suspiciously at Mitch, but she had the benefit of plausible deniability since Martha hadn't discussed the particulars with her prior to the demand.

"What kind of dessert," he asked grudgingly.

"Chocolate cake."

"You want a piece of chocolate cake?"

"No."

"No?"

"I want a whole chocolate cake."

"Where am I going to find a whole chocolate cake?"

"I suppose the same place you would find a piece of chocolate cake!"

"I'll see what I can do!" he muttered as he left in a huff.


They drove in silence to the mortuary. Reb, Lisa, the newly-hired lawyer and two special agents in charge. Every single one of them had a morose aura, just for different reasons. With everything going on, it was irritating to take care of life's demands. Reb had begrudgingly agreed with Lisa that they needed to give Miranda a decent burial, and felt guilty that she hadn't thought of it first. And although Lisa had led the way on this moral obligation, she wished instead to be by Trish's side. Everyone else in the car simply wanted to be anywhere else in the universe rather than be proxy mourners at a stranger's funeral.

"Geez, don't everybody talk all at once," Lisa said as she took the final turn into the parking lot.

"Let's just get this over with," Reb snapped and then added, "And let me do the talking, okay!"

"Fine by me. She's your family, after all."

The office was just big enough to hold the six of them, counting the funeral director. After perfunctory greetings, Reb launched into her prepared remarks.

"We, I, need to make arrangements for the burial of my niece."

"Of course. We took delivery of the body from the hospital."

"At least they got one delivery right," Lisa mumbled.

Reb's withering glare went unnoticed.

"When will you be ready for the viewing?"

"We're not going to have a prolonged memorial service."

"That's not exactly what I'm referring to. Someone needs to identify the body so that we know we are making arrangements for the right person."

"Oh, of course," Reb nodded like she knew this all along.

"And we will need to complete the paperwork."

"Of course."

The proceedings ground to a slow stop. Funeral directors were interesting people. They dealt day in and day out with people in the painful grip of sorrow. There was no such presence in this room. It felt like all duty and no compassion. Except for the cute blond with the wise crack, it was like dealing with robots.

"How, exactly, is everyone connected to the deceased?"

Every eye turned to Reb. She sighed. "I'm her aunt. Nobody else is related. These people are two Federal Agents, a lawyer and a family acquaintance."

"Was Ms. Knight orphaned?"

"Not soon enough," Lisa just couldn't help herself.

"I told you that I would do the talking!" Reb reminded Lisa, to no avail.

"Miranda tried to kill the both of us. That's why she was in prison."

Then, the impossible happened. The room got even quieter. Even the lawyer was now paying rapt attention.

"I see," the director nodded. It was the first time in his career that he had ever dealt with the victims of a crime arranging for the burial of the perpetrator. No wonder things were so awkward.

"Is that why you brought a lawyer and two bodyguards?"

"Not exactly," Reb equivocated.

"That's right," Lisa interjected once again. "They are here because of the death threats, the abduction, and the missing baby."

"A baby has been kidnapped?" he asked.

"Not that we know of, but it's within the realm of possibility, I suppose?"

"So, who was abducted?"

"Can we just get back to planning the funeral," Reb sounded exasperated.

"It was her partner," Lisa forged ahead.

"Business partner?"

"Life partner. She used to be my girlfriend."

"You two were girlfriends?" the director looked from Lisa to Reb and back.

"Good grief no!" Reb stated firmly.

"The kidnaped victim was my girlfriend and her partner. Just not at the same time."

It was beginning to sound like one of those irritating logic puzzles that were next to impossible to solve.

"Now that this gentleman knows all of our private business, I sincerely hope we can get on with what we came here to do!" Reb snapped.

"Of course. We'll get the paperwork started and then you can come back later for the identification of the body."

"Can we just do that now and get it over with?"

"We haven't completed the preparations."

"Why?"

"We were late in receiving the deceased."

"Why?"

"The autopsy delayed the process."

"Who ordered an autopsy?"

"Your niece was an inmate in a Federal prison. It's standard procedure."

Reb had never heard of this regulation, but she didn't question it. Everyone was out to protect their interests for the impending lawsuit. She was silently chiding herself for not thinking of it first.

"Of course."

"So, if you would supply us with whatever clothing you would want the deceased buried in, it will speed up the process."

Reb furrowed her brow. It was all so complicated.

"Can't we just use what she was wearing when she was admitted to the hospital?"

"You want her buried in her prison uniform?"

"Nobody's going to see her."

"I think we need to go clothes shopping," Lisa interrupted. Again.

And again, she got a look from Reb. Still, Lisa continued, "I think it's the decent thing to do. If Mitch were here, I'm sure she would agree with me."

Reb bristled when Lisa brought Mitch into discussions, like she was a mind reader.

"You don't know what Mitch would do!"

"I know that Mitch wouldn't bury somebody in their prison fatigues! I want her to be proud of how we handled things in her absence."

"Everyone wants that," Reb avoided making this issue personal for her.

"Where's the nearest mall?" Lisa asked.

"I can help with that," Mandie piped up.

That was only logical. A young, professional woman usually knew where the best shopping could be had.

"We will return as quickly as possible," Reb informed the director and she turned and wheeled out of his office.


Rose and Silver were taking turns guarding Trish and it was shift change. They had attempted to make their effort subtle. That had worked for about five minutes.

"You don't need to watch me every minute," Trish told Rose.

"I haven't got anything better to do."

"Where is Josh?"

"He's sleeping."

"Maybe we should wake him up?"

"Why would we do that?"

"Just to make sure he's okay.'

"He's fine."

"You're sure?"

"Silver, could you go and check on Josh before you retire for the evening?"

"Of course," Silver was glad to be doing something besides watching Trish.

She walked down the hallway to Josh's room. He was awake and smiling, cooing and laughing. He didn't notice Silver, so she crept back out of the room. When she got back to Trish's room, she lied to the both of them. "He's asleep."

A moment went by before she caught Rose's eye. "Let's go and let

160

Miss Trish get some rest."

At first, Rose resisted, but when she looked into Silver's eyes, she nodded agreement. Once they were out of earshot, Silver said to Rose, "You need to see this."

She led the way back to Josh's room, where he was still awake and laughing, kicking his feet and waving his shortened, deformed arms in the air.

"He's awake after all," Rose whispered. "Why did you say otherwise?"

"I wanted you to see this. It's like he's reacting to something."

"Something?"

"He usually doesn't laugh and react like this when he's all by himself. This is how he acts when someone is paying attention to him."

They watched for a moment more before they ventured into his room. Suddenly, Josh became quiet. His gaze shifted to Rose and then back to the spot he had been looking at and then back again to Rose. He looked, for lack of a better description, confused.

"Maybe we should take him to Trish?" Silver said.

"Let's do that. It might help her to relax."

Rose picked Josh up and walked him back to Trish's room.

"He just woke up," Rose stretched the truth.

At the sight of Trish, Josh began to gurgle and wiggle with happiness. It was eerily similar to his earlier reactions. Rose and Silver exchanged a glance.

"Why don't we give you some time alone," Rose suggested out of the blue.

"We'll be just fine," Trish answered, keeping her gaze on Josh.

"Call us if you need us," Silver reminded on the way out.

"We will," Trish replied dreamily.

The exchange wasn't reassuring to Rose, but she followed Silver down the hallway.

"What do you think is going on?" Rose asked when they reached the kitchen.

"I think that Miss Trish and Josh are seeing the same ghost."

It was a miracle, and even perhaps a better one than the story about

161

the loaves and fishes. Herman had found a whole chocolate cake! Chocolate cake was better than fish any old day. He had also brought Mitch's freshly laundered clothes as well. They weren't exactly soft and fluffy, but at least they were clean. Mitch changed and then proceeded to share dessert with Martha.

"I used to bake," Martha reminisced.

"What did you make?" Mitch asked, mostly to try and keep the conversation going.

"Everything! When you're poor and have a family to feed, you couldn't afford to buy store-bought baked items or already-made meals. I cooked from scratch every day. I did my baking three days a week. We never went out to dinner. Besides, my cooking was better than any diner food. So why pay extra for something that you could make twice as good at home?"

Mitch nodded between bites of cake that was far superior to anything she could've baked.

"What kinds of dishes did you prepare?" Mitch asked, now that talking about food wasn't painful to her stomach.

"Probably the same things as you."

"I don't do much cooking."

"Who does the cooking at your house?"

"Well, I guess we take turns…"

"Take turns? How on earth does that work?"

"We try and share the cooking," Mitch struggled to explain a modern concept to an old-fashioned housewife.

"I've never heard of such a thing. A kitchen isn't big enough for people to share the cooking. At least, not the kitchen I used to have."

"You mean, the one back at the cabin?"

"No. I mean the one we had in Alabama. It was a small house. A tiny kitchen. Barely room enough to turn around in. We were poor. Couldn't afford a big house. We had a kitchen, a bedroom, and that was it."

"So there were five rooms?"

"Honey, are you having ear problems? I said we had two rooms."

Mitch nodded. Further conversation was interrupted by Herman knocking on the door.

"It's lights out time," he announced like a scoutmaster at camp. His gaze settled on the remaining half of the cake. Without a word,

Mitch picked it up and handed it over to him, like a peace offering. In exchange, he handed her a sleeping bag. It was a fair-enough trade. She took Martha to the bathroom one more time and then settled in for the night.

Even in the middle of nowhere, there were malls that stayed open late. With the advent of the internet, actual brick and mortar stores needed to be more competitive. Gone were the days of banker's hours for department outlets. They were quite the group wandering around the ladies' section so late in the day. Mandie and Lisa had an instant kinship where shopping was concerned, so any attempt by Reb to rein them in went for naught.

"We only need a shirt and pants," she admonished twice to no avail.

"We want Miranda to look nice." Lisa answered back as she held up an expensive designer blouse worth hundreds of dollars.

"No one is going to see her. How many times do I have to remind everyone?"

"We will see her."

"And I think she will look fine in a simple shirt and pants. It's what she wore her entire life."

"I just don't know…" Lisa trailed off.

"I have an idea you might approve of," Mandie piped up.

"Go on," Reb encouraged her. Anything to get this over with.

"I agree in principle with the idea that simple clothing might be the best selection," Mandie paid homage to Reb's feelings. "So, what we could do is," Mandie then turned to Lisa, "if you are in the mood to shop, we could pick out some nicer things and donate them in Miranda's memory to a womens' crisis center. Women who are struggling to make ends meet could use some nice outfits to go out on job interviews and such."

Although this was a noble idea, Reb took umbrage at the notion that a complete stranger was so very willing to be generous with Reb's money. Knowing also of Lisa's penchant for shopping sprees, Reb offered a qualifier. "Let's try to keep the spending within reasonable limits. We might have unforeseen expenses down the road."

"Maybe this wasn't such a good idea after all?" Mandie offered.

"It's fine. Let's just get it over with."

Lisa sensed correctly that Reb was tiring out after a long day. She quickly selected a few things off the racks, demonstrating her excellent taste in clothing. Within the hour, they had dropped Mandie off at her office, dropped the clothing for Miranda at the mortuary and then headed back to the hotel.

"Do you need anything else tonight?" Lisa asked Reb as she was rolling toward her bedroom.

"Like what?" Reb asked back, a little too abruptly to suit Lisa.

"Well, I didn't know if you needed any help…like I could turn down your bed for you…"

"And fluff my pillows?" Reb added in a tone that Lisa couldn't read.

"I'm just trying to be nice."

"And I'm just trying to get to bed."

"Fine."

"Okay."

Reb rolled through the doorway and then closed the door behind her. Lisa waited just a tick before she turned to find the Feds watching her like hawks.

"What?" she confronted them.

They both looked at their shoes, then at each other, and then they went to their rooms as well. Lisa was left all by herself to ruminate on the day's events. She fell asleep on the couch after five minutes.


"Hello? Hello!"

"I'm awake. What do you need?"

"I need help!"

"Okay," Mitch got up off the floor and turned on the lights.

Martha was wide awake.

"Do you need help to go to the bathroom?"

"I need help with the body."

"You need help with your body?" Mitch asked, still fuzzy after being startled awake.

"No, I need help with *his* body," Martha was now whispering like it was a secret.

"Whose body?"

"That body," Martha indicated a spot on the floor that was empty.

No body. No nothing. It wasn't even the spot where Mitch had been sleeping.

"Okay," Mitch nodded. How can I help?"

"It's heavy. I need help moving it."

"Why don't we just wake him up?" Mitch suggested.

"You can't wake the dead!"

"Oh, so it's a dead body. Why didn't you say so in the first place?"

"Quiet! We don't want anyone to hear us!"

"Why not?" Mitch asked.

"Because he's dead!"

Mitch paused to think things over. Her sleepy brain was struggling to put it all together.

"Why do we need to be quiet if there's a dead body on the floor?"

"Because it's our fault."

"Why?"

"We killed him!"

"You mean, you killed him because I sure didn't do it!"

"I don't know."

"You don't know who killed him?"

"I'm not sure."

"Who is he?"

"My husband, of course!"

"So, your husband is dead over there on the floor and you don't know who killed him," Mitch summarized the conversation so far.

"Are you sure you didn't kill him?" Martha asked.

Mitch didn't know how to respond anymore. "Let's ask Herman."

"NO!" Martha fairly shrieked. "Don't tell him anything about this. He won't know anything. He's just a little boy."

"Okay," Mitch was now completely wide awake. "Why don't I take you to the bathroom and then we can worry about the body."

"What body?" Martha asked.

Mitch was stymied. If she reminded Martha about their prior dialogue, it might be the worst thing to do. So she just helped her to the bathroom and then tucked her back into bed again.

"Sleep well," Mitch said.

"You too," Martha replied dreamily.

But sleep eluded Mitch as she ran possible scenarios through her mind. Martha's husband had died years ago when Herman was

165

young, if what Martha said tonight was correct. Usually that was the case with memory issues. Short term memory was faulty while long term memory was more dependable. And if your husband had been killed and you had stumbled upon the body, or worse yet, if you were responsible for the deed, it would certainly stay with you.

But, whose part did Mitch play in this little drama? She hadn't been playing the part of Herman, since Martha had warned not to tell him. And if Herman had been a young boy, then his sister Shane had to have been young as well. It was rare, but not unheard of, for very young children to be responsible for the death of a parent. The accidental gun death happened from time to time, but a deliberate act of murder? Unlikely.

So, who had Martha teamed up with to perhaps kill her husband? And why? They would be in Alabama soon enough. Hopefully, all of Mitch's assumptions would be proven false. Martha just didn't seem like the murdering type. She looked so innocent after all. But one should never underestimate the protective instincts and strength of a mother.

Maybe it had all been just a bad dream? A figment of Martha's imagination. A night terror. Whatever it had been, Mitch wasn't about to ask Herman. She felt obligated to keep Martha's confidence. What Mitch needed above all else was another two hours of sleep.


Reb was already awake when Lisa knocked on her door the next morning. She was still under the covers, however, and irritated at the intrusion.
"What do you want and you had better already ordered room service!"
"Are you always this cranky first thing in the morning?"
"Only when I'm dealing with two kidnappings."
"Well, we may have a lead on one of them."
Reb's demeanor changed instantly. "Which one?"
"There may have been a spotting of Mitch."
"A what?"

166

"They might have a surveillance video of Mitch."

"Where?"

"Get dressed and come take a look for yourself."

For Reb, getting dressed was more involved than most people. The chagrined look on her face belied her stoic character.

"How can I help?" Lisa asked shyly, expecting to once again be rebuffed.

"Could you please get my beige slacks and blue blouse out of the closet?"

"What about your underwear?"

Reb paused before she spoke. Was there even a protocol for discussing undergarments with your life partner's prior girlfriend? Lisa sensed the hesitation.

"I guess you can view a video without benefit of a brassier."

"It might scandalize the Feds."

Despite the seriousness of the situation, Lisa managed a smile.

"Where's your bra?"

"In the nightstand. I can take care of myself if you just bring my clothes over to the bed."

Lisa did so and then left the room discreetly.

When Reb rolled out to discuss the latest developments, she looked stunning. She was camera ready in case there was going to be a press conference about the case.

"What's the latest?" she got right down to business.

"We got a tip about some cross-country movement by the suspects."

"Cross-country?"

"And we have a grainy surveillance video. We were hoping you could identify Ms. Tanner."

"Let's take a look."

The agents had the video cued up on a laptop computer. It was three seconds of an overhead view of a woman wearing a hat walking between a building and a vehicle. It could've been about a million possible people in the video, but Reb gasped. It was Mitch alright.

"Where is this location?"

"It's in the Midwest," the senior agent answered cautiously, as if Reb would immediately charter a jet to the exact latitude and longitude.

167

"We are still all on the same team, right?"

"It's in eastern Kansas."

"So, they are traveling from Colorado east through Kansas. It sounds to me like they are trying to get to where Mary is being held."

"Why would they be doing that?" Lisa asked.

"To disrupt the trial."

"But they could do that from anywhere. Why take the risk of driving there?"

"Well, if that's not their plan, why are they driving across the country?"

It was a question no one had a ready answer for.

"Did you get a license plate number?" Lisa forged ahead,

"No. It was blocked from view but we have a general description of the vehicle. It's a white van."

"That doesn't help much. There must be thousands of white vans on the road at any given time."

"At least we know that Mitch is still alive. How did you happen to get ahold of this video?"

"We have a nationwide net in place for this search. And it was also a lucky break to get a tip from the male gas station attendant."

"Why was he so observant of the ladies' room? Is he some sort of weirdo?"

"Let's just say that it was a rare sighting to have two females use the restroom at the same time."

"Two ladies?" Reb asked.

"There was an elderly woman as well."

"She wasn't on the video?"

"Not on the part you saw."

"So, there's more?" Reb's patience was wearing thin and she hadn't even had breakfast yet.

"Yes."

"Maybe if we saw the entire video, we could identify more people?"

"Unfortunately, we don't have clearance for that."

"Maybe not yet," Reb said menacingly.

"Are you going to call the President?"

"It depends on what kind of mood I'm in after I come back from the mortuary. I wouldn't bank on any improvement."

"Yes, Ma'am...Senator."

"So, let's go and get this funeral over with."

If Reb had been too direct, no one dared to say anything. Finding out that Mitch was still alive hadn't yet softened her edginess. The ride to the mortuary was somber. Reb was going to once again bury a blood relative. And even though the blood had been bad between them, it still marked a finality that carried guilt. Not only had Reb neglected Miranda, but she managed to lose track of her baby as well.

It had been omniscient of Reb to dress nicely. The media was waiting at the mortuary like someone had tipped them off to this big story. Reb had three guesses and they were all the mortuary. A free way to get publicity for their business. She didn't care. This particular nightmare was going to be over soon enough. Surrounded by two Federal Agents and Lisa, Reb wheeled into the building. Once safely inside, she breathed a sigh of relief. The funeral director greeted them in the foyer.

"Senator Fairbanks," he said.

"That was quite a welcoming committee you arranged," she replied sharply.

He mocked a look of surprise. Reb saw right through it.

"The media has its ways," he demurred.

"And so do I. Now, let's get this over with."

They went to sit in the chapel until Miranda's body was brought out for the viewing. The room was so quiet and peaceful that Reb felt her tension dissipate. It was a short term response. How many funerals do people go to where everyone comments on how good the dead body looks? And how great a job the mortician did? Words that comforted the living when we artificially preserve a body by pumping fluids into them. Unfortunately for Miranda, no miracle of modern science would have helped with her appearance. She looked sunken and ill. Even the clothes that they had picked out looked two sizes too big. Nevertheless, Reb looked on with compassion.

"Does anyone have anything they would like to say?" the director asked bravely.

Reb glanced at Lisa. "You're never at a loss for words."

"You want *me* to say something?"

"It's not like we have an audience. Is there anything you want to get off your chest?"

"Okay." Lisa inhaled. "Miranda, you probably couldn't help yourself when you damaged people." Lisa paused to take another breath and gauge how this was going over with Reb. So far, so good.

"After all, you were pretty damaged yourself from your own upbringing. You were brought up by unloving people who were more interested in following the rules than expressing affection. And maybe that would've been tolerable if the rules had been sensible or rooted in compassion. But they weren't. You were raised by stiff-necked puritans who hated themselves and everyone else."

Lisa paused again. If Reb had been displeased, she would've made her objection by now. Instead, she was sitting like a wax figure, her face drawn and pale.

"Anything else?" Reb asked quietly.

"Yes."

"Okay. Continue."

"When parents hate themselves so much, it's almost impossible to have the kind of love for their children that gives that child a sense of humanity. And when a child isn't inculcated with that kind of humanity, then they don't see the humanity in everyone else around them. So, it was no wonder that Miranda didn't see anything wrong with trying to kill you and me. I've always felt nothing but sorry for her," Lisa was now talking directly to Reb.

Tears were trickling down Reb's cheeks.

"Can you give us a minute," Lisa asked the director.

"Are you finished with the viewing?" he asked.

Lisa looked to Reb for a sign. She nodded silently. He closed the casket and wheeled it out of the room.

"Are you okay?" Lisa asked Reb.

"No. I'm not okay. All of my immediate family of origin is dead. If I was feeling okay, there would be something wrong with me."

"I disagree," Lisa challenged this notion.

"Excuse me?" Reb shot back.

"Deep down, your family of origin despised you. They despised your success. They despised your independence. They despised your sexuality. It would be okay to be okay with how things turned out."

"Well, I'm not okay. Not yet."

170

"Things take time."

"You are pretty forgiving for being the one who carries the scars from this ordeal."

"I try not to think about it."

"You see them in the mirror every day."

"I've come to terms with it. The time I spent with Mitch afterwards seems to have made my scars less noticeable."

"You think she healed them?"

"I think she healed me."

"She did that before you ever got burned."

"I'm ready to go now, if you are," Lisa changed the subject.

"Did you want to attend the burial?"

"Not particularly. I think we've done enough."

"So, now, do you think that Mitch will be proud of our efforts?"

"I do."

"I do too."


Mitch was pensive. It had been a long night of restless sleep and now they were once again on the road. When Martha had awakened, she showed no signs of remembering anything about trying to hide a non-existent dead body. This hadn't surprised Mitch. Remembering things wasn't Martha's forte.

Herman noticed the shift of mood. "What's going on?" he had asked the minute he saw Mitch's face.

"Nothing," Mitch had her answer ready.

Herman stepped closer. He wasn't buying it.

"I asked you a question," he was so close that Mitch felt the warmth of his breath as he spoke.

"I didn't sleep well. Too much chocolate cake, I guess," she refused to back down. For whatever reason, she no longer felt intimidated by him. Anyone casually observing them would wonder if they were lovers about to share a kiss.

"Get in the van," he growled.

"Thank you," Mitch replied.

Left to her own devices, she was now free to think. It had been no surprise that Herman's father was dead. No one had mentioned him before last night. The notion, however, that somehow his mother was complicit in his possible murder was the real sticking point. Unless Martha's memory was playing tricks on her, a likely enough scenario. How does someone feel guilty if they hadn't actually killed someone? Does wishing someone dead carry the guilt of the crime?

Maybe Herman's dad had simply had a heart attack? Why would Martha feel guilty about that? What had she done, fed him too much margarine? Too much gravy? Mitch wanted to know the truth. It wasn't long before the van slowed to a stop. Although it seemed a little early for a bathroom break, Mitch had learned to expect anything. The van was stopped for longer than usual. Then, the unexpected happened. Herman opened the door and asked Mitch to step out of the van. They weren't even at a gas station.
"The police want to have a word with you," he said in an even tone of voice.
At the word "police," Mitch's guard slid his gun under the seat he occupied. Mitch looked at Herman like he was kidding. He wasn't. Sure enough, there were two Alabama State police cars behind the van. Wow, they had traveled a lot farther than Mitch would've guessed with all the bathroom breaks and such. It was hot, sunny and humid.
"Morning, Ma'am," the officer was polite.
"Hello," Mitch answered back.
"We are just doing a routine inquiry."
"Okay."
"What's your name?"
"Mitch Tanner."
"What is the purpose of your visit?"
"Family reunion," Mitch answered calmly, trying her best to sound bored with it all.
"Would you mind taking off your hat."
"I don't want to sunburn my nose."
"Just for a moment, Ma'am."
Mitch looked at Herman and then complied with the officer's request.
"Thank you, Ma'am. Thank you for your time."
"Thank you," Mitch echoed the officer.
With that, the officers returned to their vehicle and awaited for

Herman to drive away. About fifteen minutes down the road, he pulled over. The van door opened.

"Family reunion?" he hollered.

"What?"

"You don't even know my last name!"

"It didn't seem to matter to them."

"Except that they now have what they wanted."

"My name?"

"A dash cam video!"

"So, if they have all that, why did they let us go?"

"They are probably calling for backup."

"So I guess our only option is to just keep going?"

"Why didn't you try to escape?"

Mitch couldn't tell him the truth. She had made a promise to Martha not to talk about the invisible dead husband. The mystery intrigued her. Deep down, Mitch wanted to know all the answers that swirled around this pilgrimage. Herman took note of the hesitation.

"You aren't getting that Swedish disease, are you?"

Mitch had to think about this strange question. "Swedish disease?"

"You know! Where people enjoy being held hostage."

"You mean Stockholm Syndrome?" Mitch tried to not laugh as she clarified.

"Yeah, that."

"I promise that's not what's going on. I just want to get to wherever we are going so that I can peacefully secure my release."

Herman simply shook his head and closed the van door.


"I think we need to have a funeral and then a memorial service," Rose said to Silver.

"Are you sure that's what you want to do, Miss Rose?" Silver answered with a question, which was not unusual for being the family bodyguard/sounding board.

"I don't want Max to wait any longer."

Silver nodded her understanding. Closure was important to people.

"Do you think Miss Trish is going to be ready?" Silver followed up.

"What do you mean?"

As far as Silver was concerned, they had danced around this issue far

173

too long.

"Miss Trish is seeing ghosts and hearing voices. I'm not sure it's a good idea to take someone to a funeral who's seeing ghosts."

"I don't think she's actually seeing ghosts. I think she's just hearing imaginary voices."

Silver wasn't much for appreciating fine points. At the risk of being stereotyped, Silver had great respect for and trepidation of contact with the afterlife. Maybe her ancestors believed too much in voodoo, and perhaps it had trickled down through her family history. She just didn't want any drama to interfere with an already difficult event.

"If you think she's going to be okay, then I'll help in any way I can."

"Thank you, Silver. I know I can always count on you for support."

"Yes, Miss Rose."

Rose took a deep breath and called the mortuary. After a brief talk with them, Rose disconnected the call.

"They can have everything arranged in three days. I guess their schedule is pretty full."

Silver nodded. Anything can happen in three days.

Chapter 8

The day after the funeral, Reb had taken to her bed to catch on her
sleep. She was exhausted from worry. Deep down in her core, she
felt unsteady. It had nothing to do with her paralysis. Half of her
was missing. In her childhood, she often heard married people refer
to their spouse as "my better half." It had seemed like a comical
affection at the time. Only now did she understand what it meant
and how it felt. It felt horrible. It felt like trying to act alive when
you felt half dead. Dealing with so many stressors at one time was
bad enough, but having to go through it without Mitch by her side
was almost unbearable. During Reb's short stint as a Senator, she
had felt all powerful. It had been like the nun's description of God
in Sunday school. All powerful, all knowing. When they say that
people are drunk with power, they are correct. It was intoxicating to
believe, however falsely, that Senators knew everything. But that's
how it felt and they did nothing to dispel the myth. There's plenty of
rarified air at the heights of arrogance. She had all the president's
men looking for Mitch and a kidnapped baby and nobody was
solving the case fast enough.

All these thoughts had raced through her mind while she had tried to
sleep. They continued through her brain as she slept until she was
awakened by Lisa.
"Are you awake?"
"I am now. Why do you keep waking me up?"
"There's been another sighting!"
Lisa made it sound like there was a water buffalo in the parking lot.
"A sighting?" Reb repeated groggily.
"They got a much better video of Mitch. Come on. Get up. What
do you want to wear this time?"
Reb thought about her wardrobe and the dwindling choices. She
hadn't packed for the long haul but hesitated to admit that for fear

that it would get Lisa all excited for yet another shopping spree.

"Running out of clean clothes?" Lisa asked.

"I'll just wear what I wore to the funeral."

"Are you sure? The press might make a big deal out of repeating the same outfit."

"Is the press in the living room?"

"Not yet. Do you want me to let them in?"

Reb looked skeptical.

"I was just seeing if you were wide awake."

"Please just bring me something to wear and give me fifteen minutes."

Lisa smiled at the word "please". If they were getting close to tracking Mitch down, Lisa wanted Reb's report to be glowing. Silly phrases ran through her mind: "Lisa was so helpful! Lisa did everything right! Lisa made this really tough situation bearable!" It all sounded so much better than, "Lisa brought me slacks and a blouse…" which was precisely what she did and then left Reb alone.

Lisa went back to the living room to wait. This must be good, she thought. The agents looked edgy, like their jobs depended on this single event. Reb rolled out in thirteen minutes, beating her expectation by two minutes.

"What do you have?"

"A video."

"You had a video last time."

"This is a better quality video."

It was like they were having a contest to see who could use the fewest words to convey their point. So far, the Feds were winning.

"Let's see it."

Indeed, it was a longer video. But what it really was defied explanation as far as Reb was concerned. It was Mitch alright. In living color. She was standing behind a white van next to a guy who looked like a hulking Jesus. Her chat with the police was brief and then she had done the unthinkable. She willingly got back into the van. She hadn't tried to escape. Reb was at a loss for words. Lisa wasn't.

"What's with that hair color? She's going to need an appointment at the beauty salon when she gets home!"

176

Normally, Reb would've jumped all over Lisa for a careless remark like that. However, she was lost in thought. Any other reasonable person would've run to safety behind two armed police officers. But not Mitch. What did Mitch know that the rest of them didn't? It seemed as though she could hardly wait to get back on the road. Reb took a couple of deep breaths.

"Are you going to pass out?" Lisa asked.

"No. Why?"

"You look pale and you are hyperventilating."

"I'm thinking."

"About the video?"

"Mitch must think she's doing the right thing. Something none of the rest of us can fathom."

"She always does," Lisa intoned.


Mitch was truly shocked that they had traveled as far as they had. Already in Alabama! Okay, so it wasn't the far side of the moon, but still a fair bit of driving. What was really interesting was that they had been stopped by the police. That must mean something. It didn't feel like an ordinary police pullover. Nobody had demanded to see her license or ID. She didn't have to walk a straight line or close her eyes and touch her nose with her index fingers. They had made no move to rescue her, and were so polite when they asked her to remove her hat. And then, it dawned on her. The dash cam video Herman had mentioned! Oh hell! Now her face and hideous red hair were probably plastered all over the news and Reb and Lisa had to have seen it by now. They must all think that she had gone half crazy. And maybe she had. She was still in a van somewhere in Alabama, going along with whatever plan Herman had up his sleeve. The van slowed to a stop. What now?

"Bathroom break," Herman announced as he opened the door.

"No police?"

"Shut up!"

"Herman!" Martha called out. "I told you to watch your language!"

"Okay."

"Okay what?"

"Okay, I'm sorry."

Mitch couldn't help but smile just a little bit. The more time she spent with Martha, the more she liked her. It made bathroom breaks so much more tolerable. When they emerged, Mitch asked Herman exactly where they were headed. Since his mother was still within earshot, he had to mind his manners.

"My hometown," he answered, trying to weasel out of answering.

"Oh really? And what is the name of the town?"

Herman didn't get a chance to answer. Martha piped up, "Klantown."

"Klantown?" Mitch was sure that she had heard wrong. There was no such place as Klantown.

"It's spelled with a C," Herman interjected.

"Huh?"

"Clantown. C-L-A-N-T-O-W-N!" he spelled it out.

"Oh, well, that certainly cleared things up! So, how much longer are we going to be on the road?"

"Not long."

"And then, what's the plan?"

"Just…" Herman was editing himself. "…get back in the van, please."

Martha smiled and nodded her head. "That's a good boy."

When Mitch got in the back of the van, Herman took his anger out on the door by slamming it three times. Mitch was convinced that the authorities were watching their every move and that it must seem quite comical to them to watch this grown man behave in such a manner.

Mitch must've nodded off again, for when they stopped, there was no bellowing about bathroom breaks. The van door opened and they were in a small town. A quintessential small southern town that smelled like barbecue, diesel fumes and puke. Once again, Mitch and Martha were escorted to a motel room. It was even worse than the previous places they had stayed, which didn't even seem possible to Mitch.

"Another night at the Ritz?"

"Sleep while you can," Herman advised.

Every night, Mitch entered sleep with innocence. No doubt, it had something to do with living in the present moment. She had made her share of mistakes in the past, but she tried to not dwell on them.

Most of them were the product of miscalculation. Those kinds of mistakes were easier to live with than the mistakes of malice. And the future? Mitch tried to not think about it too much. It would be unbearable to think of Reb getting older and frailer with each passing year. Just don't go there, she would instruct her mind. Enjoy this day. The universe is trying to tell you something. It had seemed like a pretty strange message lately. Not fearful. Just strange.

Even though she hadn't expected it, Herman had scrounged up some decent food for dinner. It had taken a while for the delivery, so Mitch was fending off reflux when Martha started yelling in her sleep again. It seemed as though the closer they got to the family homestead, the more real the past was becoming for her.

"I need help. Help!"
"I'm right here, Martha," Mitch got up and went over to her bed.
"Can you help me?"
"What do you need?"
"He fell down."
"Who fell down?"
"And he bumped his head."
"Who fell down and bumped his head?"
"I don't know."
"How can I help?"
"Where are we?"
"I think we're still in Alabama."
Martha started to cry softly. "I don't remember. I don't know. Can you help me?"
Mitch was in a quandary. She wanted to ask questions based on their prior conversations about Marth's dead husband, but was worried that they would upset Martha even more. And another part of Mitch's conscience nagged her about the ethical implications of trying to gain information from Martha to use against Herman. It didn't seem right to try and pit mother against son, if only to secure her safety. If only Mitch knew the whole story, however, she could possibly be truly helpful.

"Martha, tell me about your life in Alabama."

"My life?" she asked like no one had ever been interested in those details before.

"Tell me what you did every day."

"I was a housewife."

"Right. And you baked three days a week."

"How did you know?"

"You told me that yesterday. You said that you cooked all the meals."

"I'm a good cook."

"And what else did you do?"

Martha leaned closer. "Don't tell anyone?"

"What?"

"I killed my husband."

Mitch sighed. She knew this wasn't the truth but didn't want to argue lest Martha would stop confiding in her.

"How did you kill your husband?"

"Shhh! Don't tell no one!"

"Your secret is safe with me."

"Why did the police stop us on the road?" Martha asked suddenly.

"I don't know," Mitch hedged.

"Herman wouldn't tell me. Are the two of you keeping secrets from me?"

"Why would we do that?"

"I could be arrested, you know," Martha nodded her head.

"That's not going to happen."

"I know," Martha nodded again.

"How do you know?" Mitch was now thoroughly confused.

"Because I *know* people."


Lisa had tried and failed to talk Reb out of her plan. Even the Feds couldn't prevail.

"We know she's in Alabama. We can be there in a couple of hours."

"But we don't know if she's going to stay in Alabama!"

"Even so, we will still be closer than we are right now."

"And what do you think we are going to be able to do when we get there? Alabama is an awfully big state."

"I'm sure the police are following every move that the kidnappers are making. Just because they haven't swooped in to make an arrest doesn't mean they have lost touch. Ten damn feet," Reb finished her thoughts with an angry mutter.

"What did you say?" Lisa asked as she was packing her clothes.

"Why didn't she just walk ten damn feet to safety!"

"I'm sure she had her reasons," Lisa said.

"She could be home and safe by now! She doesn't need to save everybody or solve their problems."

"Maybe she does?" Lisa played Devil's advocate.

"I just don't understand it. Doesn't she have any regard for how worried we are about her?"

"I think it's like when Jesus got lost and they found him in the temple," Lisa put forward her theory.

"What are you talking about?" Reb sounded exasperated.

"You've not read the Bible?"

"You have?"

"Bits and pieces. Anyway, Jesus got lost when he was young and his parents found him in the temple talking with the wise men and his mom, Mary, was unhappy with him and do you remember what he said to her?" Lisa finished her long question with a flourish.

"I do."

"That's not what he said!"

"I know that's not what he said! I just meant that I do know what he said-"

"Which was, 'I'm doing the work of my father.' And that really confused Mary because his father was a carpenter, or so they thought..."

"I understand the nuance of the story. I just don't know how it pertains to Mitch," Reb stated.

"Seriously?" Lisa asked in a bemused way.

"You obviously have this all worked out. Please enlighten me."

"Do you know why you are here on Earth?" Lisa asked.

Reb furrowed her brow. It was a big question. "I imagine that my work in politics had been my driving force."

"I'm sure you are correct. You have been doing the work of your father by using your God-given talents to make things better through your career in politics."

Silence ensued for about ten seconds. Lisa was waiting for Reb to connect the dots. Maybe it wasn't as straight forward as it seemed.

"Okay," Reb said flatly.

181

"So, what do you think Mitch's destiny is in this life? Do you seriously believe that she was put on this Earth to follow you around and fulfill your every whim and wish?"

"I've never thought that!"

"Well, then, quit behaving as though you do!"

"I want her to be safe."

"What makes you think she isn't safe?"

Reb sighed. For as much as she enjoyed arguing with Lisa in order to eventually prove her wrong, it was tiring her out just when she needed to maintain her energy.

"She's still being held against her will," Reb stated.

"And I think she's doing the work of her father," Lisa intoned wisely.

"She needs to be rescued."

"I don't think so. She had the chance to escape. I think that she will be back home when she fulfills this chapter of her destiny."

"I hope you are right."

"And then, she can go back to being your *whatever*."

"My *whatever*?"

"But know this: When she's done with this odyssey, she will be a national treasure. A hero to all. Imagine all the fan mail she will get. It won't be easy to go back to a life of humdrum."

Reb didn't have anything to say when Lisa stopped for air. She was too preoccupied with her own thoughts to reply. Lisa was irritating to be sure, but sometimes she could be spot on with her remarks. There very well could be accolades for Mitch if she somehow got the best of the bad guys. But Mitch was used to that sort of thing and it hadn't gone to her head yet. However, Reb was troubled more by Lisa's intimation that Reb undervalued Mitch. This had already occurred to Reb, and it was uncomfortable to have Lisa hammer away on the theme.

"You're awfully quiet," Lisa broke through Reb's contemplations.

"I'm giving serious consideration to everything that you have said."

"For once."

Reb continued unfazed, "What you have said makes a lot of sense. But what exactly do you mean when you talk about Mitch's destiny?"

"She's a healer. She heals people. It isn't a secret."

"You honestly believe that Mitch was kidnapped so that she could heal someone?"

"It makes more sense than anything that's happened yet."

"Why?"

"The money negotiations were a sham. A bunch of silly, childish quibbling. And any concept of disrupting the trial that Mary is going to testify at has been lost in translation. So whatever else is going on is very personal as far as the kidnapper is concerned. Maybe he is sick and he wants Mitch to heal him?"

"He didn't look very sickly in the video."

"Well, maybe it's already working."

"Or maybe it isn't him? Didn't the agents mention an elderly woman on the prior video?"

"They did."

"Well, let's hope that Mitch can cure everyone and their evil ways."

"It worked for me," Lisa smiled.


Sweet Home Alabama. Mitch had been humming the tune for so long that it had become irritating to her guard. At least she knew that they were finally nearing their destination when even he was getting edgy.

When they had been stopped by the Alabama State Patrol, it would've been so easy to bolt to safety if this were just any ordinary situation. Just a few short steps. Mitch wouldn't even really had to run. Just walk kind of fast. A few short steps and this would've been all over. It had all been so surreal. Her feet had turned to stone, her legs like concrete. She was held in place by the stunning power of the universe in order to conclude whatever it had in store for all of them. Just about the time Mitch was running out of things to think about, and was on the fifty-fifth rendition of Sweet Home Alabama, the van slowed to a stop. When the door opened, Herman gestured for her to get out.

"Is it bathroom break time again?"

"We're home."

The word "home" had a lot of emotional baggage attached to it. It could be a wonderfully nostalgic set of memories evocative of a perfect childhood or a torturous jumble of horrid events seared by emotional fire into the consciousness. Or, more likely, anything in between on the spectrum. The depth and breadth of human experience is eerily both unique and similar to everyone. It's just that we usually don't figure it out until it's too late.

Mitch got out of the van gingerly. Her body was stiff, not so much with fatigue, but more with trepidation. The kind of feeling you get when you are walking toward a haunted house. If Martha had been seeing dead bodies in motel rooms, imagine what she was going to envision at the old homestead.
"Hurry up!" Herman barked.
"Or what!" Mitch shot back. She was getting tired of being ordered around.
"Just hurry, okay? Mom is waiting."
"Okay," Mitch softened her tone in equal measure.
No use picking a fight in the front yard where all the neighbors could watch. Mitch took a few steps away from the van and found herself facing a dilapidated one-story wood "house", a generous description at best, plopped haphazardly in the middle of a much-ignored overgrown-with-weeds dirt lot. Her old house in Colorado was magnificent compared to this dump.
"So, this is where you grew up?" Mitch thought she asked nicely, but her opinion inadvertently seeped out.
"Watch your tone!" Herman was already back to cranky.
"Just checking," Mitch tried to smooth things over.
"Let's get Mom inside."
"So you really still own this…place?"
"Why not?"
"No reason," Mitch replied. Maybe the real estate market was just very depressed in Alabama.
They managed to get Martha inside the house without further bickering. Mitch had taken a moment to view the street before Herman closed the door. If there were any undercover police vehicles, they were very well hidden. It was pretty clever if they were the ones on cinder blocks.

The house was sparsely furnished, but there was one comfortable-looking easy chair all ready for Martha. She settled into it, grateful to be out of the van.

"Just let me rest for a while and then I'll cook supper."

"You don't need to do that, Mom." Herman reassured.

"If I don't cook, we won't have any food for a picnic tomorrow."

"We're going on a picnic? I like picnics!" Mitch offered her opinion.

Herman glowered at her again. He really needed to expand his face-making repertoire.

"I'm just trying to be a good sport," Mitch defended her enthusiasm.

"Go sit in that chair over there and be quiet," he indicated a rather uncomfortable-looking straight-back wooden chair in the corner. If she wasn't careful, she'd be wearing a dunce cap soon.

"Can I take your mom to the bathroom before I settle in?"

Herman gave this the same consideration that one would give an intricate plotline.

"It's a simple potty break," Mitch showed her exasperation.

"Watch your language around Mother!"

"What?"

"Don't say words like that!"

"You mean 'potty'?"

"Stop it!"

"Potty?"

"I said stop it!"

Mitch went over to where Martha was sitting and asked point blank, "Do you need to go to the potty?"

"That's probably a good idea at my age."

"Okay. You lead the way."

Mitch was taking a chance that Martha, after all this time, would still remember where the bathroom was and hopefully they weren't heading outside to some outhouse. All their prior conversations had suggested that the facilities could indeed be that primitive. But, lo and behold, there was a functioning bathroom at the rear of the house. Maybe Herman had arranged for some renovations at some earlier time? Or maybe Martha's memory was so shot that she was misremembering the house entirely? Whichever was the case, it was good to have a toilet, toilet paper, and a working sink.

Martha did well taking care of herself this time. She seemed to be more sturdy with each passing day. Mitch availed herself of the modern facilities herself and then escorted Martha back to the living

185

room. Martha sat back down in the comfy chair and then asked, "What's for dinner if I'm not cooking?"

"Yes, what is for dinner?" Mitch echoed Martha.

"I'm working on it," Herman answered.

"Meanwhile, what can I do to help out?" Mitch asked.

"There's not much to do."

"I did notice that the place is in pretty good shape. Did you send in an advance team?"

"The house is looked after."

"By a caretaker?"

"Sit down and don't worry about it."

"I think we need to concern ourselves with the original issue, which is, why exactly did we travel all the way down here to begin with. We did, after all, have an objective."

"We will address that tomorrow. Mother needs dinner and a good night's sleep."

Mitch didn't say it out loud, but if Martha started seeing imaginary dead bodies again tonight, the concept of a good night's sleep was tenuous as best.

Dinner was exceptional for such short notice. Pulled pork in sweet barbecue sauce with green beans and corn bread. Most of it was store bought and then finished at the house with the exception of the corn bread. Nobody had time to bake.

"Herman!" Martha spoke up suddenly. "Next time, just buy the ingredients and let me do the baking. This corn bread is tasteless."

Mitch had thought it to be quite tasty so she was looking forward to trying out Martha's recipe.

"Of course, Mom," he said without argument. Perhaps he just assumed that she would forget all about baking by tomorrow. But the whole purpose of this trip was to fix whatever was wrong with Martha's memory. Mitch's pensive expression did not go unnoticed by Herman.

"What's on your mind?" he asked with the same dismissive behavior that he reserved for Mitch and Mitch alone.

"How did your father die?" Mitch decided to see just how far she could push him with an honest question.

"We don't talk about things like that at dinner!" he was suddenly and acutely agitated.

186

"Well then, stop asking me what I'm thinking about."

"Why are you thinking about that anyway?"

Mitch wondered if this was a trap. Talk about it. Don't talk about it. Go ahead and talk about it.

"I'm just wondering why it was so important for your mother to come back to your home town?"

"And you think my Dad's death had something to do with that? Why on earth would you think that?"

Mitch had known that at some point, she could no longer honor the secrecy surrounding Martha's memories. She consoled herself in the reality that sooner rather than later, Herman himself would witness his mother's behavior around non-existent dead bodies.

"Judging by your reluctance to answer my question, I imagine it wasn't death by natural causes?" Mitch studied Herman's reaction.

"It was blunt force trauma."

"That can happen naturally enough. Maybe he fell down and bumped his head?"

"Maybe he had help falling down?"

Mitch decided to go all in. For some reason, she felt safe doing so. "Did you kill your father?"

Herman walked over to where Mitch was sitting. He bent down until they were face to face.

"I didn't kill my father."

"But, you think someone did, right? Otherwise, your mind would be at rest."

"There was no proof. Nobody stood trial."

"Have you considered the idea that your mom knows who did it and that is what has damaged her memory?"

Herman straightened back up. "She never said anything to me."

"Maybe she thought you did it and didn't want to get you in trouble."

"I wasn't even there! There's no reason to think I had anything to do with this!"

"What about Shane? Was she there at the time?"

"We don't talk about her!"

"I'm just going down the list of suspects."

"Shane was a girl."

"I imagine a girl can kill her father, given sufficient cause. Maybe it was self-defense?"

"Maybe you need to shut your filthy mouth!"

"At the raising of voices, Martha stirred, "Herman! No arguing at dinner!"

Things had been fine until Herman lost his temper. It was hair trigger where his father's death was concerned. Which was a red flag considering how much time had passed. Perhaps a child never truly got over the death of a parent if it was by suspicious means. However, if they were going to get to the bottom of this, they would need help from the authorities. This was going to require more magic than pulling a rabbit out of a hat.

"Maybe we can visit the local police department tomorrow?" Mitch suggested.

This was rich. The same group that was being pursued by the authorities was now going to try and get an appointment with the local sheriff. It sounded like a scenario straight out of the movies. "They didn't find anything the first time around."

"Maybe they weren't looking in the right place?"


Mary had been restless. Restless as in sleepless nights restless. Serious events had occurred and she was convinced that she was still being kept in the dark about most of it. Since it affected not only her sleep, but her overall wellbeing, she decided to confront Agent Fawn about it at her next visit. As luck would have it, today was that day.

When Mary heard the knock at the door, her heart leapt. It was a physical response due to her romantic interest in Fawn. At best, it was embarrassing. At worst, it was annoying. Fawn was a married woman with children and a career. When this ordeal was all over, Mary would be back in Colorado and Fawn would be reassigned to some other secret mission and they would never see each other again. The end.

Mary opened the door. Fawn looked drawn. It wasn't nearly as poetic as it sounded.

"Come in. I'll have some coffee ready in no time."

"Thanks," Fawn nodded absently.

Mary took her time making coffee, trying to focus on her main goal of extracting information from Fawn. This was taking more courage than she had originally anticipated. Fawn graciously accepted her coffee and the stale cookies Mary had placed in front of her. But there was no smile. No eye contact.

"I want to know what's going on," Mary blurted out. After all her rumination, this was the best she could do.

"I thinking about leaving my marriage."

The sound of a door opening played through Mary's mind. Not like a squeaky, creaky Halloween door kind of sound. More just like a whooshing sound. Like fresh air. Or opportunity.

"Really?" was all that Mary could come up with for a reply.

"You think I'm kidding?" Fawn sounded piqued.

"I'm sorry. That was thoughtless. I'm just surprised is all."

"Really?" Fawn now used Mary's stalling tactic.

"As in really surprised. I guess I thought you had the perfect suburban life and marriage and all the trimmings."

"Nobody had a perfect life."

"So, what happened?" Mary somehow couldn't resist meddling now that the subject had come up.

"Everything and nothing," Fawn answered cryptically. Her agent training had kicked in.

"That bad, huh?" Mary could play this game too.

Suddenly, tears started to form in Fawn's lovely eyes. Oh damn, Mary chided herself. She hadn't meant to make Fawn cry, and hey maybe it wasn't even her fault. But, damn. A beautiful woman was crying right next to her and Mary felt frozen in place. Should she sit here like a Budda or should she reach out and make physical contact. It was agony not knowing.

Fawn came to her rescue simply by reaching out and taking Mary's hand in hers. It felt like a lifesaver tossed to a drowning person. Mary grasped back and then put her arm around Fawn's shoulders. It felt so awkward and yet so predestined. It wasn't a good time to presume to be Delphic, but maybe somehow Mary had seen this coming. In retrospect, Fawn had been shut down more and more with each passing visit. Now, the gate had opened to the most authentic expression between them. To anyone else, it was a simple side hug. To Mary, it was the beginning of something true.

"You are suddenly very quiet," Fawn remarked.

"I'm sorry. I'm not very good when it comes to surprises."

189

"You make it sound like a birthday party."

"I don't mean to. I'm just at a loss for any words of wisdom."

"You've been through a breakup."

"That was different."

"How so?"

Mary struggled to come up with the words to describe the dearth of equivalencies between Fawn's marriage and Mary and Lisa's relationship. There were core similarities yet stark differences.

"You must be in a very thoughtful mood today," Fawn was finished crying and now very curious.

"Well, for one thing, I wasn't married to Lisa."

"Does that make a difference?"

"For some people, the idea of legitimizing a relationship makes a big difference. It's a formality that adds gravitas to the situation. It's more than just about the wedding cake."

"I didn't even get a cake."

"You didn't? Why not?" Mary felt ridiculous for asking, but she couldn't help herself.

"It didn't seem important at the time."

"But, everybody gets a wedding cake."

"I think we are veering off topic a little bit here."

"Maybe it's just easier to talk about cake that the real issues."

Fawn smiled faintly. Her agent persona was quickly recovering from her teary outbreak.

"I probably shouldn't be prying into your personal life either," Fawn admitted.

That door-opening sound that Mary had heard in her head a few minutes ago was starting to sound like a door closing. It was imperative to stop it and fast.

"I'm glad that you are prying," Mary said. "My life hasn't been pried into in a long time. At least, not that aspect of it," Mary remembered all she had discussed in therapy and felt obligated to qualify her statement.

"It's never easy to talk about personal issues. That's why I felt safe bringing up this subject with you. I don't have anyone else to talk to."

"You must lead a lonely life. Needing to keep secrets all the time. Besides your husband and kids, do you have any other family?" Mary asked as she removed her arm from Fawn's shoulders.

"Not really. My parents are dead and I don't stay in touch with my distant relatives."

"That's understandable, given your line of work."

"It isn't just the work that prevents more contact."

Mary waited a beat to see if Fawn was inclined to elaborate. When that didn't work, Mary forged ahead, "Is there an estrangement?"

"Maybe more along the lines of a mutual dislike."

It was obvious from these cryptic answers that Fawn was done talking about this subject. Mary wanted to keep their new connection going, but she was quickly finding out that this wasn't the best conversation to accomplish that goal.

"Well, if you want to go back to your original topic, it's okay with me."

"I don't know. It feels like maybe I've already said too much."

That door-closing sound was back and louder than ever. Mary felt helpless. It must've shown on her face to professional-profiler Fawn.

"Are you sure you are okay?"

"No. I'm not okay. I was feeling totally out of the loop before you showed up and that's not getting any better."

"Oh, I see now. When you first asked me what was going on, you probably weren't expecting a rundown on the state of my personal life."

"It wasn't my original intent."

"This is truly awkward."

"But it doesn't need to be," Mary reassured. "It's absolutely fine that you told me what's going on with you. Have you told your kids yet?"

"Let's not get ahead of the situation, shall we," Fawn was beginning to sound annoyed, the last thing that Mary had hoped for. If Fawn didn't want to talk about this, why did she bring it up in the first place?

"Why don't we start over? If you want to talk about this, I'm happy to listen," Mary folded her hands on the table and struck a pose. She was ready, willing and able to hear the entire story. End to end.

Fawn looked directly into Mary's eyes. "I can't tell if you are being serious or not."

"This is as serious as I ever get," Mary assured her.

Fawn took her time thinking this over. Mary was so nervous, she

191

started to sweat. It was mortifying.

"I really haven't yet taken the opportunity to bring up the subject with my husband," Fawn used a lot of words to describe a simple situation.

"I'm the first person you've discussed this with?"

"Yes."

"I'm flattered."

"That wasn't my intent."

"So, you didn't bring this up to solicit my advice?" Mary sounded edgy despite her struggle to remain composed.

"Okay, sure. What's your advice?" Fawn sounded flippant at best.

"Tell him tonight. Right after you put the kids to bed. Have a backup plan in case he loses it."

"He's not that kind of man."

"You've never yet asked him for a divorce. Things can get ugly very quickly."

"You are making me have second thoughts," Fawn said quietly.

Mary felt foolish now. In her attempt to give advice, she might have just slammed shut that door of opportunity between herself and Fawn.

"Well, okay, in the meantime, can you give me an update on the case?"

"The case?"

"What's going on with the court case and Mitch and everything else?"

"Oh, that," Fawn's demeanor changed instantly. It was all back to professional in an instant. "Did I tell you yet that everyone is heading to Alabama?"

"Gee, no. I haven't heard a word about that."

"I'm sorry for not briefing you sooner. We had a confirmed sighting of Mitch in Alabama and we are keeping close tabs on developments there."

"You said 'everyone.' Who else is going to Alabama?"

Fawn broke off eye contact. This must be interesting news.

"Your mother and Lisa are heading there as well."

"Why?"

"Because no one could stop them," was Fawn's most accurate answer.

"I imagine not. What do they think they are going to accomplish?"

"Our best guess is that they want to be on scene when Mitch is rescued."

"And why hasn't that happened yet?"

"We are monitoring the situation carefully."

"Which means something important is going on that you haven't told me about yet."

"There may be a complication in the case that we are carefully monitoring."

"You just said that in your last sentence. Just tell me what's going on."

"There's also a missing baby."

"A missing baby?"

"I thought I had told you about this?"

"I think I would've remembered."

"Your cousin, Miranda Knight, gave birth to her baby."

"Okay."

"And then, unfortunately, Ms. Knight died soon afterwards."

"Miranda died and no one told me."

"I'm sorry."

"And so then what about the baby?"

"The baby is missing."

"Miranda wasn't even due yet. The baby must be premature."

"Which is why that issue has jumped to the top of the list."

"Okay, so somehow you think that my deceased cousin's missing, premature baby is somehow tied in to the abduction of Mitch," Mary put it all together in one sentence.

"We have yet to prove otherwise. I know that the average citizen believes that government agents sit around in cubicles chit chatting all day. We really do put in a lot of leg work and long hours."

Mary must've made a face like she was being chastised because in her next breath, Fawn apologized. "It's already been a long day and I'm sorry if I'm taking it out on you."

"Don't worry about it. I'm just glad that you have figured out that somehow this is all tied together."

Fawn looked at Mary. "If you ever get bored doing whatever it is that you do, you might want to think about becoming a Special Agent."

Mary didn't say it out loud, but if she ever was serious about getting involved with Fawn, it probably wouldn't be a smart idea to go into the same line of work. There would be little to talk about at the dinner table. Which sounded like what was already going on with Fawn's marriage. Silence stretched between them. As nice as it was to have company, Mary didn't have much else to say of substance and small talk would only be embarrassing.

"I guess I'd better be going."

"I guess."

"I'm working this case as hard as I know how."

"I know. And I'm sure that everyone appreciates that."

"Okay. I'll keep in better touch."

"Okay.'

Fawn left. It was just as well. Mary was practically chocking on her banal words. How much better would it be if she could just start telling the truth? Do people really want to hear that you want them to abandon their marriage just so you can explore the possibility of maybe having an affair? Perhaps Mary was being too hard on herself, but was she really ready to explore a relationship with a woman who hadn't shown any gay propensities? And with children? Mary imagined herself becoming an instant mother and the concept startled her. Love was really so much more complicated once you got past the preliminary butterflies in the stomach stage. Maybe this wasn't such a good idea after all. There was a knock at the door. It hadn't even been a minute. It was Fawn.

"I'm telling him tonight. Thanks for your advice."

"Uh. Okay!" Mary couldn't even cobble together a complete sentence after her latest train of thought.

"So, wish me luck."

"Of course. I hope it goes well."

"Okay. See you later."

Fawn left again. Mary sat down and slowly shook her head. The words, "What am I doing?" just kept going through her mind. No clear answer manifested.


Despite their guarded animosity, Reb and Lisa made pretty good traveling companions. Particularly when Reb chartered a luxury jet for the final leg of their destination. It had been quite the journey to Alabama. Not exactly champagne and caviar, but better than riding in a van.

Not only do you cross time standards, but you tend to also set the clock back as well when you travel to the Deep South. Like setting time back to the sixties when African Americans were supposed to know their "place". Or maybe even farther back than that. All these plantations didn't build themselves. Ohh and ahh all you want as a tourist, but as much blood, sweat and tears went into these buildings as the Egyptian Pyramids. Everyone felt sorry for Charlton Heston when he was forced to work as a slave in the mud pits. Where was all that sympathy when a Negro slave had to endure so much worse? America didn't invent slavery and racism, but that didn't prevent it from profiting handsomely from it.

"You seem lost in thought," Reb ventured into conversation with Lisa. A habit that she had cultivated more and more as their time together stretched on.

"I've just never been this far south." she replied.

"That sounds like more than just an observation about geography," Reb followed up.

"I've just never been this close to the area that institutionalized slavery in America."

"And all along I figured that you were simply overwhelmed by the humidity."

"That, too," Lisa was trying to be conversational, but it was a struggle not lost on Reb.

"As a former Senator, I've had to deal with many individuals who had strongly held beliefs that were vastly different from mine."

"I think that calling what went on in the south a 'belief' is too kind of a word. When this is all over, I'm going to Birmingham."

"Why?"

"To pay my respects. To educate myself. To atone for my ignorance."

"That's quite a list. Aren't you being a little hard on yourself?"

"Maybe so. But while Mary was busy exposing a network of dangerous white supremacists, what the hell was I doing? Nothing of noteworthiness."

Reb sensed that she was on perilous turf. While she hadn't exactly approved of Lisa's behavior on a variety of fronts, it certainly wasn't enough to issue a blanket condemnation. However, she was having difficulty bolstering Lisa's self-image when she too didn't work on a consistent basis to eradicate racism and bigotry.

"Life gets in everyone's way," Reb stated.

"That didn't stop Mary. She didn't let anything get in the way."

"If it had been you under the same circumstances, you would have done the same thing."

"I'm not sure I would've had the courage to carry through like Mary did. You must be very proud of her."

"I'm too busy being afraid for her right now. I'll be proud later."

"Do we have a plan for when we finally get to our destination?"

"I'm working on it."

"Work faster,"

Chapter 9

Soon after Max's death, Trish had taken to wandering the hallways on a nightly basis. Not just occasional sojourns to the haunted basement room, but a repeated ritual. It was beginning to worry Rose. She could hear the muffled footsteps and familiar creaks of the wooden floor. Even with this apparent insomnia, Trish was still the best mother ever to Josh. So much so that she had begun sleeping in his nursery. Silver had helped by arranging for a new bed to be purchased and delivered. Trish had been adamant. She didn't want her usual bed moved. It needed to stay where it was, without further comment or explanation. Rose and Silver had exchanged meaningful looks but offered no argument. Trish was a millionaire and head of the household. If she wanted a new bed, by damn, she would get a new bed!

And so, with Silver's assistance, the purchasing hadn't stopped with just a bed. Next, Trish wanted a new dresser as well. Josh's room was large enough to hold a new bed and dresser for her. Once Trish started the redecorating, it seemed as if the floodgates had opened. She bought four wooden filing cabinets complete with file folders. "That's a lot of filing cabinets," Silver had remarked as casually as she could pretend to be.
"I have a lot of paperwork," Trish explained.
"Maybe you should've bought a shredder instead," Rose interjected. All the sudden changes had affected her nerves in a negative way.
"Good idea!" Trish was enthusiastic at the suggestion. Excited to purchase still more items, she went to check out the possibilities on her computer.
The reaction from Rose escalated from nervous to outright concern. "How big a shredder can someone buy? Will we need to reinforce the flooring?" Rose asked Silver.
"I'm sure only the Federal Government knows for sure," Silver

answered cautiously, hoping to avoid sounding whimsical.

Rose sighed. Silver noticed.

"Let's go bake some cookies."

An hour later, just as they were pulling the last batch from the oven, the doorbell rang.

"Are we expecting company?" Rose asked no one in particular.

Silver and the agents stopped chewing cookies and looked at each other.

"No."

"Does this mean we need to answer the door with guns drawn?"

"Let's just see who it is before we overreact."

They went as a group to the front door.

"It looks like some construction guys," Silver had thrown caution to the wind and looked out the window.

"It could be an ambush," Vukoff said to Smith.

They drew their weapons and had them at the ready when the door swung open. The Rocky Mountain Brothers construction duo looked shocked to find themselves on the wrong end of government service firearms. Nobody said anything for a few heart beats.

"We got a call from a woman named Trish," the older brother referenced his work order.

"Trish called you?" Rose asked.

"She wants an estimate on some remodeling work."

"She didn't mention any remodeling work to us," Silver said with just a hint of suspicion in her tone.

Trish's voice from behind startled everyone. They were so busy guarding the front that they forgot all about the flank. "Is that Ronnie and Donnie?"

"Yes, Ma'am. I'm Ronnie and he's Donnie," the older brother indicated his sibling.

"Oh good! Come on in. I'll show you which walls I want you to take out."

As the three of them headed toward Josh's nursery, Rose turned to Silver and said, "It must be an awfully big shredder!"

"Let's follow along and find out!"

Within forty-five seconds, everyone was assembled in Josh's room like it was one of those mystery stories and they were going to get a blow-by-blow explanation of the crime. The only person missing was Poirot. Trish had already launched into the narrative.

"I want to know if you can knock out the opposing walls in the nursery. We need a lot more room."

"First we will need to see if they are weight-bearing walls and then-" His commentary was cut short by Rose, "Wait a second! Just hold on for a minute!"

Her commanding tone startled everyone into silence.

"How big a shredder did you buy?" she directed the question to Trish.

"I didn't buy a shredder. At least, not yet. I got sidetracked."

"By what?"

"I decided that I needed a much larger work space."

"Work space? You don't work!"

"I'm using 'work space' in a generic, abstract sense."

"I'm not sure exactly what generic, abstract work is, but are you sure it needs that much space?"

"I've been wanting to remodel for a long time."

Rose looked shaken. Just the thought of making structural changes to the mansion added ten years to her countenance. It was as if she was going to be asked to pick up a sledgehammer and do the work herself. Trish finally noticed how affected Rose was by all this, for lack of a better term, confusion.

"It's all going to be okay. I promise," Trish tried to smooth things over.

Rose looked doubtful. "It's just so much change to deal with right now."

"It's just two walls, Rose. They'll be done before you know it."

"I don't understand why you think Josh needs this much room," Rose asked. She had either forgotten Trish's prior comments or chose to ignore them.

"I'm going to be in here with him. I've been doing research and I feel it's a good idea for me to spend a lot more time with Josh. So, I'm arranging for us to have shared space."

"Shared space?" Rose asked. She had never heard of the concept.

"I'm going to in here a lot more."

"Doing what?"

"Oh, I don't know," Trish hedged. "Maybe I'll write a book or something."

"Write a book?"

"Or something," Trish was beginning to sound defensive. If she wanted to spend more time with her son and write a book or whatever, it was no one's business but hers.

"Is that why you need the shredder?" Silver chimed in.

"It's why I need a desk and a computer. And some bookshelves. And a comfy lounge chair. So, yes, I will be needing a lot of room."

"What's the book going to be about?" Rose asked.

"I don't know yet."

"Perhaps it's going to be about ghosts?" Silver wandered dangerously close to the truth.

"Perhaps," Trish said moodily and then perked right back up. "So, we need to get started. I'm going furniture shopping. Anyone want to go along?"

"Again?" Rose asked.

"Yes, again. Meanwhile, Ronnie and Donnie can get to work." Trish grabbed her purse and was out the door before Smith could stop her. A short car chase ensued until he caught up with her at the furniture store. After a short confrontation about all things protocol, things settled back down to boring as he stood around while Trish shopped. There was only Trish and the salesperson in tow to guard. And the salesperson was the most excited in the group. It wasn't every day that a customer came into the store and pointed to that and that and that. Once Trish got started, she mindlessly selected enough furniture for five or maybe even six rooms. She couldn't pass up a sectional couch and dining table with ten chairs. The variety of roll-top desks would look very stylish scattered around the mansion. She also stumbled upon still another bedroom set that caught her fancy. She liked it much better than the bed and dresser she had bought mere days ago. And, of course, she also selected a massive desk for her computer. It was the size and style that a CEO of a major corporation might have furnished their corner office with. It spoke to her in inaudible whispers, "You can write a book. I can help." And then she selected over a dozen bookshelves of various sizes and styles. If she was going to write books, she would need bookshelves.

As Trish paused for a moment, she had an inkling of why Rose was so shaken by Trish's recent actions. It must've felt like Trish was moving on too quickly after Max's death. Trish had moved on from Robbie's death pretty quickly as well. It may very well seem callous to Rose and others. A "bury your dead and move on" approach may work in the movies, but in real life, it didn't always work out that way. Trish would need to craft this message to Rose in such a way to allay her concerns.

Meanwhile, Rose had taken the opportunity of Trish's absence to tell her true fear to Silver.

"I think Trish has finally gone off the deep end."

"Why?"

"She's buying way too many things! If this was a food addiction, she would weigh three-hundred pounds by now."

"I'm not sure about that, Miss Rose. She hasn't bought enough stuff to even get on one of those hoarding TV shows."

"It's not the amount that she's buying. It's the reason behind the behavior and the rate of acceleration."

Silver wasn't inclined to argue with her employers. But as far as she was concerned, the old house could sure use some desperately-needed renovations and new furnishings. It was about time that Miss Trish started spending some of her fortune to make herself happy and comfortable. Besides, if Silver played her cards right, she might end up with a few new sticks of furniture for her room. Maybe she would get a new desk? Silver had been what people call a minimalist most of her adult life. As far as Silver was concerned, minimalist was another word for being poor. Silver's family had been dirt poor and moving from place to place only reinforced the lack of material goods for her. Working for Trish had been the most stable employment Silver had had as an adult, so it was tempting to finally desire the nicer things in life. She, for one, could hardly wait to see what got delivered to the house next.

"What do you think is the reason behind why Miss Trish is buying so much stuff?" Silver followed up, just to show that she was still paying attention.

"She's hiding from the truth and all her feelings. She never accepted Robbie's death and the circumstances surrounding it!" Rose was visibly upset, more than Silver had ever seen her be.

"You think she feels responsible or guilty?"

"Trish was wooing another woman when my daughter killed herself. Deep down she should feel something more than simply a

201

compulsion to buy more furniture!"

By the time Rose had completed the sentence, she was shaking from emotion herself. Silver noticed this and advised wisely, "Maybe you should go and rest for a spell. You won't do yourself or anybody else any good is you get yourself sick from worry."

"Maybe you are right. I haven't been sleeping very well," Rose admitted.

"Go take a nap. I'll take care of everything."

"You always do. I couldn't do this without you."

"Thank you, Miss Rose," Silver smiled.

Rose gave Silver a rare hug. They had always kept things pretty professional, but somehow this seemed proper.


Trish hadn't even noticed how long she had shopped or that the store had stayed open after closing time to accommodate her spending spree until Smith started to yawn. For some reason, she noticed this. Perhaps because he was usually the pillar of alertness.

"If you fall asleep on guard duty, do they still put you in front of a firing squad?"

"Only in war time."

"Aren't we always at war?" Trish opined.

"Technically, no. But it seems to feel like it lately."

"I guess your line of work depends on some sort of conflict."

"Sadly, yes. A tragic form of job security." Smith yawned again.

"Let's call it a night, why don't we?" Trish offered.

"Only if you think you've bought enough furniture?"

If Smith was being sarcastic, he hid it well.

"Tomorrow is another day," Trish quipped.

"We never get a guarantee."

"A guarantee for the furniture?" Trish had been distracted by the final paperwork.

"We never get a guarantee that we will have another tomorrow."

"Do you know something I don't?"

"I'm absolutely certain that I know things you don't, and vice versa."

Trish shook her head. Suddenly, she was too tired for word games. "Let's go."

Silver couldn't say exactly how long Rose had been dead. She was the first to discover her lifeless body when she checked in one last time before retiring for the night. Rather than calling for help, she got on her knees and said a prayer.

"Oh, Lord," she whispered softly, "I know that you need to bring people into your kingdom every day. But did today really need to be Miss Rose's day?"

Silver took another long minute to think things over. Rose was clearly dead. If Silver called for the ambulance, there would be six or maybe even more paramedics descending into the room. And they would have Miss Rose stripped naked and on the floor trying to pump life into her body. Possibly breaking a rib or two in the process. Try as she may, she just couldn't bring herself to have that happen. So she went quietly back to her own room to await the impending mayhem.

Chapter 10

The might had started off quietly.  Then, no surprise to Mitch,
Martha started seeing the dead body again.  There was no hiding the
reality from Herman and the guard this time.  There would be no
secret about this after tonight.
"What's going on in here?" Herman bellowed at Mitch like it was
her fault.  And, in a way, it was.  She had been complicit with
Martha in remaining silent about Martha's night terrors.  No more.
"Your mother is seeing your father's dead body.  It's been going on
since we've been on the road."
"And you didn't think to tell me?"
"Has she never done this before?" Mitch hedged.
"Never."
"So, I guess she really did need this trip to Alabama."
"You think it's a *good* thing for her to be seeing dead bodies?"
"I think it's a good thing when something this traumatic finally
comes to the surface."
"Herman!" Martha interrupted their esoteric discussion.
"What?" he answered a little too sharply as he transferred his anger
from Mitch to her.
"Don't use that tone of voice with me!"
"I'm sorry," he apologized automatically before he had to go
through the shame of being asked to again.  "What is going on,
Mother?"
"You are too young to be here.  You need to take Shane and go to
the neighbors."
"It's okay, Mom.  I'm a grown man now."
"Oh, I know you think you are.  Now run along."
"Mom!  It's Herman!  I'm an adult now!" he held her by her
shoulders until she looked squarely at him.
"Where are we?" she asked.
"We are at home in Alabama."

"Why did we come back here?" Martha asked, almost plaintively.

"Because you wanted to be here," Herman sounded dangerously close to losing all patience.

"Martha," Mitch took a soothing tone, "remember that you need to make peace with the past for you to feel better."

"I don't remember," she sounded unsteady.

"And that's why we came here. So you can fix your memory."

"What's wrong with my memory?"

"It's not working as well as it used to."

"How do you know that?"

"What's my name?" Mitch asked.

Martha hesitated. "Can I have a minute to think about it?"

"Sure. Meanwhile, was it your dead husband's body that you were seeing a minute ago?"

"He has a name!" Martha replied curtly.

"What was his name?" Mitch challenged kindly.

Martha remained silent. You could tell that it was frustrating her no end that she couldn't remember anyone's name.

Herman was standing stock still, apparently angry at everything and everyone.

"This is all your fault," he pointed an accusing finger at Mitch.

"You're right!" Mitch was agreeable. "This was my idea and I'll take the blame for everything if I can get just one tiny bit of credit if even one thing goes right."

"It's okay, Mitch," Martha piped up suddenly. "His name was Melvin. I remember now!"

Mitch looked to Herman for confirmation. He nodded.

"I have an idea," Mitch said quietly.

Silence encouraged her to continue. "Rather than us all trooping down to the police station tomorrow, why don't we see if they will make a house call?"

"A house call?" Herman asked skeptically.

"It's a lot easier to get police officers to come to your house than a doctor."

"Why would we need a doctor?"

"Are you sure you're a criminal mastermind?" Mitch asked bravely. He looked like he was just about to tell her to shut up again, but she forged ahead, "If we told them that we had a lead in Melvin's murder case, it might warrant their presence. No pun intended."

"But we don't have a new lead!"

"What if we made one up?"

"That could get us in serious trouble."

"We are already in serious trouble! You are a wanted fugitive. Your mother can't remember who killed your father."

"And what about you?"

"Oh, I'm in plenty of trouble at home. Believe me. Getting arrested for filing a false police report would be the least of my worries!"


"I have a crazy idea. Want to hear it?" Lisa asked Reb.

"Do I have a choice?" Reb was snappish as usual.

They had made the trip to Alabama, but still felt out of the loop as far as sharing of information was concerned. Sleep had eluded the both of them as time dragged on.

"Why do *you* think the Feds haven't simply descended on the house and gotten all this over with? A couple of well-placed smoke bombs would do the trick."

"I thought you said you had an idea?"

"I do. I'm just wondering if you, given enough time to think about it, would come up with the same conclusion."

"Your idea must really be way out there, because I haven't figured it out."

"Here's a clue: Why do you think, despite all those phone calls to all those hospitals, there was no new information on Miranda's baby?"

"I don't know."

"Seriously, are you that intellectually lazy?"

"I can always put you on a plane and send you home."

"That's your answer for everything, isn't it? Use your money and power instead of your brain."

"If you have the solution for this, I think you better start telling it to the authorities."

"I think they already know what's going on and they just haven't told us. That's why it's so important for us to figure this out for ourselves."

"You think they haven't told us everything they know?"

"I'm sure of it. You've gotten on the wrong side of these Federal agents and now you are the last person they would share anything

206

with."

"So, what is your theory?"

"Why do you think the Alabama State Patrol just stood there and let Mitch get back in the van?"

"I guess they thought she was in danger if they made a rescue attempt?"

"Ten damn feet."

"What?"

"Remember, you kept saying ten damn feet."

"Right…"

"It wasn't like a car chase or an armed standoff! It would've been easy for the police to draw their guns and take care of everything. But something prevented them from doing so. Remember when you said that Mitch didn't need to protect everyone." Lisa said.

"I remember."

"Well, maybe she isn't the one doing the protecting. Maybe the authorities are doing the protecting."

"But what about the elderly woman that they mentioned?"

"If the police thought that the elderly woman was in any danger, they would've taken action."

"So, who are we protecting?" Reb was by now exasperated.

"I've already talked about that! Weren't you paying attention?"

"I'm sending you home!"

"No, you're not. But you need to be sending me to the store to get you some new wardrobe essentials! This is turning into one long trip."

Reb became sullen and pouty. Always a good look for her but entirely lost on Lisa. She was tired of verbally sparring with Lisa, who was obviously determined to demonstrate her intellectual superiority. If Lisa had indeed figured it all out, she was derelict in her duty to have a serious discussion with anyone who would listen to her.

"Why don't you ask the agents to join us and you can explain everything to them?"

"I have a better idea. I'll write down the solution to this entire case on a piece of paper and seal it in an envelope and give it to you. Then, when this is all over, you will see that I'm right."

"That won't help in the short term."

"Nothing is going to help in the short term. Only Mitch can ensure that this is successfully resolved. Meanwhile, what color underwear do you want me to buy for you?"

Trish was tired after all her shopping. In her frenzy to fill all the voids in her life by spending money, she had neglected to see to Josh's bedtime ritual. She checked in on him and then went to have a word with Rose. Her screams woke the entire household. Agents Smith and Vukoff were right on the spot while Silver, dragged down by a guilty conscience, was the last to arrive. And then, as Silver had feared, those half a dozen paramedics showed up. Mercifully, they realized in short order that Rose was beyond help. So, rather than transport her body to the hospital, they called the coroner. Events and time slowed to a crawl. Although they had just been through this with Max, every individual death brought shock and dismay.
"We're losing all of them," Trish remarked quietly to Silver and they waited in the fireplace room for the coroner.
"What do you mean, Miss Trish?" Silver asked reluctantly.
"All the survivors of the Holocaust. One by one, they are dying. We are losing the witnesses of history. One by one." Trish stopped talking when she realized that she was repeating herself.
"Oh, I thought you meant that we had lost all the Goldsteins."
"Did Rose show any signs that she didn't feel well?" Trish asked. It was the next logical question, but Silver suddenly became reticent.
"I'm not a doctor," she answered curtly. An attitude totally out of character for her.
Trish made eye contact. "What happened?" she asked like she suspected that she wasn't going to hear anything close to the truth.
"Miss Rose just seemed more tired than usual," Silver told part of the truth.
"And?" Trish wouldn't let up.
"And she was more upset than usual."
"We are all more upset than usual."
"Miss Rose was upset that you were carrying on with Lisa while Miss Robbie was killing herself."
"Oh," Trish said and then became defensive. "If that were the case,

Rose would've died a while ago. Right when things were happening."

"I'm just telling you what she told me right before she died."

"She said that to you right before she died?"

"It was her theory about why you were cracking up!" Silver hoped that she hadn't given away her timeline.

"Cracking up?"

"Yes! Cracking up! You know, hearing voices, seeing ghosts, buying furniture."

"Buying furniture is normal," Trish deflected.

"Not at the breakneck speed you were doing it at," Silver sounded like an expert.

"Well, now we have one more funeral to plan," Trish was ready to change the subject.

"I can help."

"You might need to do it all if I'm cracking up," Trish muttered.


After they had gotten Martha tucked back into bed for the might, Mitch and Herman had a heart to heart talk.

"You should have told me sooner!" Herman started loud and only settled down when Mitch pointed to Martha's room and shushed him.

"Don't wake her up again!"

"You could've warned me," Herman said quietly.

"I think you need to tell me a few things as well," Mitch intoned.

"You know everything you need to know," he groused.

"I think it would be good to know who had a motive to kill your father."

"No one killed my dad! He died of a blunt force trauma."

"Then why does your mother think she's responsible?"

"She doesn't."

"Yes, she does! And I think that's what's wrong with her mind and memory. So, if we are going to heal her, remembering that this was the whole point of this entire endeavor, you need to start telling me the damn truth!"

It all came out a little more forcefully than Mitch had intended, but to her surprise, Herman didn't have his usual adverse reaction. A moment passed.

"We were just kids when it happened."

"You and Shane?"

"Me. And. Shane." Herman spoke the words slowly, loath to even say his sister's name.

"What happened to Shane?"

"She disappeared. We don't talk about it."

"You mean she was a runaway? Or kidnapped?"

"She left home."

"At what age?"

"Why does that matter?"

"Why won't you give me a straight-forward answer?"

"It's family business."

"I'm trying to help you solve this problem. Was Shane sexually abused by your father?"

"Shut up!" Herman pounded his fist on the table so hard that it shook to its foundation. By only a miracle, Martha slept through the racket.

"Was your dad abusive to everybody?" Mitch figured she was getting closer to the truth with every question.

"My dad was a typical southern redneck husband."

"So, what does that mean? Did he slap your mom around when she got out of line?" Mitch asked the question in the only way that she felt would elicit a truthful response from the southern redneck sitting across the table from her.

Herman was quiet for a moment. His eyes had that ten-mile stare that people get when they are seeing visions from their childhood. "It didn't happen very often," was his rationalization for male-on-female violence.

"Often enough that you saw it."

"So what!"

"So, imagine what went on that you didn't see. How many times did he beat her up while you were at school or at a friend's house?"

"I didn't have any friends."

"Probably why," Mitch remarked offhand.

"Shut up!" Herman's wounded child came to the forefront.

Mitch ignored the command. She needed to know the extent of the damage, "So, did your dad beat you up?"

It was a full two minutes before he answered.

"Yes."

It was a short answer that spoke volumes. In the tragic scenario that is generational violence, Herman was a true victim.

"Do you have children?" Mitch asked suddenly.

"No."

"Why not?"

"Children aren't safe in this world."

Mitch didn't know if she entirely agreed with his surmise, but chose to not argue the point. Instead, she asked a question that she herself hoped to survive.

"What else did your dad do to you?"

Five minutes passed. Five whole, entire minutes. Five minutes is three-hundred seconds. Mitch inhaled and exhaled. If these were to be her final moments on the planet, then she wanted them to be honored. How many times do we fritter away time? Five minutes here, five there. Never thinking that it could be the last five minutes. It gave her something to think about while Herman was forming his response.

"Does it really matter?" Herman finally spoke. His voice was surprisingly vulnerable.

"It does to me," Mitch replied honestly.

"My father was a pedophile."

Mitch almost fell off her chair at his answer. "A pedophile?"

"That's right. Before they had a fancy word for it or a law against it, he raped every boy and girl he could get his filthy hands on."

Mitch had no words. The horror was palpable.

"So, are you happy now?" Herman said.

"He raped you as well?"

"That's right."

"I wish you had told me sooner."

"It isn't something that normally comes up in daily conversation, is it?"

"I'm very sorry for what happened to you, Herman." Mitch could only shake her head in sorrowful slowness.

They sat like estranged relatives at an uncomfortable family reunion for another full five minutes. There was one silver lining in this otherwise dark cloud. Herman noticed Mitch's countenance brighten just a bit.

"What?"

"The only good outcome of this terrible truth is that there are now plenty of suspects in your dad's murder. At first, I thought it was your mom."

"And now you think it's me?"

"Oh for heaven's sake, Herman. It's not you. But now, we have a whole town full of suspects from which to choose. Don't you see? Anyone who had a child victimized by your dad had a motive for murder! We are *this* close to solving the case!"

"If anything, we are farther away. Too many people to choose from."

"Only a select few would take the law into their own hands. That's why we need to have a conversation with the local sheriff."

"I'll see what I can arrange."

"The sooner the better."

"In all your questions, you didn't ask the one I thought you were going to ask."

"Which was?"

"Why didn't the State Patrol rescue you when they had the chance?"

"I didn't ask because I already know the answer. You think I've just been sleeping in the van this entire trip!"


Mary didn't know what to expect the following morning. When Fawn did stop by, if she even would, what would Mary's response be? Would there be a lot of chit chat about marital relations? Or just more guessing games. For once, Mary wasn't looking forward to the visitation. She was even more uneasy when Fawn showed up wearing sunglasses. God forbid there had been violence.

"What happened to you?" Mary blurted out.

"What?" Fawn answered with a question.

"What are you hiding behind your sunglasses?"

"Oh, these. I forgot I had them on," Fawn removed the glasses to reveal nothing more than red-tinged tired eyes.

"I was worried," Mary admitted sheepishly.

"About what?"

"Nothing. Never mind."

"Okay, well in my continuing effort to keep you updated on events, something has happened."

"What?" panic started turning Mary's stomach cold.

"Rose Goldstein died last night."

"What happened?"

"She died peacefully in her sleep."

"Well, I'm blaming Trish for this!" Mary retorted angrily.

"I don't think you can blame someone for someone else dying in their sleep."

"Watch me!" Mary challenged.

"I know you don't like Trish," Fawn tried to talk.

Mary interrupted, "I despise Trish! She was supposed to be taking good care of the Goldstein family and now, all of them are dead!"

"I think we should arrange an emergency session with Dr. Anna."

"Why? I'm not the one causing problems! I'm just the one who is brave enough to tell the fucking truth!"

As Mary finished up her tirade, she was fairly shouting. The effect was not lost on Fawn and her tired eyes. "I'm only trying to help."

Mary fell into a sullen silence. Grief comes in all varieties of surprising packages and only the brave choose to unwrap them in the proper order. Where was Mary's compassion for what Rose may have been experiencing during her final moments on Earth? Did she suffer despite what Fawn had reported? Did she even know the end was near? Did she fondly think of Max and Robbie or was there even time for that? Did it matter that she died alone?"

And what had been Mary's first response? Mary's primal reaction was to cast about for someone to blame, and Trish made an awfully convenient target. Mary had a lot of bottled up, corrosive anger and it was bound to start leaking out sooner rather than later.

"Maybe an appointment would be a good idea," Mary conceded the point.

"I'll see what I can do. Also, your dad is on the way and will be here soon."

"Thanks for arranging for that. Meanwhile, how are you holding up?"

"I just need one good night's sleep. I'd give my eyeteeth for a vacation."

"How did he take the news?" Mary drilled down to the conversation she really wanted to have after all.

"He cried like a baby all night."

"And?"

"We're going to get some counselling of our own."

"That's probably best," Mary could only be this truthful.

It was enough for Fawn. Enough for right now, anyway.

"You haven't asked about the rest of the case?"

"I don't need to. I know that Mitch has taken control of the situation and everything is going to work out okay."

"You are closer to the truth than you could ever imagine," Fawn nodded her head.

"Of course I am. In the end, Mitch gets everything to go her way."


The news of Rose's death traveled just as quickly to Reb and Lisa as it had to Mary, however with quite the opposite reaction.

"Poor Trish!" Lisa had said in front of everyone.

Reb didn't give much credence to this sympathetic response, but had the good grace to keep it to herself.

"It's a good thing we sent Smith back," was all Reb had to say on short notice.

"Maybe we should go back as well?" Lisa was fishing about for the best plan.

"I'd be happy to charter a flight for you, but I'm staying here."

"Then I'll stay as well. You need my help."

"I don't need your help," Reb practically laughed and then reminded herself of the sanctity of the moment.

"I have a feeling we're not going to be here much longer anyway," Lisa ignored Reb's remark.

"Why do you think that?"

"Haven't you noticed how on edge the Feds are? Something is going to happen real soon."

Chapter 11

Sheriffs of small southern towns indeed still made house calls.

When Martha had awakened the morning after Herman and Mitch's dialogue, she noticed the subdued atmosphere. The absence of hostility didn't necessarily usher in peacefulness. In this case, a vague uneasiness seemed to be enveloping everyone. It was like everyone was in on the secret but her.

"The sheriff is coming over for a visit," Herman told Martha over breakfast. Her response was to drop her coffee cup, shattering it into a dozen pieces. Mitch looked from Herman to Martha as the guard cleaned up the mess.
"Who called the sheriff?" Martha asked with a shaky voice.
Mitch wondered which decade Martha was mentally living in. Was it present day or years ago when Melvin was "found dead'?
"I called Sheriff Howard," Herman started to explain but was interrupted by his mother.
"Oh! Sheriff Howard! I should bake some cookies!" Martha exclaimed.
Mitch looked over at Herman. Was it typical southern hospitality to bake cookies when the sheriff paid a visit?
"The sheriff wants to talk to us about the day Dad died."
"There's nothing to discuss about that! I'm sure it's just a social call," Martha was trying and failing to hide her real emotions.
"I'm sure everything is going to be just fine," Mitch soothed.

Then, Martha did the inexplicable. She rose from the table like she was forty years younger and went almost in a trance to the bedroom to begin preparing for the arrival of Sheriff Howard. It was like she was getting ready for a date. She picked out her prettiest dress from the meager selection. Then, she washed her face and combed her hair. All by herself. It was spooky to witness. Mitch wondered if, when Martha looked in the mirror, she saw her contemporary self or herself when she was twenty-five. Which countenance was looking back and smiling? She came back out to the main room and sat in her comfy chair to await her visitor.

Mitch could tell that Herman was unnerved. He had never before seen his mother behave this way. Martha was slowly losing her social filters and this was telling. The story was becoming clearer to Mitch, but Herman struggled to keep up.

So, when Sheriff Howard showed up, a young-looking, pasty-faced middle-aged man, Herman was totally unprepared for what followed. Herman ushered the sheriff into the house and across the room to where Martha was presenting herself as the closest rendition of a coy schoolgirl that an elderly woman could manage.
"Well, good day, Sheriff Howard," Martha trilled. "You are as handsome as you ever were!"
Mitch was waiting for the "fiddle dee dee" but Herman interrupted. "Sheriff Howard is here to talk business!"
"Oh, nonsense, Herman! Go and fetch Sheriff Howard a cup of coffee while he and I get reacquainted. Run along!"
At the word "reacquainted," Herman and Mitch exchanged a look.
"I'll meet you in the kitchen," Mitch gave Herman a sideways nod.
"Yeah," he said reluctantly.
When they were out of earshot, Mitch asked, "Who was the sheriff when your dad died?"
Suddenly, the light came on for Herman. "Sheriff John Howard."
"And who is here now?"
"Sheriff John Howard Junior."
"Your mom thinks she is talking with John Howard Senior."
"They look enough alike to have her make that mistake."
"Did your mom have a crush on the sheriff when you were a kid?"
"How the hell would I know?"
"We'd better get back out there before Junior gets any wrong ideas about your mother."
"Like what?" Herman was still befuddled.

216

"Let's begin by reassuring him that she just doesn't throw herself at every handsome man who walks through the door."

Mitch took the lead as they reentered the living room. Although Junior acknowledged their presence, it appeared that all his good police training was serving him well. He was patiently listening to Martha go on and on about the good old days. Junior didn't show any signs of pulling his gun to arrest Herman or anyone for that matter. Martha still looked like a giggly school girl, trying her best to recapture Junior's full attention.

"My mom thinks that you are your dad," Herman explained quite succinctly.

Junior nodded like he had already figured that out. "Will that help her to remember who killed your father, or will she need to talk to him personally?"

"He's still alive?"

"He's still breathing," Junior replied cryptically.

"Is he in a nursing home?" Herman followed up like he was some kind of social worker.

"He's still living at the lake. I keep an eye on him when I can," Junior replied.

It didn't sound to Mitch like there would be an issue getting Martha and John together to hash out their personal history. "Maybe we could all go to the lake for a visit?" Mitch wanted to move forward now.

Usually, a suggestion as bold as this would've drawn a rebuke from Herman. However, it seemed as though they were running out of options.

"How soon can you be ready?" Junior asked.

Mitch shrugged her shoulders. Herman was running through the options in his mind. Mitch could tell by the frowny face he was making.

"Is your dad up for a visit?" he finally asked Junior.

"Dad is always up for a visit."

"Well then, let's go."

Chapter 12

Trish didn't need to be told twice to start spending money on another casket. Once she had gotten in the habit of spending money, she hadn't been able to stop. However, it was her next suggestion that surprised Silver.

"Let's move."

"Move what?" Silver thought they were talking about rearranging furniture. Again.

"No, I mean let's relocate."

"You mean, get a new house?"

"Right!"

"Why?"

"Why not!"

Silver stopped asking questions. Trish was only able to give simplistic answers at this point, which made it obvious that she hadn't thought this through.

"Don't you want to move?" Trish asked.

"I've moved around a lot in my life," Silver avoided answering the question.

"You don't want to move," Trish picked up on Silver's mood.

"I would do whatever you ask me to do," Silver wanted to be as cooperative as possible.

"I want you to be happy," Trish said sincerely.

"Why do you want to move? You just started renovating this place. Tearing down walls…" Silver trailed off.

"I just don't want to be here anymore. I tried to make it work and look what happened."

"What happened, Miss Trish?"

"The dead don't stay dead in this house."

In a way, Trish was correct. They had already solved the hauntings of the Livermore Estate's original ghost. The lesbian daughter of Benjamin Livermore had been given a decent burial after her skeleton had been unearthed in the basement. But everyone else who died was either buried properly or were about to be. Now that Rose had passed away, the brakes were temporarily on concerning Max's final journey as well. Truth be told, it wasn't Max or Rose who were causing Trish's uneasiness.

"You think that if we move out of this house, that you won't see Miss Robbie's ghost anymore?" Silver did her best to avoid putting too fine a point on the topic.

"It might do the trick."

"What about Josh?"

"What about Josh?" Trish repeated a little on the sharp side.

"He sees Miss Robbie's ghost too."

"He does?"

"Yes..." Silver hadn't realized until now that this was news to Trish.

"And nobody bothered to tell me?" Trish was downright snappish.

"I guess we thought you knew?"

"We?"

"Miss Rose saw it, too."

"What exactly did you and Rose see?"

Silver practically reenacted the entire scene where Josh was reacting to nothing and then changed when Silver and Rose apparently scared off Robbie's ghost.

Trish didn't say anything at first. She was hovering between disbelief and concern. How could she possibly disbelieve what Silver was reporting when she herself had heard voices? Apparently, Josh was much more receptive to visits from Robbie. After all, he didn't carry the guilt that Trish did.

"Could it have been something else?" Trish asked.

Silver didn't answer.

"Did you or Rose see anything yourselves?"

"No."

"Maybe it was a dream?" Trish was grasping at straws.

Silver knew why.

"If you move Josh out of this house, you'll be taking his mother away from him all over again."

Trish finally nodded assent. "Could you get Ronnie and Donnie back here?"

"Why?"

"Well, if we're going to stay here, I'm going to redo the place from top to bottom."

Silver didn't say it out loud, but she sure hoped she would get a bigger bedroom out of this remodel.

Chapter 13

Viewing the grainy surveillance video of Mitch, Herman, Martha, the guard, and Sheriff Howard file out of a dump of a house and get into the white van was one of the strangest things Reb had ever witnessed in her life. She was pleased that the Feds chose to share it with her and Lisa. But damn! What was going on? Nobody seemed to be in any particular rush. There had been no secret hand signals that Reb could discern.
"He looks just like Jesus!" Lisa had exclaimed.
"No, he doesn't!" Reb had argued.
"Yes, he does! Just like every picture of Jesus at the Vatican."
"You've been to the Vatican?"
"I've seen pictures in travel brochures."
"The elderly woman must be his mother."
"There is a family resemblance."

When Reb had inquired where the troop was heading to, the Feds had demurred. They wouldn't put it past Reb to get in her vehicle and try to get there first.
"Mitch had better be in no danger whatsoever," she warned the agents.
They seemed nonplussed. How much danger could someone be in as they were being escorted by one sheriff to visit another sheriff?

By force of habit, Mitch settled in for a long ride. She was surprised when the van jolted to a stop after about ten minutes. Apparently, it didn't take long to get to the country when you already lived there. The house on the lake was much nicer than Herman's homestead. Sheriffs did pretty well for themselves in the south. If Mitch had been a suspicious person, she would've figured that this place had

221

been built by payoffs and graft. Seriously, you could run a bed and breakfast in this lodge.

Everyone regrouped outside the van and walked single file to the front door. At least, it looked like a front door. When no one answered, Junior signaled everyone to follow him around to the lake side of the house. It was slightly reminiscent of summer camp for Mitch. She had gone to summer camp once as a kid and once was enough. It wasn't at all like Hayley Mills movies. It was more like a mosquito-infested sunburn endurance test. Beyond that, it was the first time Mitch had truly come to terms with her sexuality. While all the other girls were enthralled with boys, Mitch had no similar enthusiasm. It became awkward in a hurry to remain mute when others were sharing stories.

When her parents had first suggested the idea of summer camp, it had all sounded so exciting. Beautiful color brochures had arrived in the mail. In a time long before the internet, people actually requested information over the phone or by mail. It had been a feat of research on her parent's part to even find camps to contact. A few were local calls, but most were long distance. Mitch hadn't truly appreciated how much effort her parents had spent on this project until much later in life.

So, after they had gawked at and admired the selections, they chose a camp with rustic-looking cabins and pristine lakes in another state far away from home. While other parents were wealthy enough to buy airline flights for their children, Mitch's parents were forced to be more economical. They took a family road trip to Michigan where, after getting Mitch checked in to camp, they settled into a roadside motel a few miles down the road. Just in case camp didn't work out.

Once Mitch had had her fill of boy-crazy females, she found her niche with some rowdy boys who were more interested in cannonballing into the lake than flirting with girls. Being called a tomboy was a small price to pay for escaping an otherwise untenable sexual outing experience. And although the week passed without major incident, when Mitch's parents brought up the idea of going again next summer, Mitch politely declined.

Wise people that they were, her parents accepted Mitch's decision without asking a thousand nosy questions. The following summer, they traveled to the Grand Canyon. It was hot as Hell and still an improvement over camp.

As they approached the lake, Mitch caught sight of an elderly gentleman in a rocking chair. Apparently, Sheriff Senior preferred to spend his time outdoors. Junior called out to announce their arrival.

"Hey, Pop!"

Senior didn't say anything as he glacially turned to look at where the sound was coming from. He sure looked about the same age as Martha, but appeared to have lost a step or two along the way. At least Mitch had gotten Martha up and walking around. Sheriff Senior didn't look like he was even willing to stand up for company.

Maybe she was being too harsh. Or, maybe even worse, judgmental. Then, Mitch picked up on something like a vibration. It felt like, for lack of a better word, heaviness. She almost stumbled into Herman as she was being pulled to be at the center of this area as if it were a black hole.

By now, Senior had turned his head enough to see the approaching party. His gaze settled on Mitch of all people. The Universe was not wasting time. "Who the hell are you?"

"That's your best southern gentleman charm?" Mitch stalled for time. She was feeling light headed and hadn't counted on being the center of attention this early in the encounter.

"I don't care much for strangers sneaking up on me. This is private property."

"That works out just fine since we have private matters to discuss," Mitch retorted. Standing in the hot sun wasn't improving her mood. When in the hell did people forget basic manners, like asking a traveler to take a seat in the shade!

"Do I know you? Do I know any of you?" he asked gruffly.

Mitch looked over at Junior. How were they ever going to get to the bottom of this mystery if the two principal players couldn't remember much of anything?

"Sheriff John Howard!" Martha's shrill voice broke the silence. Both John Howard Junior and John Howard Senior jolted, but Senior was much more affected.

"Miss Martha? Is that you? He turned his gaze toward her.

"Well, of course it is, silly!"

"Come over here and sit yourself down. Junior! Don't just stand there all slack jaw! Get Miss Martha a chair!"

It's important to note here that Junior wasn't averse to being ordered around by his father. He was just temporarily taken aback by the animation Senior was displaying. He hadn't seen his dad this lively in a long time.

Mitch relaxed a little No longer being the center of attention helped her regain her balance, literally and figuratively. She hadn't yet figured out what was causing this imbalance, but had a feeling that all would soon be revealed.

Junior, meanwhile, had the good common sense to find everyone a chair, and they were now seated in a haphazard circle, like a prayer group.

"Where have you been all these years, Miss Martha?" Senior asked. She couldn't answer correctly because she couldn't remember. So, she vaguely answered, "Oh, here and there."

Mitch thought it interesting that Martha had so quickly transitioned her attentiveness from Junior to Senior. It must have showed on her face.

"What's wrong with you!?" Senior fairly barked at Mitch.

"You did it, didn't you!?" Mitch shot back, surprising even herself.

"Young lady!" Senior became as animated as a man half his age. That's not something people discuss in mixed company!"

Mitch had to think for a second. Then it dawned on her.

"I'm not talking about you and Martha having an affair."

Things got cricket quiet, but it was too hot for chirping.

"But I could," Mitch added. "Is that what was going on?"

At this question, Herman and Junior simultaneously took umbrage.

"Shut your filthy mouth!" Junior stepped way out of his professional capacity.

"Why would anyone consider sex as something filthy?" Mitch asked in return.

Junior became curiously quiet all of a sudden. And pale. Very pale.
"Uh oh," Mitch said so quietly that no one heard it over Junior's surprising swoon and subsequent thud as he hit the ground.

Maybe everyone else thought it was the heat, but Mitch knew better. She looked around. No one had made a move to help, so Mitch went over to where Junior was sprawled awkwardly on the ground. She knelt down and lifted his head. When his eyelids fluttered, she helped him into a sitting position. His police training kicked in as he held onto his holstered gun, making sure no one could now take it away from him.

"Could someone please get him a glass of water?"

"A shot of bourbon would be better," Senior remarked.

"Well, maybe after we get Junior into a chair," Mitch replied.

Without further prompting, Herman recovered from his temporary mental paralysis and lifted Junior into a chair. He was strong and graceful from his years of practice on his mother.

"Water please. No bourbon," Junior whispered.

Nobody moved. And why would they. There were two senior citizens, a criminal mastermind used to giving orders instead of taking them, and a guard with a gun.

"Okay. I'll do it," Mitch sounded piqued.

"No!" Herman fairly shouted and then turned to the guard. "Get water!"

The guard looked peeved, like it was below his station in life to be the team's water boy.

"Go!" Herman wasn't kidding.

Reluctantly, the guard took off toward the main house. Hopefully, he knew the way around a kitchen. Mitch figured that now was as good a time as any to take Senior and Martha down memory lane as gently as she could. She sat between them while Herman was propping up Junior.

"You two kids were in love, weren't you?" Mitch asked as she took both of them by the hand like they were participating in a séance.

In a way, they were. Only instead of communicating with the dead, they were going to have an honest conversation with the ghosts of the past. Senior shifted uncomfortably while Martha kept her gaze on the ground.

"It just sort of happened, didn't it?" Mitch asked quietly.

Surprisingly, Senior spoke first. "Junior's mother had gone to the

Lord," he began with a trembling lower lip.

"Mother died too young," Junior nodded along. His color was slowly returning.

"And I still had Junior and my job and I tried to convince myself that that was all I needed."

"He was the most eligible widower in town," Martha piped up.

Mitch mused about this. Was Clantown full of eligible widowers back then? How tough would the competition be?

"Oh, Miss Martha!" Senior was on the verge of wiggling out of his chair from embarrassment.

"It's the Lord's truth!" Martha wasn't about to let up.

Herman looked uncomfortable, but he would just have to live with it. Mitch was doing what she was brought here to do. Telling the truth was the only way to heal everyone.

"So, Martha, you were still married to Herman's dad."

"I was," she answered with a bitterness new to her tone of voice.

"Was he mean to you?"

"He was mean to everyone. Nasty to everyone."

Mitch was listening to Martha, but also watching Junior and Herman. Neither one looked well at this point. She couldn't explain why she, the stranger to the situation, saw the raw truth so clearly. Herman's dad had figuratively poisoned the well and they were all sick from being forced to drink from it.

"So, how did it happen?" Mitch purposely phrased her question vaguely.

After a while, Martha broke the silence.

"I gradually found out about Melvin. I didn't want to know. But I did. And if Jesus Christ feels it necessary to send my soul to hell for eternity, I'm sure I deserve it."

"So, you killed Melvin?"

"No!"

"But you feel so guilty. Why?"

"All the little children…" Martha's voice broke.

"How many?"

"All the children. All the Good Lord's children. All the…" Martha started to cry now in earnest.

"Look what you did!" Senior was upset. "You made her cry!"

"It's better that she cry now rather than damage her mind even more by trying to bury the truth."

226

Herman looked at Mitch. "Is this your idea of healing my mother?"

"It's a damn good start."

"Miss Martha didn't do nothing wrong!" Senior blustered his way back into the conversation.

"What was your part in this murder mystery?" Mitch countered.

Senior made eye contact with her. He was now fully aware of the seriousness of this dialogue.

"Miss Martha contacted the sheriff's office that night. I was on call. She needed help."

"What kind of help?" Mitch prodded gently.

"Help with a drunk, abusive husband kind of help! Normally, back then, we didn't interfere in what your modern world refers to as domestic disturbances."

"Why not?" Mitch couldn't help but ask.

"Because they were usually settled by the time we got to the house."

"Settled?"

"Yes! Settled!"

"Like, 'the wife was taught a lesson and didn't want to press charges' kind of settled?"

"We were trained to allow married couples to work out their differences with as little interference as possible."

"However, Miss Martha's situation was different because you were in love with her."

"I just didn't want to see her get hurt anymore."

"Did you know everything that Melvin was guilty of?"

Things got very quiet again. Junior was looking pale again. Where was the guard with that water?

It was at that exact moment when Mitch realized they were running out of time. Obviously, the Feds had intercepted the guard during his water run.

Herman's stare was drilling into Mitch's eyes. He had simultaneously come to the same conclusion. The only person who had a sidearm now was Junior, and he was on the verge of another fainting spell.

Mitch knew that she wouldn't be able to win a wrestling match for the firearm, so she conceded as much to Herman.

"Go ahead," she nodded.

"Doesn't matter. I'm not getting out of here alive."

"Okay, so will you please tell me where the baby is before you die?"

Reb and Lisa had watched in awe as the Feds had taken down the water-fetching guard. Against all the rules, and at the personal behest of the President, Reb and Lisa were allowed to go with the agents as they infiltrated the premises for the final showdown. Reb's logic had been that there may be information that she could provide to be helpful to the situation. It had been a feat to smuggle Reb and Lisa into the house without attracting attention, but once they were settled, they literally had a front-row seat.

When the guard had come to the main house to get the water, the ensuing takedown was more like a slow-motion ballet than a routine arrest. The agents were casual in their process. Instead of yelling at the guard to get down on the ground, a move certain to immediately alert Herman, they simple puffed some substance from a canister into his proximity and then cushioned his collapse. A wordless, soundless procedure. He was handcuffed in an official vehicle five miles down the road before anyone had even mentioned the missing baby. When this topic came up, Reb was fully alert.
"Are you surprised?" Lisa asked Reb.
"Shush! We promised to be quiet!"
"I'm not hollering."
"Shhh."
"You really hadn't figured that out yet?" Lisa wouldn't let up.
"You're telling me that you knew about the baby all along?"
"I figured it out. Mitch figured it out. Even the Feds apparently figured it out."
"And your point is?"
"You're supposed to be the smart one."
"Herman doesn't have the baby!"
"Of course not. But he knows who does."
"Okay, Genius, who has the baby?"
"I'm going to tell Mitch that you actually called me a genius!"
"I'm so looking forward to not seeing you after today is over."
"Okay. I'll write down on a piece of paper who has the baby and then I'll fold it up and scotch tape it and then you can read it after this is all over. Anybody got a piece of paper? Anybody?"
The agents were peeved but still looked at each other like they were going to get still another call from the President unless they could

produce paper, pen and scotch tape.

Meanwhile, Mitch and Herman were locked in a stare down. No one had spoken. Thankfully, the Feds hadn't missed anything.
"When Mom is cured, you get the baby back," Herman made his final offer.
"So, I need to keep you alive."
"That's correct."
"If I were you, I wouldn't make any hasty decisions. Let's just finish what we came here to do."
Herman nodded agreement. Everyone took a collective deep breath in the house.

Sheriff Senior had taken this lull in the proceedings to do some serious reflecting. Years ago, he had started to hear rumors about Melvin. At first, he had chalked it up to town gossip. Folks in small towns made up all sorts of salacious stories to alleviate the boredom of living in a rural setting. But then, something had occurred. Young Junior's behavior had begun to change. Most parents would've acknowledged the change as just part of the rebellious stage most kids go through. However, Senior was an officer of the law and well-trained in behavioral science. Junior was acting guilty and masking it in recalcitrance. It had stumped Senior for a while. After all, there were matters criminal and otherwise to occupy his time. Then one day, it all came together like a thunderclap. One jarring, ugly, unfathomable thunderclap. The hazy memories became cut-glass sharp.

Junior had come home more angry than usual. Senior hadn't had a direct conversation, but he remembered hearing Junior's bedroom door slam shut and music loud enough to melt wall-paper paste emanate from his room. Senior, for the hundredth time had contemplated knocking on the door. And for the hundredth time, talked himself out of doing so.

Instead, he chose to answer a police call from Martha and Melvin's residence. Once again, Senior had arrived for another domestic disturbance call. He entered the residence to find Martha cowering in a corner and Melvin in a drunken rage. As usual, the call had come from concerned neighbors.

"Whadya doin here!" Melvin slurred his usual greeting.

"Official business," was Senior's curt reply.

"Git outa my house!"

"Not before I talk to Martha."

"Git out now!" Melvin bellowed as spittle sprayed from his mouth.

"Why don't you just go sit in the kitchen and have some coffee and sober up."

"Why don't you go the hell home and mind your own family business."

"It isn't my family who needs help."

Melvin got this look in his eye like he knew something that nobody else knew.

"You sure about that, Mr. Lawman?" Melvin taunted.

Senior looked Melvin in the eye. Pure evil was looking back.

"My family is fine," Senior kept his voice steady.

"Yeah," Melvin took a step forward. "Your boy. What's his name again? Oh, yeah. Junior. Yeah, Junior is fine. Real fine."

The emphasis on the word "fine" was not lost on Senior, but he kept his composure.

"Miss Martha, so you want to file a complaint?" Senior asked without taking his eye off Melvin. He already knew the answer and it would break his heart to witness her answer.

"No," was her meek reply.

"Are you sure?" Senior would've given anything to hear a different response.

"She is sure!" Melvin interjected. "Now, Mr. Lawman, you run along home with your tail between your legs just like you always do."

Melvin was calm by now. He was even more frightening when he let go of his rage. Senior knew it was hopeless to stay at the house. He headed home.

Home. Senior pondered the concept of home. After the death of his wife, Senior hadn't really felt at home in his house anymore. The spirit and spark of his wife had been the true foundation of their family unit. He and Junior had muddled along and it was only tonight that Senior realized how absent of a father he had been. This realization caused him to smolder in anger and self-loathing.

230

He knew what he had to do when he got home. It would be his most challenging hour as a parent. It would be absolutely necessary to get the truth from Junior for both their sakes. When he walked down the hall to Junior's room, he noticed the house was quiet. He knocked on the door. There was no response. He knocked again. Still no response. Senior swallowed his pride and anger and opened the door. Either Junior was asleep or he was pretending.

"Son," John said.

No response.

"Wake up, son. We need to talk."

Junior opened his eyes. Senior knew that he had only been pretending to be asleep.

"Are you awake?"

"Yeah."

"I want to take you to the hospital."

Naked fear suddenly possessed Junior's facial expression.

"I'm not sick!" Junior blurted out.

"I know you're not sick," Senior kept his voice steady.

"Well, then, why?" Junior's voice betrayed his young, tough resolve.

"I want to make sure that you are…okay."

"I'm fine."

"Get dressed."

"No."

"So, you'll be going in your pajamas."

"Okay! Okay…" Junior sat up.

"I love you, Son," Senior stepped closer.

Junior cowered back. "Don't touch me!"

Senior never could've guessed that he was capable of feeling so much anger as he was experiencing at this moment. He had to hide it from Junior in order to not frighten him anymore.

"Okay, I'll be at the front door when you are ready."

The ride to the hospital was quiet. There would be time for talking when Senior knew the truth. Back in the day, a rural hospital didn't have a million rules and regulations. When Senior pulled up to the emergency room entrance in his squad car, there wasn't someone waiting to demand his insurance card or extract upfront payment. After a brief but frank discussion with the doctor, Junior was taken to a private room for an examination. Senior only waited for about fifteen minutes before the doctor came out to break the horrible news to him. Senior nodded along like it was just another case, but his guts were twisting with every revelation.

"Would you do me a big favor and keep him overnight? Just so he can…be safe?"

"Sure," the doctor nodded. He was going to suggest as much anyway before the request. There would be many more steps in this process. An overnight stay was just the beginning of the healing.

Senior waited until Junior had a room and then went in to say goodnight.

"I'm sorry, Dad," Junior did his best to hold back tears.

"You have nothing to be sorry about," Senior replied. "Sleep good." If he said anymore, he'd start crying himself.

Senior then went to retrieve his patrol car and sped off into the night. It only took ten minutes to reach Melvin's house. John got out of the car and silently approached the front door. The house was dark. He went around the back entrance where the kitchen door was. He saw a glimmer of light and heard a muffled noise. He tried the doorknob and the door opened with an irritating squeak.

"Who's there?" Martha cried out.

"It's John.'

"Don't turn on the light!"

"Why not?"

"He's bleeding!"

"Who?"

"Melvin!"

John scanned the room with his flashlight. Sure enough, Melvin was face down on the kitchen floor in an apparent pool of blood. Head wounds always bled badly.

"How did you know he was bleeding?"

"I saw it with my flashlight," Martha answered as she produced her own electric torch.

"What happened?"

"I thought you would know," Martha answered vaguely.

"Why would I know?"

"Same here. I just found him!"

In the almost romantic aura of flashlight illumination, they studied each other. If they hadn't been so much in love, they would've suspected each other of the crime.

"So, you just found him like this?" Senior asked.

"John! We need to do something and fast!"

"What do you suggest?"

"Maybe we could hide the body?" Martha was now in full panic mode.

"Why on earth would we want to do that?"

"Well," Martha started to fidget from one foot to the other. "Because!"

"Because why?"

"It was an accident! That's what happened. I'm sure of it!"

"What kind of accident?" John was having a difficult time forgetting that he was the sheriff.

"I don't know! Why do you think I would know what happened?"

"Because…you live here. And you were the first person to discover the body."

"No, I wasn't. You were here first!"

"No, I wasn't."

"Why are you here anyway? Why did you come back?"

John paused to ponder his dilemma. He didn't want to talk to Martha about his discovery of Melvin's criminal activity with his son. It was too early for him to be able to do that.

"I was worried about you," he skirted the issue.

"If you were so worried about me, why didn't you stay in the first place?"

John used the flashlight to illuminate Martha's face. There were fresh bruises and contusions.

"What happened after I left?"

"What do you think?"

John hung his head. Even though Melvin had done the beating, he felt responsible.

"I should've stayed," John admitted even though he remembered that Martha had indeed dismissed him earlier in the evening. "I should call in my deputies."

"I'll go to prison if you do that!"

"Did you kill him?"

"No. It was an accident."

"Then you have nothing to worry about."

"I know how the law works. I can't prove I'm innocent without a witness."

"Still, I need to follow procedure."

Martha sat dejectedly at the kitchen table while John radioed for help.

Clantown was a small burg, still it took a while for reinforcements to gather. It wasn't exactly the group from C.S.I. They dusted a few key items for fingerprints and then took a statement from Martha. It was barely a paragraph. There weren't too many ways to say, "I found my husband dead on the floor and I didn't do it."

They called the coroner and when the body was packed up and carted off, everyone dispersed as well. Left to her own devices, Martha drew a bucket of soapy hot water and started to clean the floor of Melvin's blood. She didn't want the children to see it first thing in the morning.

Even by small-town standards, the investigation was brief. Melvin had most likely fallen in a drunken stupor and hit his head on the stove. Nobody got too terribly excited over the fact that there was no hair or blood evidence on the stove. By the time they had come up with that theory, Martha had cleaned the stove a dozen times.

Due to the fact that they had assumed at the crime scene that the fatal blow was caused by the floor, no one had bothered to investigate for other murder weapons, either stationary or portable. If the deputies had been compared to the Keystone Kops, the Keystone Kops could've sued for slander.

And John Senior? He just kept tabs on the group. When the medical examiner had found a head wound consistent with some sort of attack with a hard metal object, John had led the group on one more sweep of the crime scene disguised as a social call on the Widow Martha and the orphans Herman and Shane. Martha was distant and the children were like sentries flanking each side of their mother to protect her from this latest intrusion. After opening and closing all the cupboards in the kitchen, John waved off the rest of the search. The deputies were happy to oblige. It was a miserably hot day and all they could think about was getting back to the station. They headed out, leaving John to finalize the process.

"How are you doing, Miss Martha?"
"Why don't you leave my mother alone!" Herman's young voice came as a shock to everyone.
"Now, son," John started to speak, but Herman interrupted him.
"My Mom didn't do anything wrong, so leave her alone!"
Rather than be angry, John appreciated young Herman's defense of his mother. Families needed to show up for each other. If John had been more available to his own son, maybe none of this nightmare would've happened.

John Senior's rheumy eyes focused on his grown son as he came back to the present moment. As the memories of the tragedy had unfolded, regret rather than insight had dominated.

"So! All you fuckheads decided to have a family reunion and not tell me, huh!"
This pronouncement startled everyone. Like automatons, their heads all turned in unison to where the voice had emanated.
"Well, you don't look too bad for a presumed-dead heroin addict," Herman shot back as he stood up, hardly out of respect.
Mitch was confused. "Who is that?" she asked Herman,
The same sentiment came out of both Reb and Lisa, only directed at the Feds.
"Where did she come from and how did she slip past the guards?"
"She's our ace in the hole. Now, please be silent. We need to be ready for the ambush."
"The ambush?"
"Hush!"
Reb had never in her entire life been told to hush. She followed the rude directive only to help save Mitch's life.
"Well, that's a helluva way to greet your long-lost sister, you asshole!"
"You better watch your mouth, you stupid slut!" Herman wasn't backing down.
Reb looked at Lisa and mouthed the word, "Sister?"
Lisa shrugged her shoulders, trying hard to respect the need for silence.

Reb poked the Fed closest to her in the ribs. "You found Herman's sister?" she whispered.

The agent glowered but whispered back, "We have been doing more than just sitting around watching you."

The sharpshooter who had been pointing some very official looking long rifle in the general direction of the family gathering raised his left hand. It was an ominous signal. Now was the time to remain silent.

"Call me whatever you want," Shane continued after a pause, "But you are nothing more than a disgusting, repulsive Nazi!"

"At least I believe in something. It's better than sleeping my way through my entire hometown!"

"Hey, Junior!" Shane approached the only person who had a gun. "Are you going to let him talk to your old girlfriend like that?" Obviously, this hadn't been Junior's best day in a while and it sure didn't seem to be turning the corner just yet.

"Everyone, shut up!" Martha's voice cut through the insults and innuendo. Now that she had everyone's attention, her feelings became clear.

"Family doesn't talk like that to family and acquaintances!" When it looked like Shane and Herman were ready to talk over her, she held up her hand just like the sharpshooter had done a moment ago. The universal signal for utter silence worked. Mitch marveled. When Mitch had first met Martha, she acted like a frail, old woman. Now, she was sitting in a chair commanding the attention of people. Holding court was an apt description.

"We didn't come here to fuss and fight. We came here to solve a murder!"

"Wow!" Mitch blurted out despite the call for quiet.

"What?" Herman hissed.

"I did it!"

"You? You couldn't have possibly committed the murder!"

"I'm not talking about the murder!"

"What are you talking about?"

"I cured your mother."

"No you didn't."

"Yes I most certainly did! Look at her!"

236

Everyone, even new-to-the-party Shane, was now watching Martha. Shane found her voice first.

"What the hell is going on here?"

"It's a rather long and complicated story," Mitch dove in. "It all started with a plot to overthrow the United States Government by Herman here."

"It wasn't just me," Herman inadvertently incriminated himself.

"Oh, I understand that you had help. Lots of it. But, you were the brains behind everything."

In a sick, twisted way, Herman was flattered.

"And then," Mitch continued, I was abducted for what seemed to be an effort to influence the Federal trial. But then, thing changed."

"There's a Federal trial?" Martha was taken aback.

"One of my best friends is in protective custody," Mitch intoned the seriousness of the situation.

"Herman! Is that true?" Martha directed her extreme displeasure toward her only son.

"There was a misunderstanding," Herman replied vaguely.

"How did things change," Shane wanted to get back to the original train of conversation.

"Well, when nobody decided to pay the ransom for my return, the real reason for my abduction came to light."

"Which is?"

"The rumor is that I'm some sort of famous healer. Somehow, Herman here found out about that. Whether before or after my kidnapping is beside the point. So, the focus shifted from influencing the court case to healing Martha."

"What was wrong with her?" Shane asked.

"Oh, fuck you, Shane!" Herman interjected forcefully.

No matter how many instances, it was still jarring to hear such language from a man who resembled Jesus.

"You watch your mouth, little brother!" Shane shot back.

"You've got some nerve to be *oh so concerned* after all these years," Herman sneered. "You went off and screwed around and left me to take care of everything. So, don't embarrass yourself now by pretending to give a shit about anyone but yourself!"

Mitch didn't know if she should continue speaking or not. It had gotten really quiet here by the lake.

"Mitch?"

237

"Yes, Martha?"

"What are you talking about? And if anyone interrupts you one more time, I'm giving Junior permission to shoot."

If there was ever a time to choose one's words carefully, this was it. Mitch decided to direct her next exposition to Martha.

"When I first met you, Martha, you seemed frail and bedridden. Look at you now! Before, your memory was failing you. Not a little bit either. It was like you had an advanced case of dementia."

"Am I doing better now?"

"You are getting my name right first time now."

"I'm sorry if I got it wrong before."

"It's okay. However, I don't think it's just a coincidence that your memory has improved as we've gotten closer to solving your husband's death."

"But she hasn't had dementia her entire life!" Herman couldn't control himself to stay silent this much longer.

Junior put his hand on his holstered gun, but Martha gave an almost indistinct shake of her head. It was oddly comforting to Mitch that Martha's protective nature of her son ran deep.

"I agree," Mitch interjected, only to hurriedly placate Herman. "I'm quite certain of a few things now. Your mother hasn't had dementia all these years, but I know that your father's death had a profound influence on her psyche. People get damaged after a series of horrific incidents."

"My Mother didn't go through a lot of horrific incidents," Herman even had the gall to use air quotes when he said "horrific incidents."

"Shut your fucking mouth, Herman!" Shane now chimed in on what was supposed to be Mitch's monologue. While her vocabulary hadn't expanded much, Mitch felt this was an important interruption.

"Go on, Shane," Mitch encouraged.

"Herman and Martha are the living, breathing examples of what chronic abuse can do to a person. Their only difference is that Martha internalized the abuse while Herman externalized the abuse."

Mitch nodded along but Martha seemed confused by this sudden shift in thought process from the usual "fuck you" Shane personality.

"What's she talking about?" Martha directed her question to Mitch.

"At the risk of gender-stereotyping people, women generally punish themselves for abuse, while men punish other people. After all, how many mass shootings are perpetrated by women?"

"Right!" Shane chimed in. "Herman here turned into a real asshole white-supremist Klansman and you lost your mind, Mom."

Martha started to weep.

"What's going on with you, Martha?" Mitch asked kindly.

"She called me Mom."

"She also said you lost your mind," Herman added snidely.

"You just can't help yourself, can you?" Shane shot back.

"So, tell everyone, Shane. Did you handle Dad's abuse by turning into a whore or a heroin addict?"

Just when you thought that things couldn't get any quieter, all of a sudden, the softest sounds of nature were amplified. A rustling leaf. A distant bird caw.

"Dad never abused me."

"I don't believe you!"

"I don't care if you believe me or not."

"So you decided to just go and fuck up your life for no good reason?"

"You certainly seemed preoccupied with spinning falsehoods about my life. Are you that jealous of me for escaping this hell hole?"

Despite the fact that Mitch had appeared to be simply listening along, she was also carefully observing Herman. He was now clenching his fists and looked like he was ready to lunge for Shane's throat.

"Does anyone want to hear the end of the story?" Mitch asked quietly.

"Make it quick!" Herman ordered.

"I'll bet you a million dollars that I know where the baby is. Are you a betting man, Herman?"

He stopped clenching his fists.

Lisa nudged Reb. "Here it comes," she whispered.

Martha asked, "What baby?"

"You couldn't possibly know anything about that!" he sputtered.

"Herman, it's always bad form to suggest or assume that other people, especially women, aren't as smart as you."

"You would need to be psychic to know."

"Being psychic has nothing to do with it. I'm just using logic."

"You tell him!" Lisa muttered under her breath.

"The baby is where the baby has been all along. When this is all over, some Federal Agent needs to have a serious discussion with the hospital administrator."

Martha seemed content to hear that a baby she had never heard of was in a hospital. Shane, not so much.

"I'm sure all of this is just fascinating to the two of you," she interrupted. "But you still haven't solved our father's murder!"

"Martha has," Mitch said quietly.

"What?"

"Martha knows who killed her husband. Isn't that right, Martha?"

Martha started to nervously pick at her dress.

"You! Shut up!" Senior stirred from his stone-like silence to confront Mitch.

"The two of you were so in love," Mitch turned her calm attention to Martha and Senior. "I can't imagine how painful this was for the two of you. Here you were, in a small town. How does that old song go? A town without pity. It was probably even worse than that. A town full of stiff-necked sanctimonious people who created a cottage industry out of judging people and destroying their lives."

Martha stopped picking at her dress and took Senior's hand in hers. Mitch continued, "Senior, you had lost your wife, and your son had been abused by Melvin. Martha, you were married to a truly terrifying, evil man who abused you night and day. Who would have blamed the two of you if you killed him?"

At the worst possible time, Junior decided to rouse himself out of his compliant stupor and pull his gun. It was aimed directly at Mitch's head.

"Relax, Junior. No one is accusing you. You were in the hospital at the time."

"Shut up!" he hollered with a barely discernable shakiness in his voice. "Nobody accuses my dad of murder! Especially some Yankee like you!"

Junior was waggling the gun around like he hadn't used one in years. Not even for target practice.

Of all people, Shane the Agitator went slowly over to him. "Put the gun down before you accidently shoot someone."

"My Dad didn't kill Melvin!"

"Yes, I did," Senior looked at his beloved son.

"No!" Junior shook his head.

240

"You are right, Junior," Martha said slowly. "I killed Melvin."
Mitch looked around in a rather exaggerated fashion to see if anyone
else was going to confess. When no one else spoke up, Mitch
continued, "I think that what happened was an unfortunate accident."
"What do you mean?" Herman asked, still eyeing Junior and the
wiggling gun.
"Here's what I think happened," Mitch was ready to wrap this up. "I
think that Melvin continued to abuse Martha after Senior left the
house that evening. After Senior secured Junior in the hospital, he
went back to the house. Melvin was really drunk by this time and
was verbally harassing Martha in the kitchen when Senior came in
the back door. Words were exchanged and then Melvin attempted to
hurt Martha, perhaps something along the lines of a choke hold.
Somehow, Martha finally found enough strength to try and fend him
off. This was made easier by the fact that Melvin was blind drunk
by now. Senior witnessed them lurching around the kitchen and in
his attempt to help, pushed Melvin off Martha. Melvin stumbled, hit
his head on the kitchen stove, and died in a pool of blood."
"So, it was all an accident?" Shane asked.
"The real crime was the cover up. And there's nobody better than an
officer of the law to destroy evidence, is there?"
"So, nobody killed Melvin?" Junior was in disbelief.
"Alcohol," Mitch said. "Alcohol killed Melvin."
"But you are still blaming my Daddy for a crime!" Junior's voice
was almost as plaintiff as a child.
"Well, I guess the only thing that your Dad and Martha are guilty of
is cleaning the stove. I guess if we really wanted to pin the fault on
anyone, it would be those town folk I mentioned a few minutes ago.
What would have happened if John and Martha had told the truth?
They would have been condemned in the court of public opinion.
Isn't that right, John?"

Senior nodded his head slowly. "I had already lost my wife. I
nearly lost my son. I couldn't afford to lose my job. It really was an
accident. It really was," he said as his lower lip started to tremble
again.

Mitch continued, "Still, it was a trauma that took its toll on Martha.
Facing and admitting the truth has been nothing but beneficial to her.

241

So, my work here is done. I've helped Martha heal her memory. May I be excused?"

Mitch had hoped it would be that simple. However, she had been witness to far too much criminal activity to be allowed to walk away. Just like in the movies, events started quickly and then de-evolved into slow motion. Both Shane and Herman went for Junior's gun. This seemed surreal. Mitch had expected this from Herman. But Shane? Shane had positioned herself strategically closer early on, so she easily won the lunging contest. It was like she had planned this all along.

It still didn't make sense, but before Mitch could stand up, she was dragged out of her chair by Herman and put in a headlock. Junior was protesting that he no longer had his gun, so Shane cold cocked him hard enough to knock him out. She sure hit hard for a girl.

As Mitch's brain was being starved of oxygen, her last observations were of a lot of shouting between Shane and Herman as well as shouting and gunshots from somewhere behind her. She had the sickening sensation of being whirled around, pushed down, and hitting her head against something very hard yet smooth. Everything went black.

Chapter 14

First, there was light. No. That wasn't right. First, there was pain. Then light. Then more pain. Then nothing. Then, everything repeated. Pain. Light. Nothing. Then, something new. Images. Fuzzy images. Like space aliens. Only they were speaking words that sounded like English. There was a repeated word. Sweetie? Something like that. And then, quiet and darkness. Darkness was good because there wasn't any pain or light.

And then, there were those fuzzy images again. And that word "Sweetie" again. Time went by. And then the two images came into sharper focus. They weren't so bewildering now. And then that word again. "Sweetie."

"Are you awake? Sweetie."
"Don't bother her, Lisa!"
"Rebecca, I'm not bothering her!"
"Well, Lisa, you are bothering me!"
"Quiet, Rebecca! I think she can finally hear us!"

They had stopped talking. Finally. One of them was tall and blonde. One was short with dark hair.
"What? Where?"
"Oh my Lord, she's talking!" the tall blonde said.
"Are you Lisa or Rebecca?"
"I'm Lisa," the tall blonde answered.
"So, then you must be Rebecca," she looked at the other one.
"That's right. So you know who you are?"
"Of course I know who I am. My name is…Sweetie."

www.ingramcontent.com/pod-product-compliance
Lightning Source LLC
Chambersburg PA
CBHW072224170626
46813CB00003B/1078

*   9 7 8 0 6 9 2 9 9 0 5 6 8   *